Poor Man's Galapagos

by

Christopher Canniff

Dedication

Soli Deo Gloria

For Roxanne, the love of my life, and Colin and Abigail, who continually teach me the value of fatherhood.

For my parents Craig and Barbara, who have loved me unconditionally and supported me in all my endeavours, and my brother Benjamin, who has done the same.

Other Works by Christopher Canniff

Novels

Abundance of the Infinite

Short Stories

Solitude

Clean Conscience

The Russian Soldier (excerpt from a previous version of *Poor Man's Galapagos*)

Table of Contents

We seemed to breathe more freely, a lighter air, an air of adventure. Faraway countries, heroic deeds, beautiful women whirled round and round in our turbulent imaginations. But in tired eyes which nevertheless refused sleep, a pair of green dots representing the world I'd left mocked the freedom I sought, hitching their image to my fantasy flight across the lands and seas of the world.

Ernesto Guevara de la Serna

Las manos que dan también reciben

Hands that give also receive

Ecuadorian Proverb

1. Molotov Cocktail

August, 1987

TÓMAS MONTGOMERY HARVEY was given a lighter and a Molotov Cocktail and told to await the approach of the armoured military vehicle that passed by periodically firing tear gas bombs over concrete walls. He sat on the ground, removed the rag from the cocktail and took a drink of the bitter Caña Manabita sugarcane alcohol inside. Then he set the bottle aside and produced his copy of the island's most current Diario Hoy newspaper.

As he waited, he read the article accusing his 70-year old father Montgomery of being a thief. He flipped to the section indicating that, at age 18, Tómas Montgomery Harvey was now conscripted into the Ecuadorian-Peruvian border war being waged over oil and uranium. This senseless war had lasted half a century and had littered the border with landmines. His days of cautious isolation were over. He was no longer a boy, but a man being thrust into the harsh realities of public humiliation and certain death.

The front page article describing the protests to overthrow the president for alleged incompetency, three months into his four-year term, no longer interested him; except for the burning tires blocking the main road into town and the thick, black smoke billowing over the university walls and poisoning the air. And his father was surely innocent of the allegations that he had embezzled millions of American dollars from a government investment account. He had to be. There was good reason to trust a man who had never done anything dishonest, who had never lied or cheated anyone, and who had never taken a single Sucre he didn't rightfully earn.

Past the agronomy building, the library was empty, the books no longer guarded by vigilant and watchful librarians. The bicycle racks were now unoccupied outside a closed steel door in an area where students ordinarily consumed carbonated beverages and candy caramelos. The gate beside him was closed and secured with a padlock attached to a heavy chain. Several young male protestors in bandanas, shirtless and wearing black makeup, stood looking out onto the street. For now, there was a subdued silence.

A short time later, gunfire sounded. Tómas rose as students ran toward the main university gates. Then, there was quiet again before an armoured military truck came into view, camouflaged green against the brown surroundings. He crouched behind a bush, beside the gates that the military were bound by edict not to enter, observing a vehicle he had not seen before except on television because Veronica, his father's wife, had insisted he stay inside during these protests. Tómas had obliged, not wanting to participate in the fighting, but wishing to observe from a distance a part of what his father had seen in his brief occupation as a war correspondent. His forced military duties had changed that perspective.

This vehicle appeared smaller than those in the television newscasts, including an undersized turret in front that was not being used. Its 12 wheels bounced unevenly over the dirt road. A slotted window was open on the vehicle's side and a wide-mouthed barrel had been pushed through, aimed to clear the height of the university walls. There was a loud *thwump* as if an oversized cork had popped. A dark object flew through the sky and over the wall to land squarely into the centre of student activity. Now the space was vacant, as the object began spinning and spitting smoke wildly before exhausting itself.

A noxious odour sucked the moisture from his eyes and replaced it with a stinging, burning sensation. The scent invaded his nose, and dryness permeated his nose and throat. His instinct was to run, to escape, but he found that he could not move his legs. The corner of his blurred vision caught a flash, which he thought to be the fire of a Molotov cocktail.

One of the protestors had thrown a bottle through the bars of the gate and the homemade bomb had blasted against the side of the vehicle. The small explosion sent shattered glass in all directions and made a thunderous noise, but the transport still bounded down the road, seemingly unaffected.

Tómas wanted to strike out against that armoured vehicle with a single, swift action of his arm, adding his Molotov Cocktail to the chaos. The resulting explosion would leave him sweaty, shaking, and feeling as though he had finally fought back against something. Only he could not throw it. He sat there with the unlit bottle in one hand and a lighter in the other until he heard the rickety wheels travel far into the distance. At once weak and defeated but finally able to stand, he was relieved that his lack of action had gone unnoticed by those around him.

Tómas headed home. Everyone in the family would be there. He walked by Isla de la Plata's only cliff overlooking the Pacific's great plain. His shirt stuck with sweat to his lean frame, the business end of a carbon-filtered cigarette crunched between his fingers in one hand and the bottle of sugarcane alcohol with its rag fuse coddled in the other. Twenty metres below, the sea splashed against convoluted rocks alive with cangrejos, crabs that climbed and receded with the waves of the outgoing tide. His mother Violet had come to this spot often before she left the island, and she must have contemplated her departure while sitting on these same rocks, thinking of leaving her newborn son behind with the gift only of a name. It was easier for her to leave,

Montgomery told Tómas, as Violet never once allowed herself to gaze into her baby's eyes. There was no chance for feelings of protection or maternal love to emerge. She could learn to forget his tiny hands, his facial contortions, and his minute arms stretching toward hers. But his eyes, Montgomery had always said, his eyes she could never forget. Nothing would burn itself into her memory like that.

Now he could see fishing boats returning to their ports, followed closely by an array of sea birds. The nets glimmered with picudo fish, the fishermen wearing the same hats that protected them from both sun and rain. The setting sun cast stretched shadows beneath a long line of clouds, where northern and southern air currents collided to flow inland and create the island's only seasons, wet and dry.

Tómas tossed his cigarette into the surf and pulled out his lighter. With a quick flick of finger on flint he ignited the white rag in the bottle's mouth, dropped it, and watched the sea of flame splash onto the rocks below. A strange sense of relief overcame him at the sight of fire, which extinguished promptly under the modulations of the sea.

Soon darkness would descend and the moon goddess Mamaquilla would appear, volleying herself among a thousand stars as she pondered why the Inca who once worshipped her had disappeared. As he continued home, he wondered whether he would be left alone, without his only known blood relative once again, and whether he would spend his nights considering why, if the accusations against his father were not true, Montgomery would have run away so quickly.

2. The Chinchila Lagoon

THE NEXT MORNING, Tómas walked beside his father along a wide expanse of barren beach. Montgomery's eyes shone a rich azure, a colour mimicking the sea around him as though the hue, continuously absorbed over decades of peering into the water's depths, now emanated from his gaze.

Montgomery was still active after 70 years of life, manual labour seeming more a requirement of good health than a burden. The strength of his sun-baked limbs fought his hunched stature with every step. He was still slender, his physical appearance the same as that of the island's farm workers, and Tómas never remembered him otherwise. But Montgomery was a traveller, a writer, an occasional farmer, with protruding ears trapped between the large, turned-up collar of his grey shirt and the wide brim of his sun-bleached Panama hat. His worn sandals revealed crooked toes at the end of long, leathery feet. Miniscule sand crabs scattered away as they walked, burrowing back to the safety of waterlogged homes.

"The newspaper accusations, they are chisme," Tómas said. "Worthless gossip."

"I'm glad someone thinks so," Montgomery replied, smiling. "But really, they're more important than you know." He spoke in English, in a faded British accent which Tómas had been told also permeated his own speech.

Tómas tried to comprehend the meaning of his father's words as he looked out over nearby fields, illuminated by the morning sun, fields that had occupied Montgomery's time between travel-writing assignments over the last 50 years.

"You remember," Montgomery continued. "We once worked those fields out there, together, until we were forced to stop. We collected bananas and plantains along with my greatest friend Eduardo Delgado, removing them from palm trees using blades tied to poles made of caña sugarcane shoots."

"I remember the heavy poles," Tómas replied. "And how heavy were the straw baskets to collect red coffee berries and yucca."

Tómas also remembered that Human Rights Watch had launched a campaign against the practice of employing youth for the harvest, and Montgomery had been forced to send the children home, Tómas included. But they never talked about that.

Looking around, Tómas saw that the same type of heavy caña poles, split down the centre, had been tied loosely together to form walls, and then placed between straw roofs and sand floors to produce the few distant residences within view. Both the building materials and the land beneath them were free of cost.

"You know, Tómas, this section of land from the cliff down to the area of the Chinchila Lagoon has been for sale for many years. It was the only land the government ever tried to sell on this island, and the most pristine plot of land here."

"I know. You told me before. But you said this chisme is important? For what?"

"Well. What you don't know is who bought the land."

Perhaps Tómas's father had acquired the funds to purchase the land. Maybe he was not as trustworthy as he would have his son and others believe. Conceivably, the allegations could be true.

"Not you?" Tómas asked.

Montgomery grinned. "No, not me. This land you and I once worked together is now desolate and unfarmable. The albarradas built here a few years ago by that international organization, they never worked. Instead of collecting rainwater runoff for the crops, they've back-flooded so all they collect now is seawater. And now this land is all Eduardo's, ready for the hotel he's always wanted to build on it."

Eduardo Delgado, Montgomery's friend of 50 years, had political aspirations beyond his current position as the island's mayor. And perhaps also a part of Eduardo's plans were this proposed hotel and this newly acquired land with its ancient and new albarradas: artificial u-shaped embankments capturing rainfall runoff to transform normally arid landscapes into tropical sanctuaries suitable for a wide variety of crops. Tómas had studied them for years by collecting soil samples and perusing aerial photographs.

They continued walking in silence, feet dragging through the sand. The last of the black smoke from protest fires was still visible on the horizon, most of the fires extinguished immediately following the morning announcement that the seat of interim presidency was occupied, the former president having fled the country with several of his cabinet ministers.

"I'm leaving soon," Montgomery said, the light of the sun displaying etchings of age on the corners of his face. "I'll be going to Quito."

Now that his father had declared his decision to retire, Tómas never expected they would be apart again. A lifetime of separation was finally over and their relationship was supposed to begin anew. He had overheard Montgomery telling Veronica that he would help look after Tómas now. 'Tómas is 18,' Veronica had replied. 'He can take care for himself.' Her words were spoken mockingly, in observance of the fact that everyone except Montgomery realized that this resolution had come too late.

"*Your travelling will be left to the printed page,*" Tómas continued. "You said that. And now, with the newspaper article about you, the people, they will think—"

"Damn what people think," Montgomery interrupted, suddenly angry. "You know, you worry too much about that. And that's no way to speak to your father. If I ever spoke to my father like that, he would've clubbed me so hard I wouldn't have been able to talk for a week. Respect ... that's what you lack ... and discipline. You need the opportunity to take new chances instead of hiding in the house with Veronica, afraid to face life. The army—even though I oppose this war and you'll need to find a way to complete your military service without being sent to fight at the border—it'll be good for you."

Montgomery paused for a while, looking out over the land. Tómas's cheeks warmed as his eyes surveyed the beach. He had not challenged his father before, and had only seen this same anger directed at Veronica. Until now, he had always avoided being targeted himself. And he wanted to retract his statements, if only he could.

"But it's true," Montgomery continued after a moment, calmer now, picking at his teeth. "This will be my last trip."

They started walking together toward a pathway leading home.

"You know, I always thought when Eduardo would talk about it, that building a hotel here was a selfish and shallow ambition." Montgomery turned to Tómas. "You know, the one-time farm worker who dreams of wealth and its consequence. Until I found out what it was."

"What?" Tómas asked quietly, almost inaudibly.

"Well, he has a vision to build a hotel unlike any other. A hotel that will bring tourists. And that is the only vista on the island that will work."

Montgomery pointed to the cliff in the distance as they continued toward the pathway. He stopped abruptly before a thicket, turning to walk toward a sparkling lagoon a hundred metres away. Tómas, eager to avoid another confrontation with his father, followed closely behind without speaking.

The sound of birds in the trees grew louder with every step. The noise of a hundred Tijeras, huge birds with red tails like open scissors, emanated from a tree resembling an open sun umbrella. A sign in a thicket beneath the tree read: 'protected area.'

"Part of Eduardo's land is here," he said loudly once they reached the pool of water. He stomped one foot on the damp earth. "Here, on the Chinchila lagoon. Shamans once considered these waters to be magical, using them to cure sicknesses of the body and maladies of the spirit. The sick would arrive to ask favours of the lagoon and the shaman would offer the mystical waters gifts of scented oils, flowers and coins. Then the shaman would use tobacco, alcohol and special amulets as cures. I once wrote an article about this. All of it is interesting, all of it sold magazines and newspapers, but all of it is nonsense."

Montgomery coughed, and he suddenly appeared very frail in the stark sunlight.

"Why Quito?" Tómas asked softly.

Montgomery began to walk away as he replied.

"I have a presentation to attend there, for an honorary degree. I'll go to my office first to collect my files, and then I'll close the place for good. Then I'll go to see an old friend. Yup," he said, grimacing. "Tomorrow I leave on the ferry."

Montgomery continued toward the thickets and the birds. He was heading home.

Tómas could insist on travelling with him this time, only his persistence would likely invoke his father's anger again. Too bad he couldn't ask the mystical waters of the lagoon what he should do. But perhaps he could.

Montgomery ambled slowly away and stopped to look at the top of the cliff. He often told Tómas his itinerary, when he would leave and when he would return, and he did not give more than a cursory explanation of what he would be doing while away. But to Tómas that didn't matter anyway. He only cared that his father would not be here.

Tómas reached down to pick the head from a pale wildflower, white and in mid-bloom, its fragrance sweet, the petals wilted from the wet salt air. The flower smelled like the sand, like the sea, like the smell that permeated the streets of the island. The lagoon shimmered in the morning light as he bent over and set the flower onto its waters in his own personal shamanistic ritual. The crumpled petals floated away quickly into the sea, to the west, toward the mainland.

"I will go with you," Tómas shouted.

"You've never accompanied me before," Montgomery replied, turning back and wincing in the light of the sun. "And you've been called for military service. The hotel, too, you'll become important to its construction. You must finish your schooling. There's a great deal of work to be done, and going to Quito is not among your tasks."

"For how long will you be gone?" Tómas asked.

His father looked out toward the sea without answering. Tómas caught up to him and stopped several metres away. Confronting his father was becoming easier now.

"You were a war correspondent," Tómas said.

"Many years ago, yes."

"You have seen war up close. And yet, you ask me to go to this border war? For certain I will be killed, for reasons against mine and the country's interests."

Montgomery shook his head. "No, no. I told you I oppose this war, but you'll need to complete your military service. And besides, you're mistaken, and paranoid ... there's no fighting any more, only isolated skirmishes. The war's been going on for so long without end. You'll serve your year, and be done with it ... and what would you do, run away as I did? Trust me when I say you'd regret that." He paused, coughing into a handkerchief before continuing. "No, you'll do well in the army. It'll give you the direction you sorely need."

"You know there is fighting. You see that in the papers as I do. You only want reasons to stay away from me. You always have reasons."

Without responding, giving only a glancing look, Montgomery crept through the sun-scorched underbrush, walking past the tree with its Tijeras above and below, carefully sidestepping small mud puddles. In his wide-brimmed hat and with his crooked walk, it was as though he was in pain, an injured rice farmer carefully avoiding marked landmines left over from a war long forgotten.

Only after watching the ferry diminish into the sea the next morning did Tómas have the strange sensation that he might never see his father again. There were so many questions he had wanted to ask but had not: about the circumstances surrounding these accusations of embezzlement, how he could help to prove his father's innocence, and more detailed information about his mother. All of these were inquiries that no one else on the island could answer, and some of which he had never even contemplated until now.

3. An Honorary Degree

MONTGOMERY HARVEY SAT near the stern of the ferry Santo Domingo as it carted passengers from the island to mainland Ecuador, the strong smell of diesel fuel lingering despite the wind. The vibrations of the vessel resonated through his seat, the engine growling and stifling the noise of screaming toddlers, windblown children running through the aisles, and those somehow conversing. These families would all be meeting with relatives, he thought, trekking to the Andes or venturing to the beach in the cab section of pickup trucks filled beyond capacity. They would take a trip to the mitad del mundo, one of the world's only monuments to the equator, or swim in the cool ocean waters and eat fish and shrimp ceviche. They would bask in the glory of nature and family.

Montgomery had left his family forever. His departure had been sullen, as though everyone knew this would be their last sighting of him. And even though only minutes had passed since he had gone, he already perceived in himself a sharp, stinging sensation that made him want to return on the next ferry back to the island. But he could not. He would clean out his office and then receive his honorary degree from the University of Quito before telling Eduardo that he would be leaving the country. This is what he had resolved to do. He would then hide away in the vastness of the capital city before seeking political asylum in Peru, where he would die, his name no longer printed in the newspapers and magazines as it had been nearly all of his life. After news of the accusations against him was no longer news, there would be a few articles written sporadically about him. Some might postulate theories of his sudden disappearance. Others might discuss his asylum, some calling it political, others dismissing such claims as unsubstantiated rumour. Gossip. Chisme. And by leaving now, he would avoid an investigation into the allegations against him. His name and his memory would simply fade away.

Wiping the sweat from his forehead, he turned back to envision the opulent hotel that would be built on the island's westernmost point. The hotel's shiny white umbrellas would line the beach, and the cliff and its extension of large rocks would sit below the magnificent façade of floor-to-ceiling windows and oversized chairs illuminated with lavish chandeliers. To the east was San Cristobal, where his family lived, the island's only population apart from the countryside area of Monte Cristo; what islanders referred to as the campo. The island had not changed for a hundred years with few exceptions, among them the unreliable phone system and the diesel generator that was now connected to a small electrical distribution system on the island. The hexagonal spires of San Cristobal's only church were still there as they had been a century ago, scrubbed clean by the constant rains of the wet season and looking oddly luminous in the morning sun.

Over the line of sight of the campo was a small, snow-capped volcano, Mount Pichincha, looming over the skyline. The last steam eruption, five years ago, had made headlines in the newspapers as two volcanologists, who were on the summit at the time of the eruption, had disappeared. Although no magma had escaped from its mouth since the time of the Conquistadors, when Pichincha had waged the only defence against what was happening in its home, the islanders nevertheless said that the entire island was doomed for disaster, and that the recent deaths on the volcano should be enough warning to convince any detractors. As he gazed towards Pichincha, he thought he saw a trace of smoke escaping its peak. Smoke? Or cloud, or his aging eyes playing tricks?

The ferry docked nearly an hour after departure near the barren city of Guayaquil, families reuniting and heading off together beneath a sea of wailing sea birds. Montgomery searched through his pockets to produce a note he had written to Tómas, which he had originally intended to leave for him as a sort of final goodbye.

You think you're old enough to take care of yourself. But you need a family. I've left you with the only family I could ever give you, in the past, and now. I want you to finish your degree and complete your military term. I want you to help Eduardo build the hotel, our island's future. These are my wishes. I don't want you to look for me, or to be concerned with where I am, or why I left. Just know that I've left as a result of a chain of events that I myself, and no one else, initiated.

Even now, reading through the contents of the wrinkled page again, his words seemed too resolute, too final. The letter almost dared Tómas to search for him, and to seek out answers only he possessed. But still, he should have left this message behind, if only to reinforce his desires.

Before he could change his mind he sealed the envelope, wrote Tómas's name on the outside, and made the ferry driver promise he would deliver the note to Tómas upon returning to the island.

An hour later, Montgomery boarded the bus for Quito, which ascended along winding mountain roadways rich with vegetation. The rusty green bus took them over cliffs that seemed to slide into verdant valleys, the bottoms of which became increasingly distant, until the bus finally arrived at its destination in the cradle of the Andes sitting at an elevation of three kilometres above the sea. He felt the familiar tingling in his fingers and toes caused by the lack of oxygen at this altitude and tried not to think of its obvious association with a stroke.

He ambled slowly down Avenida Universitaria, past restaurants with clanging dishes and bars proclaiming their presence with loud salsa music, past hostels swarming with foreigners examining oversized maps. All of these voluntary exiles lined the streets with their Tilley hats, guidebooks, backpacks and language tapes. The passing years had changed the city, and it was better this way. The tourists' love of adventure, of a gateway to other lands even more exotic, had brought them to the heart of Quito, to Gringolandia, land of the Gringo foreigners. And the city sector was alive with their influence, welcoming these unknown societies and traditions, letting the solitary wander about its avenues in a veritable sea of anonymity.

Tómas had once told him that Quito sounded as though it catered so much to other cultures that the locals were overwhelmed. Tómas did not want to visit this city; so it seemed strange that, on the beach, he had asked to come. Perhaps he had intuited that his father would never return, and he wanted to ensure that the trip was a vacation and not a life decision. From walking around, it was obvious that the island would become much like this place. Tourists by the boatloads bypassed the island each June in search of the humpback whales that spawned and entertained before returning a month later to the icy waters of the Antarctic. Instead of staying on the mainland, the whale enthusiasts could remain on the island once the hotel was built and replace the island's only current tourists, Mormons dressed in dark suits and bowties who spent the day carrying ice cream cones that no other adults ate and talking to people who didn't care to listen. The island could one day be infused with this same barrage of street vendors selling knitted caps, sweaters, necklaces and umbrellas, the same buffet-style dinners, coffee shops bustling with readers silently sipping frothy drinks to the music of Schubert and Brahms, pool halls, nightclubs, and wooden carts on street corners pedalling unripe mangoes sliced, bagged, salted and peppered and ready to eat. The island had avoided change and remained in isolation far too long and everyone, including Tómas, would have to accept that.

Montgomery passed by a frail toothless woman sitting on the pavement, her dirty kneecaps buried in her chest, a thin blanket beneath her. She sent a tiny child about three years old, perhaps her granddaughter, toward him. The girl was dressed in rags, and she kept pace beside him with an outstretched hand. She spoke in the slow vernacular of the Sierra region. "I have hunger," she said in Spanish, repeating it as she pointed to her open mouth. Stopping and turning toward her, he reached into his pocket and gave her a fifty thousand Sucre note. The girl quickly ran back to the woman, who snatched the prize, equivalent to ten American dollars. Staring back with a startled expression and then examining the money, the woman sent the girl away for more. The girl eagerly repeated the same plea to Montgomery, who donated again, and then to another foreigner, a man who passed by pretending not to notice her.

Later that day at his hotel room, he wrote and mailed one last article, about that girl, for publication in Diario Hoy. He wrote that he wished to bring that child back to Isla de la Plata, to see her beside trees teeming with enormous Tijeras birds, their black tails opening up in scissor formation of black and red above her, and to watch her toes being licked by salt water tongues lapping to shore. He wanted to watch her reaction to the pescadore fishermen pulling shrimp larvae out of the ocean with fishing pole antennae protruding from the sand. But he knew that this girl would only be content running through crowds to satisfy her grandmother's covetousness. She would dream of that toothless smile, and of the only home she had ever known.

Montgomery sat on the bus to his mainland office. Everyone was staring at him. They once stared at his red hair and mocked him for his height and freckled spots, evidence of sun exposure on alabaster skin that also distinguished Tómas from every other islander. Montgomery's red hair had now turned to white, his freckled spots having become a speckled and splotchy mess, and the people's gazes, once simple curiosity at those characteristics they had never seen, were now mistrustful and apprehensive.

The bus passed between office buildings, malls and banks, spaces between the structures periodically revealing distant Andean peaks covered in lush green forest: a snapshot of serene, untouched wilderness amidst crowds navigating through a concrete jungle.

The building housing Montgomery's office was ten stories tall, in the desolate perimeter of Quito, the concrete building arbitrarily placed among dimly lit dwellings and litter-strewn alleyways. Children chased dogs and each other through the moonless night time streets. A group of women discussed where their husbands said they were, and where they actually believed they had gone.

The hallway was engulfed in blackness and he felt his way down the hall to his office door, accustomed to patting the unpainted wooden surface to locate the door lock. The door had been left open.

Flipping the light switch did nothing, and so he set a match to the candle he left on the shelf for when the power went down. The dim illumination revealed his usually meticulous office with file folders on the desk, scattered apart. His written reminiscences and photographs taken in the foothills of Italy, on the Swiss Alps, in front of a monastery in China, in the middle of a square in Germany where books were once burned, beside bubbling pools of mud in New Zealand, near a castle in Spain, and during a royal wedding in Oslo were all here, strewn haphazardly together. His desk drawers were empty. His life's work had been violated at the hands of an unknown prowler.

Surveying quickly, he estimated that most of the contents of the room, as he remembered them, were still here. All, that is, except for his most important file that had been left in a locked file cabinet. It had to be here, and yet it was not. He checked back again and again as he swept through the rest of the room, his eyes darting everywhere, lighting and re-lighting the candle until he finally picked up his chair and sat down, exhausted, the candle sputtering out again. All of his files and photographs, most of which had been published through the years, the originals of which were of no interest to anyone but him, had been callously ransacked.

Striking another match, he saw that his calendar with meetings, travel dates and appointments marked in red ink had been removed from the wall and was now on his desk. His tattered, leather-bound journal was on the dusty floor, and he knew that whoever had rummaged through this place would have as easily thrown his years of memories in the garbage as tossed them on the floor.

This thought made him want to comb the streets looking for the perpetrator, to find out who had taken the yellow file folder. Picking up his journal, he placed the carefully preserved old volume on the desk so he would not forget it.

Swivelling the chair around revealed four pictures, neatly pinned to corkboard on the wall. They were untouched and he was grateful for that, and for any distraction from thoughts of yellow file folders. These were among the best travel photographs he had ever taken. Each of the images was captured by way of an elaborate set of rods and wires, of his own design, that extended out from nylon straps crossing his chest and housed a camera that was placed and activated from an assortment of different locations. Using this apparatus allowed him to photograph himself at various distances and angles. Two of the photographs he had always admired for their aesthetics. In one, he was parasailing off the Argentinean coast, the rainbow colours of the full sail reproduced in vivid colour and gleaming in the scorching afternoon sun. Another was a deep blue depiction of himself scuba diving off the coast of Cozumel among parrotfish and giant crabs hiding in coral reefs. The other two he acknowledged as his most beloved, but more for the bravery they invoked in him, a conquering of the fear of his feet being anywhere other than firmly planted on the ground, than for the pictures themselves. One showed him rock climbing high in the Austrian Alps, proudly displaying his carabineer and crampon for the camera. Another light blue photo showed him skydiving, plummeting toward a French drop zone at 125 kilometres per hour, thinking that any one of the hundreds of plane flights he had taken in his lifetime could have accidentally ended with him barrelling toward the earth this way, looking at his watch, holding firmly on to his ripcord that he wouldn't have had if his fall had been from a commercial airliner and, as he recalled now, praying aloud.

The candle went out with a draft, and he lit another match. He carefully removed the photographs from the corkboard, placing them on the desk.

On the corner of his desk, atop a pile of mail, was an engraved invitation to receive his honorary degree tomorrow, as well as the announcement of a press forum for Eduardo Andre Briones Delgado, in Quito, in two days. He took both documents, along with the photographs, and left the room.

After driving through the streets of Quito in the back of a taxicab for a time, Montgomery realized this search for the person carrying his yellow folder was in vain. He would have to inform Eduardo at the press forum that his original mayoral financial records, the ones retained in Montgomery's office for safekeeping, the records that really should have been destroyed, were now nowhere to be found.

Montgomery walked through Old Quito, towards the university campus. He had accepted this honorary degree—unlike some philosophers and playwrights such as Sartre and Shaw—not as a service to others after him who might actually aspire to obtain such an honour, but because it provided him with a sense of closure to a lifetime dedicated to photojournalism.

He had written about this place before, the part of the city that reminded him of Paris and Amsterdam with its narrow cobblestone streets and its unique architectural artefacts. The houses here were crowded together indistinguishably and built on steep roadways that only saw pedestrian traffic. Here, he felt as though he were visiting all three cities, Old Quito, Paris and Amsterdam, simultaneously, as if he could defy the banalities of space and time by walking past the gothic churches of Old Quito to the Louvre as a medieval fortress, sauntering down the Champs-Elysées to see Hitler and Mussolini parading in victory, and over to the Latin Quarter to visit student ghosts stuck there for seven hundred years. He found himself at the inauguration of the Van Gogh museum and walked down to an assembly of Technicolor coffeehouses full of pungent smoke.

The university courtyard where he was to receive his degree was sparsely occupied, and surrounded by a wire fence. As he walked through an opening in the fence, a thin man in a grey collared shirt standing behind a podium, before a dozen empty folding chairs, suddenly cleared his throat. The man placed his hands on the podium, and those few students who were loitering about quickly sat down.

After Montgomery sat in the front row, the man introduced himself as an Adjunct Sociology Professor at the University of Quito. Reading from a typewritten page, the professor elucidated in a slow drawl the beginnings of a 50-year career that started with Montgomery's Uncle, Devon Harvey, who trained Montgomery as a war correspondent in the Spanish Civil War. Devon and Montgomery were imprisoned by Spanish fascists, Montgomery moving to Ecuador after being released and returning to Europe at various times throughout the Second World War to document and photograph its battles, and later, those of African nations.

"This honorary degree in Journalism and Photography, Photojournalism, represents a lifetime of achievement in two fields of art," he said. "In his early war writings, Montgomery Lionel Harvey shows what unites the people of all nations. Not only a lust for personal gain, the root of all immorality, but love and duty, the root of all selflessness."

As he continued, Montgomery was reminded of a recent conversation with Tómas. Tómas had said he didn't know what love was, any more than he knew what it meant to have faith. The two were identical, Montgomery had replied.

The professor outlined how Montgomery's earliest photographs were taken without concern for personal risk. He referred to the most famous of the repeatedly-published pictures, obtained after parachuting over the beaches of Normandy with Allied paratroopers. A young French woman at the beach's edge stood in front of an array of floating Allied helmets; Canadian and American troops in the foreground helped the wounded ashore. The article accompanying the picture presumed she was challenging the belief that it was a victory. The Regina and Royal Winnipeg Rifles of the seventh Canadian Brigade had broken through German defences at the cost of a thousand lives: a thousand helmets floating to shore, parting sand, or landing on green grass. And this was only a tiny section of the coast stretching from Havre to Cherbourg.

"The woman's eyes," the professor said, pausing to look into the eyes of the crowd for the first time since he had started speaking, "they showed a lack of understanding of what it meant to possess such a great sense of honour and duty."

Montgomery stood on an overcrowded bus, grasping a metal railing to maintain an unsteady balance on the way back to his hotel. He hadn't thought of his mother and two brothers in England for countless years. They had lived together in London before the Second World War, and he had left them to travel to Spain with his Uncle Devon. Devon's final act, before dying of typhoid, was to secure a visa for Montgomery to a South American country. It was the only way out of the Spanish prison camp and from conscription back home.

Montgomery had left his family in England and run away, the only way he knew how, returning to Europe as a war correspondent whenever he needed money. He did not return to his London home until after the war.

On his first trip back, he had wandered the streets of London, streets he did not recognize because of buildings that were no longer there. He came across his old neighbourhood and located where his house once stood, at 21 Grove Street in Whitechapel. All that was left was a collection of rubble. The war office records clearly indicated what had happened to his mother and two brothers. Their names were listed in a war office logbook under "casualties."

Gone from his dreams were the memories he had of them—their wonderful summers at his Uncle Devon's cottage in Northaw, the look on their faces when he told them he was leaving for Spain just as his father had left to work in the mines of South Leeds, never having returned. He had forgotten about his mother and two brothers and discarded them from his memory, the same as his father had.

Perhaps he lacked an understanding of what it meant to possess a sense of honour and duty. He had abandoned his family and his British homeland when they needed him most. Now he had left Tómas, Veronica and her mother Flory, his Ecuadorian family, and the land he had called his home for so long to live out the last days of his life in Peru. They did not know that his departure was permanent. His actions were disgraceful, those of a pitiful coward who had forgotten how much he regretted leaving England so many decades ago and how horrified he had been at the sight of his British family's names in the war office listings. And yet he wanted his son to stay and join the army, and pay for his own acts of commission.

He again contemplated returning to the island, his resolution more forceful in his mind. But the accusations against him, and the file that had been stolen from his office, were enough to keep him away.

The honorary degree, in an envelope under his arm, suddenly sickened him. And so he disposed of it in the trash as he stepped off the bus.

4. Dream-like State of the Present

TÓMAS WALKED DOWN the dusty Avenida Che Guevara in the early afternoon, his back soaked with sweat. After passing by the Place San Cristobal and the gated walls of the university, he arrived at the office of the island newspaper Diario Hoy.

As he approached the nondescript brown building his heart beat rapidly at the thought of confrontation with Juan Carlos. Montgomery had told Tómas, long ago, that both of his grandfathers had suffered from heart troubles and that he would consequently have difficulties, too. Tómas found comfort in knowing that this is how he would likely die, as though knowing a facet of one's own death is preferable to knowing nothing at all. Now, recalling his father's words, he knew he would simply have to calm down, the anticipated tone of his speech having to change from spastic to a firm and menacing calm.

Last night during a period of sleeplessness, his heart beating the same as now, he realized that a door had been opened without hint of when it would close. When Montgomery told Tómas the exact day of his return, he was rarely late. The itinerary given was to revive him from the weeks and months of melancholy that followed each of his father's departures. While an absence of six months in Italy or Spain, or a year in Africa, China or Indonesia might be imminent, he would have the exact day of his father's homecoming to mark on his calendar. And now, even

Veronica did not seem to know. Juan Carlos, however, who had written the article about his father, and who had been frequently with Montgomery just before his departure, must have some answers.

After passing through the front doors, his breathing now slowing, Tómas saw Inés: a young brunette señorita with dark freckles and thick, shining lips who was always hungry for conversation and laughter, mostly her own. Rising from the desk to kiss him on both cheeks, she revealed a tight-fitting red dress with straps falling down over her thin shoulders. She smiled and replaced the straps as Tómas asked to see Juan Carlos.

"Now, we practice my English," Inés said. "I saw Veronica at the market, yesterday. I read about your father. I am sorry for him, and for you. Do you have a novia, a girlfriend, yet?"

"No."

"My novio, my boyfriend, he is a mujeriego, a womanizer, and no good for me."

"At this moment, he is fortunate to be with you."

Inés frowned. An elderly man eyed her from the corner of the room, and she excused herself, speaking rapidly in Spanish now, citing a looming deadline and a nasty editor with a disagreeable wife.

She made a quick phone call and returned to her electric typewriter, directing Tómas to the adjacent waiting area littered with newspapers. Inés's long nails clattered on the keys, the sound accompanied by hushed conversations that echoed throughout the office. Newspapers were stacked to waist height on the floor and piled on tables and chairs. The scent of ink and paper was in the air. Grabbing a newspaper from the stack, he sat down and looked over the front page. His father's name was all over the cover. Tómas began to feel his heart rate increasing until he saw that these were reprints of articles Montgomery had written, and not news stories about him.

Tómas read through his father's article on Russia, one that he had read many times before. The overall impression he was left with was that this was different from his father's other articles, and somehow different from the last time he had read this particular article, in that so much of his father's life was written into it; as if someone, eager to tarnish Montgomery's image further in the eyes of the islanders, had rewritten the original document. Perhaps Juan Carlos was to blame, but toward what end, Tómas didn't know.

Another piece in the corner of the front page had his father's name attached to it, an article about a pandering girl and her toothless grandmother. Tómas reasoned this was written out of remorse for having left his only son behind on his travels over the years, Montgomery declaring how he wished to see his son wading over foreign lands with him and reacting to places he had only read about. Maybe this article was his father's clandestine explanation of the reason why he had always left his son behind: because Tómas, who knew nothing of life away from his island home, would only be eager to go back. He would dream of returning to the only place he had ever known.

The phone rang. "Juan Carlos, he will be here shortly," Inés said in Spanish, putting the phone down, and returning to her typewriter clattering.

Tómas sat on one of the stacks and found the newspaper article indicating that he was being conscripted into the Ecuadorian-Peruvian border war. The letter in his pocket stated that he was required to report to the base in the Ecuadorian mainland city of Guayaquil within thirty days.

He reread through the article accusing his father of embezzlement, the news piece explaining that Montgomery Harvey had arrived in Ecuador from his native England during, and not after, the Second World War. The piece written by Juan Carlos, a man Tómas had always considered until now to be his closest friend, was intended to disparage Montgomery's character and to show that if he was capable of running away from his country when he was of age for active service, in a time of war, then perhaps these accusations of embezzlement of millions of American dollars from a government investment account were true. Other people had told him over the years, but Tómas had never listened, until now: Juan Carlos was not to be trusted.

Looking up, his heart began to pulse rapidly as he saw Juan Carlos, whose forehead dripped sweat beneath a pile of matted, neatly trimmed hair. Juan was stout, dressed in tight jeans and an oversized crimson shirt, and his face looked punched flat by an invisible hand.

"Compadré," Juan Carlos said with an elongated smile, leaning over and embracing Tómas, who stood up and dropped the newspaper onto one of the piles.

"Take it," Juan Carlos said in Spanish, releasing his grip and handing the paper to Tómas. "I wrote an article about the border war, in this edition. Some Peruvians ... they must have been Peruvians ... they destroyed our hotel room while we were staying near the border. They broke our equipment, and robbed my notes and tape recordings. But still, I finished the article. At the end, even though I never saw them, I still wanted to find them and break their heads."

"You disrespected my father," Tómas said in English, standing up and feeling his heart racing as he extended a finger in Juan Carlos's direction. "You, my *friend*, you called him a coward and a thief."

"I do not know what you heard, but—"

"You are a seller of lies. A gossipmonger capable, with your typewriter, of reaching too many ears. You need to recant that article, and also the Russian article you just printed and added more gossip to."

Juan Carlos wiped the sweat from his forehead with the back of his hand. "You are drunk?" he asked, speaking in English now as he examined Tómas's face.

"No."

"Then I do not know why all this anger? People here, they do not have good feelings about your father, for the same reason they do not have good feelings about me. He left his wife and son behind for years so he could write articles that, to be true, not many people here read."

"Not true."

"They are more agreeable to him on the mainland. I do not think they would offer him an honorary degree here on the island. I am so sorry to say this. I am sorry I had to report the story the way I did—and I tell you, I added no gossip."

"How do I know?"

Juan Carlos wiped his forehead again with a rag he produced from his pocket, and then he dabbed his neck.

"Maybe you think I was not right, reporting the story of your father. Maybe you think it was cruel. And maybe some of it was. But I tell you this: I am a reporter for this small newspaper with a ... how do you say in English ... circulatory? A circulatory of one hundred on an island with two thousand people. I must to write what I know is the truth, no matter if it hurts; and sometimes, I know it hurts. Your attack on me is proof."

"All truth as you see it?"

"As others see it too. Listen to me; we should not be fighting as we are now. We are friends, you and I. Good friends. The best of friends."

"We *were* friends. And you cannot say to the world what you think is right, when everyone knows it is wrong. I sent letters to the editors of the island and the mainland newspapers. I was telling them that the article is not true. I disrespect you, the same as you do my father."

"Why?" Juan Carlos looked intently at Tómas for a moment, his eyes squinting as though trying to discern something. Sweat was forming on his forehead.

No answer came, and after a few moments, Juan Carlos continued.

"You are angry with me. I am sorry for that. But let us talk of other things. And in Spanish, por favor." He began speaking more rapidly in his native tongue. "I saw your name on the list. You will have to report for military duty soon, and you will be sent to the border."

Tómas sat down, clutching the newspaper in his hands. "I know."

"I will help you. I will tell you about that place. There, at the border, there are too many land mines to count. Soldiers return with no hands and feet, or they return dead, just for stepping out of camps to urinate or to follow marching orders. I tell you because I know. I was there. This happened to many of my close friends."

"Really?"

"So you must say you do some sort of work for the government, and make an exemption claim on that basis. You can say you are against the war instead, or that you cannot kill. If that does not work, say it is against your religion. If they do not like that, say you have no religion. Then, see what they say. Eventually, they will have to give you a conscientious objector card."

Juan Carlos sat down on top of a pile of newspapers, which shifted slightly under his weight.

"I cannot imagine killing some Peruvian soldier, recruited like me, only to defend land," Tómas said. "All for the cause of some uranium and oil. But still, I know my father regretted not serving his country—"

"You should not feel such a need to go. I will tell you what I know about conscientious objection. You know, if I was ever drafted, that is what I would apply for. Immediately. I would not waste a minute. Look at your time. You have only one month? Time is short. You have heard of Alejandro Pédro Juarez Jiminez?"

Tómas paused for a moment, listening to Inés's clicking typewriter that stopped, giving complete silence, before starting up again.

"He was a conscientious objector," Tómas said.

"Yes," Juan Carlos said, fluttering his shirt to induce a cooling wind.

"He has been fighting in the courts for many years. I read about him. Without his military certificate or conscientious objector card, he could not leave the country, or work, or go to school."

"I was his lawyer," Juan Carlos said, shaking his head. "I could not help him. I wrote an article on a housing plan that did not show Eduardo and his friend, the President, in a positive way. The judge was a supporter of the President, end of the story, and end of my practice as a lawyer."

"Just because of that?"

Juan Carlos shifted his weight on the newspapers.

"There were other things involved," he stammered nervously. "Things I will not talk about. Things that were not in my control."

"What things?"

Juan Carlos paused and then began speaking calmly a minute later. "Like the military not responding to my filings," he said, "even when they were ordered to do that, many times, by the courts."

"Why?"

Juan Carlos smiled. "You too should be a reporter," he said. He waved his hands expressively as he continued. "The military never said anything, except for their official words that the only people exempted from military service are those men with jobs who support their families, or ... married people, students of the church, or the police ... those who cannot physically do the job, those with problems in the head, or what else?" He rubbed a finger on his chin. "I am missing something ..."

Juan Carlos blinked quickly, his eyes surveying the room again before his gaze attached to the secretary, who was walking by with some files, her rounded, slender form silhouetted against the dirt-brown walls.

"Ah, ya ..." he said, looking back at Tómas. "There are Ecuadorians living outside the country, too. So the only way to claim this exemption, if you are living in Ecuador when you are drafted, is to escape the country somehow. Then, you can say you do not live here."

Someone dropped a glass, which shattered loudly. There was a smattering of applause, and some stifled laughter. The newspaper stack Juan Carlos was sitting on shifted slightly, and he moved to prevent the weight of the pile from falling over.

"I provided statistics in the court," he continued, "such as only sixty percent of those called up report for duty. Of the sixty percent, only forty percent perform military service. The other twenty percent are exempted, many for reasons different from those I have just said. But the judge, he would not listen to me."

"Because he supported the President, and you did not."

"Well, you know, it is like some of our card games. They go by different names. They are all the same. They always seem so very complicated. The rules of the game change depending on whom you play with."

Tómas nodded his head. "Exactly," he said. There were obscure rules, depending upon who among their group of friends—Raphael, Alfonso, Rodolfo, Hector, Johnny, Willy and Julio—they played cards with.

"*There is a rule where you cannot put down eights or spades after the next deal, if the person on the right took cards last round,*" Tómas said. "Or *there is a maximum three times you can take cards in a round; other times cards go to the dealer.*"

"Exactly. No one knows all the rules. They are always different, and you do not learn them until you are in the middle of the game. We play such games at parties all the time. Making up obscure rules is most of the fun, and it makes me wonder how much the military enjoys changing the rules to suit themselves."

"I heard that paying a 'Compensation Quota' can get you out of conscription."

"Yes. But it's very expensive. And those who have been conscripted, such as you, cannot do this. Such rules often come with much complicated explanations to justify, because they do not apply to anyone with connections in the government or the military. Then, they do not have enough people for military service and then, do you know what they do?"

"No," Tómas said.

"They drive pickup trucks around, taking anyone who looks suitable to fight."

"But that happens in Colombia, more than here, supposedly."

"True," Juan Carlos said, his forehead shimmering now from the light of a nearby window. "But still, it happens."

"This is too complicated," Tómas said, pausing. Then, an unexpected thought occurred to him. "You would have, as a client, someone who was once your friend?" he asked.

Juan Carlos stared over at the secretary as she walked down the hallway, her dress sandwiched tight to her body, the straps falling off at the shoulders again.

"As I have told you, we are still friends. Best of friends. And I have many times thought about beginning the case again." His eyes returned to Tómas. "... starting over another time, with what I know now. Because I must tell you ... being a reporter is interesting for many reasons, but being a lawyer ... standing before the judge and the people, making laws of the country instead of writing articles and hoping that will make a difference ... that is when I feel truly alive."

"There are many things similar between being a reporter and being a lawyer."

"No, I do not know what you mean," he said, shaking his head. "But to begin the case again ... that would depend on my client ... Alejandro Juarez Jiminez acted against me in many ways, writing letters I did not agree with, making claims to the Pichincha court that I did not support. Why, you know, he even wrote a letter to the Director of Mobilisation of the Armed Forces demanding a Conscientious Objector card immediately, so he could leave the country for some conference in Brazil ..." He paused and smiled, before adding: "You, however, are not so much with the head of a pig. And you are my best of friends. If I would be representing you, I would have to consider it ..." He leaned over and patted Tómas on the back.

The pile of newspapers Juan Carlos was sitting on suddenly slid out from beneath him. He fell to the floor, remaining motionless for a moment before rising up and gathering the papers with a laugh. Tómas, bending down to help, abruptly remembered one of the reasons why he was there.

"My father was going to his office in Quito," Tómas said, straightening a new mound of newspapers between them. "To receive an honorary degree there. He said that he would see a friend."

"Yes," Juan Carlos said, pushing some papers into a corner. "And so?"

"I think he may not come back."

Juan Carlos stopped and looked over at Tómas, asking: "Why?"

"I never asked to go with him, to be a fisherman's son, until the time before he left."

"A fisherman's son? Of what are you talking?"

"Travel writing was the only way he knew to earn money. But there were other ways. I saw a fisherman's son come to class with a smell of fish, after a morning on a boat with his father. I wondered why my father could not be a fisherman, too. But I never asked to travel with him, to be a fisherman's son, until I saw him the final time."

"And?"

"And he would not let me go with him. He did not say when he would be back. He always told me, every other time I can remember ... and, did he tell you?"

Juan Carlos rose as Tómas stacked the last of the papers into tidy piles.

"No," Juan Carlos said, swiping the dust from his knees and pants. "Why would he tell me?"

"I saw you together, many times, lately. Before he left, you went on his morning walks on the beach. I saw you at the market with him. I thought maybe you were friends, until I read the article calling him a thief. I thought maybe he told you more than he told me."

"I accused him of nothing other than what he did."

"You are convinced he is guilty?"

"I am. And he told me nothing more, other than what was printed in that article. And I saw Eduardo around your father many times too, just before he left."

"You think he might know something?"

"Eduardo is on the mainland."

"How do you know?"

Juan Carlos smiled before continuing. "I am assigned by my editor to go to a press forum in Quito tomorrow, at the Santa Rita de Cascia. You can ask Eduardo yourself. I want to talk with him, too; I have a friend, a fisherman. You know Raphael."

Tómas stood up and brushed the dust from his pants. "For certain."

"He has a boat. He was going to take me only, but now he will take us both to Guayaquil. We will take the bus to Quito."

"I have not left this island," Tómas said. "Not once."

"I know, but you have read your father's articles."

"Some, yes."

"Then really, you have some travel experience," he said, smiling. "Tomorrow, we will leave. It is time you learn to experience a different place for yourself, apart from your father's imagination. To be a fisherman's son."

The next morning Juan Carlos and Tómas sat on Raphael's boat on the beach, with four logs beneath them. Raphael's lean upper body, shaded partially by his broad hat, pushed the boat over the tree trunks and worked quickly to take them from the back of the boat and place them under the front, beneath the hull, as he rolled the boat out over the beach and toward the water on its bed of uneven wheels.

The vessel hit the water and began floating, the wood bouncing on the waves beside them. Raphael waded into the water up to his waist and grabbed the logs, one by one, rolling them back to their original location beneath a wooden hut at the edge of the beach.

As they sat in the boat waiting, Tómas contemplated that he would have to object to fight against mandatory military service; if only he had the compulsion, the persistence, and the recklessness to reject any deliberations of what other people might think, what the islanders might talk about in the privacy of their homes. He wondered if the people of the island might speculate about his inability to find and assist his father, and whether they might reason that, like his father, he had simply resigned to haunting the streets of the capital city like a ghost; caught in the space between the reality of his past life and the dream-like state of his present.

5. Hotel Santa Rita de Cascia

THE HOTEL SANTA Rita de Cascia in Old Quito had a rusty brick façade. Its wrought iron balconies were garnished with French windows resembling those of a building from another part of the world. The building's sixty rooms could have overlooked the canals of Venice, or the Roman Coliseum. Its overhanging flowerpots and golden signs normally attracted tourists, whereas today this Ecuadorian replica drew only those attending a forum for the press.

Tómas and Juan Carlos walked down a busy street approaching the hotel. Tómas had never seen such crowds of tourists, so many strangers, and so many businesses catering to them. For a moment he thought he heard the word 'payaso' from a man passing in the street, his eyes turning toward him as he walked by.

'Payaso, clown, your hair is on fire,' the other children would say to him when he was a boy, when his hair was redder than it was now, back when it had the tinges of orange he would eventually outgrow. Payaso con la cabeza y el cuerpo del zanahoria: clown with the carrot stick head and the tall, slender stature of a carrot. Tómas could have run away as the boys ridiculed him, and he could have fought back. But he would always stand with clenched fists, his face reddening, his heart pounding, not challenging them, his feet rooted to the ground as his hair was rooted to his scalp. El payaso asustado, they would call him. The cowardly clown. He had questioned Veronica about why he was different. It was through this questioning that he had first learned his parents were not originally from Ecuador, and that his biological mother was not Veronica but a woman named Violet who had moved to Canada shortly after Tómas was born. It was the first time he had sensed that he didn't belong here, and that maybe his father was never around because he shared this feeling, too.

Here in Old Quito, though, regardless of what he had just heard, he was no different. Here, he was the same height as the tourists, and he no longer looked down on a collection of black and blonde heads. He was just another face in the wave of different faces, another head of hair among a plethora of odd and distinctive colours.

They entered the lobby of the hotel through ornately carved doors, passing into a decorated foyer. Juan Carlos gave his press identification to a man in a suit at the entranceway, and both he and Tómas were outfitted with tags to identify them as reporters from Diario Hoy. Walking through a portico, they entered a massive room.

The walls were adorned with mirrors supporting half-chandeliers made whole by their reflections. The carpeting was woven with intricate, gold-laced patterns and was identical to the ceiling tiles, mirroring each other. It all combined to create an imposing symmetry, augmented by elongated, framed picture windows positioned in the centre of each wall. Government officials and military men lingered around the entranceways in immaculately cut suits and tailored uniforms, all laughing the same laugh as if to complement the equilibrium. It was a balance somehow disturbed by his presence here.

"I do not like this place," Tómas said.

"It is beautiful, but excessive," Juan Carlos replied as they sat down among a sea of folding chairs.

Tómas stared at a decorated and unoccupied podium at the front of the room before looking around at the men in military uniforms. His fight against military service would be from necessity. Others would think what they may. But he could not fight alone.

"And so when I am your client," Tómas asked quietly in Spanish, after ensuring no one else was close enough to hear, "you can say I will not consent."

"I will," Juan Carlos replied softly. "But you know what problems you will face."

"No. I leave that to you."

"I did research at my office, after we talked. The September 1984 Law of Compulsory Military Service has been changed. It now says in time of war or an emergency, National Security Law applies."

"What significance is that?"

"The army can now make the reserve forces mobile. When you are between twenty-six and fifty-five, even if you do not perform military service now, still, you will be part of the reserves. We may win conscientious objection after years of fighting, but then you can be called into reserves. And you will have no time to file an objection. I have read they might conscript women also. Our mothers and wives may soon be marching off to fight for all that land Peru is claiming."

A group of men and women, talking loudly and laughing, sat nearby. Tómas turned away from them.

"Women will not go to war," Tómas said, lowering his voice. "But if what you said about the reserves is true—"

"It is."

"Then I would not be in the reserves for another eight years. By then, the border war might be over."

"And if reserves are made mobile after that for some other emergency, it could mean you help evacuate towns when a volcano erupts, or keep peace after a president is impeached. That, you could do." Juan Carlos nodded, as though agreeing with his own conclusion. "But still," he continued, shrugging his shoulders dismissively. "I see no end, in our lifetime, to this 150-year war ... but there are always other ways ... let me see ... you are a student at the university?"

"Yes, and?"

"Let me see what I can do. I remember something, I think of it now, from many years ago. Students, they can put off military obligations for two years to finish their degree. Yup, that is what we will do. There is a provision for students. Your fight, at least for the next two years, it will be easy."

Tómas raised his eyebrows. In three weeks, he would have to report, regardless of what Juan Carlos could do. The letter in his pocket mandated that. He would not get an answer so promptly.

Chilled air began flowing in through overhead vents. Air conditioners were normally only in banks. The frozen air peeled over his skin like a spiritual presence, reminding him of an article his father once wrote about George, a spirit who resided on the third floor of this hotel and who was known to fold shirts and silently cover hotel guests in blankets as they slept. George was the first owner of the hotel who, until the last years of his life, lived tragically alone, caring for the place as though it were his only child. George was not the only ghost in the area, but he was definitely the friendliest of them. To the east, down the Avenue of the Americas, near the city centre, resided the Jamaican ghost of the most powerful voodoo woman ever to set foot in the city. Her puissant force continued after her death, her spirit able to spit in the faces of those who mocked her memory: those whom she might have called the 'unbelievers.' Her voodoo magic still filled the streets. And off the west end coastline, toward the Isla de la Plata with its sparkling waters and cliffs jutting into the Pacific, pointing the way to Indonesia and New Guinea, flew the flag of the Spanish ghost ship wrecked off the island's coast nearly 500 years ago. Its phantom sailors were forever doomed to search through the night shadows for their destination port. There was something otherworldly about this city and its history that his father might describe as nonsense, despite having written and thought about and researched it, but that Tómas believed was more than just stories from the past.

Members of the press began entering the room, congregating near the front in tattered clothing with identification tags and cameras wrapped around their necks. Some of the newsmen's wives, older women too young to be considered elderly and too old to be seen as youthful, took their assigned seats at the back of the room. They were dressed in sagging clothes with droopy faces, wearing thick coats of makeup that seemed to cascade slowly down their cheeks. The chairs around Tómas and Juan Carlos were being filled.

Eduardo Delgado appeared in the corner, approaching the podium in a dark, shimmering suit and a wide tie. The only anomaly in his attire was the collection of multicoloured papers protruding from his jacket pocket that blended in with the wrinkled gold, blue and red flag of Ecuador behind him, the flag's coat of arms signifying dignity, victory, protection, fraternity of its people, harmony and trade, independence and the blood shed for it, the sea and the sky, ample crops and fertile land.

"If this was a fundraiser," Eduardo began in gentle, melodious Spanish, pushing the papers into his pocket. "I would say how great is the honour to charge you so much for your dinners." Stifled laughter reverberated throughout the crowded room, followed by a sustained silence.

"But there is no dinner," he continued, his voice firm now. "I chose this place for the forum today because it is similar to the hotel that will be built on the island. That hotel, too, will be glorious."

Eduardo's dark eyes contrasted with the pallor of his skin. He had a rigid stance over the microphone, his head hunched slightly forward, and he dabbed his neatly cropped moustache with the back of his hand. His face looked chiselled rather than fleshy and his dark, greased hair stuck to his scalp. Tómas was reminded of a wooden sculpture formed by an inept artisan, to be preserved for posterity and unvisited in some obscure museum.

"The threat of military dictatorship, it no longer haunts Ecuador," Eduardo said in a rapid Spanish. "We chose democracy, just as Haiti, too, has done. This democracy has given what is called free enterprise, which gives opportunity for new projects like the island hotel. What will this do for the island's people? This, you may ask yourself. Low-cost food items: rice, milk, lentils and cooking oil, to start. Reduced telephone prices, making telephones accessible to everyone on the island. All from increased subsidies, from investors and government, once the hotel builds the tourism industry there."

Juan Carlos took notes feverishly, capturing words as Eduardo spoke while other reporters held tape recorders high in the air. Juan Carlos repeatedly underlined the last part of his transcription.

Eduardo concluded his short speech by pointing out similarities between Haitian, Peruvian, and Ecuadorian history. There was a brief ripple of applause. Eduardo answered a few questions quickly before announcing that the press forum was over.

He began gathering up his papers from the podium as the crowd dispersed.

Juan Carlos suddenly raised his hand, his face flushed red. He stood up as Eduardo looked over and smiled.

"Yes, Juan Carlos?" Eduardo asked.

"Several years ago," Juan Carlos said loudly, his tone harsh. "You said at a fundraiser that increased subsidies from the government would follow, once the *low-cost homes* were built. The homes you proposed, too, for the island."

"I am sorry, the questions are over," Eduardo said, his smile dissipating, his moustache drooping like fangs. "And apart from that, what you said was not a question."

"I wrote an article on that low-cost housing plan," Juan Carlos continued. "I was against the prices of houses not staying stable, the rich buying them by the dozen and selling them at higher prices. I researched the history of South American housing projects to come up with my conclusion. I commented on each of them in my paper. Maybe you read this. I explained why those projects did not work. My article was part of what ended the housing plan. Because the public was not liking the idea. And now," he said, his face shimmering with sweat in the lights, "now I am against this hotel, as I was against the housing plan."

Eduardo turned away, waving his hand dismissively, saying nothing. He walked toward the door as newsmen regrouped around the podium, activating their tape recorders. Just as Eduardo was opening the door to leave, Juan Carlos spoke again.

"And you were involved in the scandal that sent Montgomery Harvey away from the island and his family," he said. "How do you answer *that?*"

"Finally," Eduardo said, turning around. "A question. A good reporter always asks many questions, instead of making comments without sense. The housing plan was not realistic. That is why it ended. Not because of your newspaper, despite what you might think. And I know nothing of Montgomery leaving, or how temporary or long his absence might be."

"And a luxury hotel in one of the poorest areas of the country, which will be funded by —"

"It will increase the living standard of the islanders," Eduardo said quickly, interrupting him. "Tourism is a powerful force to make change happen, Juan Carlos. It surprises me you do not know that."

The meeting room began to clear. Tómas's eyes were drawn toward a familiar apparition standing at the opposite end of the room; a spirit with white hair and a recognizable, hunched physique. Montgomery.

Eduardo exited through the door. For a moment, Tómas paused, watching the white door close slowly behind him. He had come here to talk with Eduardo about his father, but that was no longer necessary. He would speak with his father directly. But when he turned around, Montgomery had vanished.

Tómas ran outside.

The street seemed even more crowded than before. He pushed his way through the crowd of brightly coloured scarves, shawls and hats of the indigenous whom Juan Carlos had said were from nearby Ambato. The traffic on the street comprised a donkey carrying sticks and baskets of fresh fruit, a few taxis sputtering noisily by, a scooter and a green-white bus. The lingering smell of exhaust fumes was everywhere.

The bus was overcrowded and techni-coloured with indigenous patrons. Amongst the colours stood his father, holding on to a railing inside. Tómas could not be sure, but he thought he saw Eduardo in a seat nearby, obscured by those standing. Montgomery was looking ahead, his gaze as intense as it had been in the Hotel Santa Rita de Cascia.

Tómas stood motionless, watching the bus speed away, before starting after it. As he ran behind, the vehicle accelerated away rapidly in a puff of black smoke and turned on to another busy street. His father was gone.

6. Self-Imposed Exile

THERE IS ONLY one reason why I have decided to leave the island, never to return. I could give any number of explanations to any number of people: to my family, to the press, to others I know. But, in the end, they would only believe what they wanted to. And what they chose to comprehend as my motives for leaving would be different from what I had offered them.

It once terrified me to live apart from England where I was born. But my Uncle Devon convinced me that living in exile would prove easy. And it did. But, through the years, I was the one who chose to stay away, the same as I have remained away from Ecuador through the decades since. This new voluntary exile should seem natural to me, an extension of the life I have lived for the past fifty years. Yet it does not.

I have never felt a part of the places I have lived in or travelled to. In my past decades of travel I have sought out other expatriates, to identify with some commonality that had brought us there. Some never wanted to go back to their homelands. Some that intended to return never did. We wandered in search of something different, some unique aspect of our lives that had led us to the same place. Maybe it was rejection of our former lives, our responsibilities, and the ideals and futures we had once envisioned for ourselves. But it was abandonment that led all of us away from our homes: we were all abandoners in our own newfound lands, together.

But why am I finding it so difficult now, to stay away? I must do so, and as I have seen in the news so many times before, if I am not available for trial, I cannot be tried. The crimes of which I am accused will remain only unproven accusations. My family will not be disgraced and ridiculed and shamed because of me.

I once wrote about exile, on the boat taking me to Ecuador for the first time, which went from Portugal through the Isthmus of Panama and further south to Guayaquil. It was written in the format of an Ancient Greek oratory. The Athenians used exile as punishment for those considered a nuisance or a threat. As I wrote that article, my own exile escape from the Second World War, I considered myself to be a nuisance and a threat, refusing to embrace duty to family and country, and leaving my mother and younger brothers behind in London to fend for themselves while my father lived and worked at the mines apart from them. Neither myself, nor my father was there to help them, to save them.

And now at this part of my life five decades later, as an absent father and husband, I have the realization that no man wants to face, but one which I will have to accept, one that gives me the reason why I decided to leave the island forever: the knowledge that leaving my home will be better for everyone. While some would consider this letter a bit self-glorifying if written into one of my publications, this shall go no further than from my pen to this paper, to be destroyed before my death. No one shall see this except me.

I will rewrite that article and send it to Diario Hoy under one of my pseudonyms, the fabricated pen name of Señor Galo Cordoba, that the editor, and perhaps no one else, will recognize. Perhaps this will be my final piece of writing.

I have heard of a man in Aguas Calientes outside of Machu Picchu in Peru who helps people such as me, people seeking asylum, political or otherwise. I must find him soon, for as my breathing becomes more difficult, my vision is also quickly deteriorating. All of the places I am visiting become blurrier each day.

Perhaps I will ask my family to visit me in Peru, once I have visited this man and settled there for what little is left of my life ...

7. Bliss

TÓMAS TOLD HIS father, before he left, that he didn't know what love was. What it meant apart from the standard interpretations of the term, or what it meant to have faith. Montgomery told him that an instant of truly experiencing either is the height of what one can ever hope to achieve. Equating it to Dostoevsky's statement, who he said elucidated it best, he explained how one moment of bliss, only an instant, is like the moment before an epileptic seizure that very few get to experience—the moment that is sufficient for the whole of one's life. Montgomery said to Tómas's confused expression that, one day, he would understand.

Tómas searched through the city streets, thinking of what his one moment of bliss might be, what truly experiencing an instant of love or faith could possibly mean. He spent a week with Juan Carlos, searching through Montgomery's mainland office—where Tómas pocketed a small journal that he found on top of Montgomery's desk—then through Quito's city airport, the bus station, travel agencies, taxi stands, and car rental companies.

At first, Tómas reasoned that his search was simple curiosity. He wanted to find his father and help him however he could, even if the only assistance he could provide was to tuck him away in a hostel in some obscure area of the city. His father would then have the time to write the letters and do the research that would exonerate him, as Tómas would hand-deliver all of the letters that would prove his father's innocence, over the course of days or weeks—whatever it took—while disregarding his military obligations. But what frustrated him was that the curiosity driving him to find Montgomery and the lack of expectation that he actually would, were mixed with thoughts of a love he had never felt and could not contemplate. He even had a sudden longing for a beautiful young woman such as Inés - was that love? Missing his father, wanting to be with him, always occupied his mind; he had a deep sense of commitment to Veronica and Flory, and a yearning to know about his mother; but nothing he would describe as love. Would his one moment of bliss come from finding his father—his last hope for finding out more about his mother, a subject they had rarely discussed?

Tómas continued in frustration as they travelled to Guayaquil for another week and visited the same exit routes there. Montgomery must have travelled one of these ways if he was on his way out of the country. Regardless, he had to get out of Quito where he would certainly be recognized, Juan Carlos said, and he might have gone through Guayaquil if he were headed south to Peru. But maybe, Tómas thought, Montgomery was planning to remain in some obscure area of Ecuador: in Salinas at a house near the beach, in Cuenca with its European air and cobblestone streets, or in Baños in a hut at the edge of the jungle.

"When he wants to be found, he will find you," Juan Carlos said, waving his hand resignedly. "He will return to the island when he is ready. For now, we will wait and talk to Eduardo; he is returning to the island in a few days."

But Tómas was not ready to accept that his father could not be found, nor was he prepared to acknowledge that Montgomery had left the country. So remembering something his father had once told him, he talked to people who did not recognize the name Montgomery Harvey, who claimed to have never read any of his travel articles, and who directed Tómas and Juan Carlos to a dozen places a foreigner might go. They went to the gardens, where busloads of tourists arrived to watch the wild iguanas perched in trees, sunning themselves on rocks. They went to the base of Quito's volcano and talked to tour guides sitting on bicycles. They went to busy malls and congested street corners, and to Gringolandia. They talked to police on the streets and to a woman in an enormous golden headdress at the mitad del mundo, the country's monument to the earth's equator.

"This has no sense, visiting these tourist destinations," Juan Carlos said in the midst of a crowd gathered around techni-coloured aboriginal dancers at the mitad del mundo. "He would not be here."

"No one thinks to find any locals, except guides, at a place like this," Tómas said. "My father told me once that if he ever had to hide, that is how he would."

After a while, Juan Carlos said: "He might be doing that. Only not in *this* country."

After days of empty searching, Tómas realized that Juan Carlos was right. Montgomery might not be in Ecuador at all. And when he wanted to be found, he would make his presence known.

The next day Tómas and Juan Carlos returned to the island.

It seemed like weeks since Tómas had been in his own bed. Unable to sleep, he turned on the light and opened the small, leather-bound journal he had found on Montgomery's mainland office desk. Beside the journal, he placed a waterlogged and ink-stained note from his father, given to him by the ferry driver on the return trip. He underlined a portion:

> *I want you to finish your degree and complete your military term. I want you to help Eduardo build the hotel, our island's future. These are my wishes. I don't want you to look for me, or to be concerned with where I am, or why I left. Just know that I've left as a result of a chain of events that I myself, and no one else, initiated.*

He flipped through the journal to see if anything had been written about his mother. The writing was miniscule, difficult to read in places, and was mostly about events in Montgomery's life between the world wars: growing up poor and without a father, sneaking out every night to explore the city on his bicycle, spending summers at his Uncle Devon's cottage, and reminiscences of his brother who was always sick, and an actress at a local theatre with whom he had been infatuated. But there were more recent entries. They were mostly random thoughts and written sketches of places he had been, writings that formed the basis of his travel articles.

Tómas found himself getting drowsy as he read the words: *secrets are what one has when there's nothing left to cling to. When all that remains is yourself in your solitude, all you have are your secrets that can only be shared with strangers. Unforgivable, otherwise untellable secrets.*

He shook himself up again to the words: *Isla de la Plata or the Isle of Silver, more aptly designated la Isla de Mil Sombras de los Azules or the Island of a Thousand Shades of Blue, was instead named for the precious metal found by Spanish soldiers shining from native necks and buried beneath inherited earth. The Spanish Conquistadors battled the islanders, their firearms pitted against spears. Conquistadores. Conquerors. They brought no women with them. In North America, those from the European continent who had brought their women were known as Settlers.*

The Isle of Silver and the Poor Man's Galapagos. Notions embedded in history and geography. The former from its prior abundance of a precious metal, the latter from its close proximity to the mainland in comparison with the Galapagos Islands; Isla de la Plata is thirty miles from the coast, the Galapagos Islands six hundred. Charles Darwin's flawed theory evolved from the more isolated environment of the Galapagos, with its blue-footed boobies perched above sun-heated rocks, sea lions barking their husky songs on huge expanses of beach beside giant tortoises dragging their weight through the sand, marine iguanas diving to clear blue depths in search of aquatic plant life, and a hundred different species of finches. Only some of this splendor, a few varieties of finches, blue-footed boobies, some sea lions, but none of the famed giant tortoises, has been bestowed upon the few visitors to Isla de la Plata, mostly Ecuadorians, who lack the money to travel more than thirty miles from the coast ...

Tómas woke up, hours later, his lamp still illuminated, and he looked with renewed interest at the book. Among the pages, wrinkled and stained with age, he came across the following passage: *Violet told me last night, as we sat in front of a fire on the beach, that I think too much as she does. She said that this is the source of our unhappiness, that we are too much alike.*

The fact that his mother Violet had sat together with his father on a beach in front of a fire produced more of a visual image of a time and place that they had shared, than Tómas had ever thought of before. Tómas's confused anger at her abandonment of him seemed to dissipate, by knowing such vivid details as what they actually said to each other on this specific night. The scattered reminiscences he had obtained from his father about Violet over the years suddenly formed into a cohesive whole on this page, becoming a part of the reason she had left the island without her son, making her real.

He put the book down. If there was more written about his mother, he couldn't read it now. Why hadn't Montgomery told him about the root of her unhappiness? Why had this been kept from him for so long?

Tómas turned out the light and, thinking of his mother and a frustration with his father for all that he did not disclose—his suppressed knowledge, his unforgivable, untellable secrets no better than lies—Tómas drifted into an uncomfortable, dreamless sleep.

8. Destroyed Paintings

DARKNESS WAS BURDENED by intermittent light reflecting in from the intricate open-air masonry work at the abutment of the roof and the walls of the house. Silence was laden with cricket song.

Just as the ancients of the world who believed everything visible to them—the sun, the moon, the stars, the trees, bodies of water, even stones—were alive and in possession of a jealous, spiteful and oppressive soul, Tómas saw the insects passing between his room and the light outside, unimpeded, as all indignant toward him; as were the gold, blue and red flag of Ecuador and its coat of arms hanging on the concrete wall, and Montgomery's only paintings barely visible in the faded light, as well as the thin blanket covering him, and the heat of the night air and the mosquitoes buzzing at the netting covering his bed.

Tómas, his eyes wide open, examined Montgomery's only paintings: a series of eight tall, narrow pieces of art that had given him nightmares as a child. The subjects seemed to be spirits caught in a limbo world of blackness, each of the images apparently representing a different stage of confinement, their figures disproportionately elongated vertically and darkened so that their limbs appeared to be made from slender, charred tree branches.

He suddenly recalled a passage he had seen while skimming through his father's journal. Pulling the lamp switch on, opening the book again and flipping through it, he found the page he was looking for:

There was no colour anywhere in that cursed prison camp where my Uncle Devon died and I was left to fend for myself among the other "political prisoners." It was all greyness and blackness like the black and white photographs you have seen. I have made paintings of it. It has been my only expression of that, the worst time of my life. Various shades of terse grey brushstrokes depict an elongated young man slumped over in a paltry wooden chair, naked. His head rests on his chin in the first of the portrayals, a man contemplating his own escape, believing his situation unavoidable but still possessing hope. The other paintings represent a man with glints of optimism at contemplating a liberation of the camp, then thoughts of complete desperation when offered black bread to eat and blood to drink; his thoughts varying from desire to inflict the same pain on his captors, to thoughts of the meaninglessness of such an existence and then, inevitably, to considerations of inflicting pain on himself and then ultimately, suicide. Each of the stages of confinement spans a week, then a day, then an hour, the stages alternating between compressed and elongated time frames. There is no background in any of them, as there was nothing around me during my incarceration but the greyness of sensory deprivation. The young man in the paintings has, as his only escape, his introspection. Something no imprisonment could take from him.

Tómas walked out into the kitchen, and found a copy of the Diario Hoy he had been reading earlier that day. Returning to his room and skimming through it, he found the article and the passage he was looking for: *My thoughts will run with distant memories of times long past, leaving me in a different state of anxiety, despair, frustration—each instant, each day, each week, each month—as in my only paintings made from my memories of a prison camp in Spain.* The author's name, Galo Cordoba, was familiar. After searching through a pile of paper clippings in the top of his dresser drawer, he found what he was looking for. Confirmation, from another article, that this was one of his father's pseudonyms.

The truth of the news item's narrator had been suppressed from him, and the impersonal impressions of the spirit world that he had always envisioned these paintings to be were actually portraits of his father's anguish. He had not been told of his father's or his mother's unhappiness, the reasons for it, or why Montgomery chose to live apart from his English or his Ecuadorian family. And the image of his father's Quito bus speeding away as he gazed intently forward seemed a final garrulous act in a lifetime of silent, despicable lies.

He now wished that his father, instead of putting these paintings in Tómas's room, maybe so he wouldn't have to look at them himself, had destroyed them.

Looking at these creations now in the shadows of the room, Tómas rationalized that he would have to do the job. Ripping each of the canvases apart with his hands, one by one, he suddenly stopped at the last of the series and held the head of the figure, torn at the neck and seeming to stare up at him. Focusing on those eyes, repentant and sorrowful, he wondered about the young man whose only escape was his introspection, desperate thoughts, and a sense of timelessness. In his anger, Tómas had mutilated this symbol of his father's pain.

Veronica called for him, and then her light illuminated upstairs. Extinguishing his lamp without saying a word, his heart thumping in his chest, he closed his eyes while thinking of the benefits to having prisoners' thoughts and imaginations subdued by elaborate machines—whose memories of the past, and whose potential promise of freedom, would be stifled.

As Tómas awoke the next morning, he looked at the floor and suddenly recalled what he had done. Lowering his head, he crossed his arms and sat staring at the remains. It was as though Tómas had done this in a dream subconsciously knowing, but without consciously accepting, that Montgomery would never return to find his paintings under the bed mutilated and in pieces. And since he had done this, he had the odd feeling that somehow, in some strange way, he had ensured that Montgomery would forever remain away from this house.

But he would have to continue searching for him, and to find him one day.

As Montgomery's profile had retreated down the streets of Old Quito, Tómas thought he had seen someone in a seat near his father: someone he could talk to, and in whom he would need to confide despite the taint of wrongdoing exposed by Juan Carlos, despite the fact that he should not seek out a potentially devious man to tell him where his father had gone. The only man whom he could think might tell him something, anything, and who, according to Juan Carlos, might be back on the island today.

9. Unfulfilled Obligations

TÓMAS WALKED BETWEEN grey concrete buildings; a chicken ambled by and pecked at the ground before a few children playing on the road chased the clucking bird away in a cloud of dust.

A voice shouted from behind him. Stopping to turn around, Tómas saw Juan Carlos approaching. He was bruised and limping, and dressed in a brown t-shirt and slacks. Tómas, afraid that Juan would not stop, attempted to move back. Juan Carlos's weighty stomach almost knocked Tómas against the wall.

"I was very sad with you," Juan Carlos said in rapid Spanish, swallowing hard and pausing to breathe between sentences. He was perspiring heavily, his face wet with sweat. They began walking together between the buildings, emerging on the street alongside playing children and cyclists.

"I saw the letters you sent to the editors of El Comercio and Diario Hoy," Juan Carlos said. "My editor showed me—and I was very hurt."

"I was angry when I sent them," Tómas said. "And apart from that, I told you I sent them."

"You must understand one thing. You may think the best of your father. I know you do. But I am not the only one who says he is guilty. And his running away, for certain, did not help. I did not destroy his image as you think; he did that by leaving after the accusations were printed—"

"And he told you nothing of leaving, and you told him nothing of the article you would write. I do not believe that."

Juan Carlos continued as though he had not heard him. "Do you not hear the people on the streets all the time, as I do, talking of his guilt? And your letter talks about the hotel and Eduardo's political aspirations. About printing rumours as facts. And calling me a gossiping liar with a typewriter. All full of hate. I never have heard such things from you. Except once in my office recently, when you must have been drunk. We are friends, are we not?"

Tómas did not reply, focusing for a moment on a man riding a rusty bicycle who weaved deftly around the children, and then around the potholes that littered the road.

"I have some information to show you," Juan Carlos continued. "You will be not happy with your father, and you will understand me then. I will show you the paperwork and tell you everything, but not now. Now, I am too angry with you."

Tómas examined the bruises on Juan Carlos's face, and then observed his stature. With his limp, he seemed unable to put weight onto his left leg.

"What happened to you?" Tómas asked.

"Ah, ya. Well, I am sure it was Eduardo ... the police came to my apartment. Eduardo is very angry with me. My words from the press conference are in many newspapers."

"I saw the accusations of embezzlement are connected to him now."

"Yes, you are right. The police, they told me to leave the island, to collect my family and leave the country. I refused, and they did this."

Juan Carlos stopped to exhibit his face, a swollen ankle, and he lifted his shirt slowly to show contusions on his belly.

"So what will you do?" Tómas asked, at a standstill now beside him.

"I moved. But you must tell no one. I live in a boat in the bay. The one with the stilts. I bought it from the man who owned it—he has not used it for years—in trade for a roasted guinea pig and some beers. I think, from the stench in that boat, that he has the better part of our deal."

They moved out into an open area with scrub brush and a few houses lining the roadway. A taxicab drove by very close, at high speed, churning dust. They stepped over to the side of the road, coughing.

"I am sad because all I wanted to do is help your father," Juan Carlos said. "And to help you."

"You have not helped my father, or me, or Eduardo, with your lying typewriter. Your injuries are the result, and the fault of your lies."

"These are not the words of a friend. And let us not argue about this now. I have news about your application to postpone your military service because you are a student; but I am reluctant now to give you this news."

"Tell me."

"You will send more hate-letters to my editor?"

"No."

"Good. I thought he would fire me. He made me give proof about the accusations against Montgomery, as you asked for in your letter. He wanted to publish what I showed him, along with your letter, and I said he should not. I repeated my request over and over until finally, he agreed. But still, the editor of El Comercio, I see that he has printed your letter, so all of my pleading to my editor was for nothing. Except for now, I am not forced to publish the proof."

"Proof my father is guilty?"

"One day soon, I will show you, the same as I showed my editor. He wants desperately for me to publish it. I told him I will not, and he said he will fire me. Then I told him I will publish, one day soon, when the time is right. That has made him happy for now. But, I must return to my news."

A woman came out from the back of her house with a pile of wet clothes, and began beating them against the side of a huge rock. Juan Carlos lowered his voice, and continued speaking.

"What I wanted to tell you," he said, "was your application to postpone military service as a student was denied, immediately. I do not understand why, and they did not say. I went to the recruitment office and said you would be studying abroad. They said they would deny that also, saying I provided no proof ..."

"I thought it was to be easy."

Juan shook his head. "I have not looked at the Constitution yet, to see if it says about conscientious objection. But still, there is article 108, but I would not want—"

"What is article 108?"

"One moment, please." He produced a folded paper from his pocket, wiped his forehead with the back of his forearm, and began reading: " ... *if sufficiently motivated, conscientious objection may be accepted by the Director of Mobilisation of the Armed Forces.'* Article 93 tells what you need to do to apply." He paused, and took a deep breath.

"Apply? This gets too confusing to me."

Juan Carlos sighed. "We will need to fill out a special form. But first, we must decide on what basis you will apply. Article 108 does not address that."

"I can say I have an objection that is religious, that I belong to no organized religion—"

"No," Juan Carlos interrupted, shaking his head. "It is odd, I must admit. Everyone here is Roman Catholic, you say you are not. But for that, you will need a signature from a clergyman, maybe even a bishop. Let us not decide now. I will get the application form, and we will fill it out together. We will need to be very careful in what we say, and to think about this more ..."

And with those words he walked away in a different direction from which he came, speaking to himself as he sauntered down the road, looking at all those around him. The woman cursed at a chicken and a mouse darting through her yard as she continued her housework.

Eduardo Delgado's mayoral office was in a building overlooking cliffs that formed the west end of Isla de la Plata. From the outside, Tómas always envisioned this building as ready to fall to its death, its impending destruction heralded by the early morning shadows that seemed to want to drag it down the steepness of the hill and out into the sea. Its exterior was grey concrete, and devoid of any refinements that would make it architecturally interesting.

Tómas walked through the painted white front doors and past an open door bearing Eduardo's name. Tómas had been here many times with his father, but he had never been here alone. Entering the room apprehensively as an uninvited and unannounced guest, he felt a slight breeze that brought the scent of mangoes and stale tobacco toward him.

A set of large, open windows offered a unique, though distant, view of where the hotel might be built. The island Centre of Recruitment and Reserves was also visible from here. Eduardo stood rigid in the corner, his crimson shirt, floral print shorts, and brown sandals producing a collage of a man who might be a tourist in his own country.

"Enter, enter," Eduardo said in English, smiling as he moved toward Tómas. "I just was thinking of you now. I am very happy to see you. I thought to come to your home to discuss a matter with you. But you are here; therefore we can discuss it now ... yes, please enter, sit down ..."

He shook Tómas's hand firmly, before supplying a chair from the corner. Uncertain as to what Eduardo wished to discuss, Tómas forgot his own intention in being there. He remained standing as Eduardo reached into a drawer of his desk, produced a knife, and began removing the bright orange skin from an overripe mango.

Russian matroyshka grandmother dolls were displayed in a shallow bookcase while Italian marble statues, Egyptian papyrus, long-faced African masks, and watercolours of unnamed French streets papered the walls. These were items collected as souvenirs, items once in Montgomery and Veronica's room. They were remnants of a life spent abroad. The life of Montgomery Harvey.

Remembering now why he was here, unsure of where to begin, Tómas contemplated asking Eduardo whether he knew how to contact his father, and whether he had sent the police after Juan Carlos. But before Tómas could speak, Eduardo interrupted his thoughts.

"It is strange, no?" Eduardo asked in a leisurely, methodical Spanish, the blade of his knife flashing at Tómas in the light. His breath was pungent even at a distance.

"What is?"

"Your father could have stayed here. To face the accusations against him. But instead, he wanted escape."

"Escape to where?"

"He asked me to tell no one. Not even his son."

"Do me a favour. I need to know."

"Yes, I suppose it can do no harm now ... Peru. He went to Peru."

"Where in Peru?"

"To a town near Machu Picchu. He said he would not be back, although still, I do not believe it." A yellow section of mango slipped from the edge of his knife and disappeared between his teeth.

Tómas sat down in the chair, surprised that this information was so easily obtainable. Was it reliable?

"How do you know this?" Tómas asked.

"He told me before the press forum on the mainland. Yes, you were there. I saw you next to that monkey Juan Carlos. I thought your father was just talking nonsense, that he would not leave for long, but I have not seen him since I left him in the main bus terminal in Quito."

"Why Peru?"

Eduardo shrugged. "Because of the accusations, he might have wanted to leave the country. Or do some more travelling."

"And he gave you no reason."

"Take care how you talk to your elders. But I remember asking whether he was still retired. Instead of answering, he talked about you and Veronica, and how sad he was to leave. He continued on about regrets, on and on without stopping, as he does when he is nervous."

"And he did not say when he would be back."

"I do not think he ever wants to stop travelling. He wants to escape his fears. You know, to travel as much as he has, it is a luxury most of us can not afford. I have many times wished I had his life. But still, I think, one day he will return."

Eduardo paraded slowly by his matroyshka dolls displayed in a large bookcase, and stopped before a framed and matted print identified as Velasquéz's Las Meninas. He slipped another slice of mango between his pursed lips, and offered Tómas a piece. Imagining the sweetness of the moist fruit shocking his tongue he accepted, depositing the wedge carefully into the corner of his mouth. The flavour was slightly sweet, but more sour and acidic.

"The personal library of Velasquéz, after he died, they found books on almost everything," Eduardo said. "Nothing on God, though. Much like your father's library. I have many times wondered what Velasquéz, and your father, could have done with God's help, knowing what they did without His blessing."

Eduardo retreated from the print and placed the partially consumed fruit and the knife on his desk. As he lit a cigarette and held it between his lips, Tómas saw that his skin at this proximity, and with the sunlight glancing off his face, resembled windblown sand.

"Whisky?" Eduardo asked, offering a glass with a small amount of brown, transparent liquid.

"No," Tómas said. "Not during the day."

"But it is almost evening."

Tómas never drank whisky at any time of day. He did not want Eduardo to know that he was accustomed to imbibing the poor man's drink: sugar cane alcohol, a beverage that rotted his gut. And he did not wish to divulge that he had watched his friends turn recently toward a more intoxicating substance, the yellow powder derivative of the coca plant that putrefied their minds with an overpowering sickness requiring more, a more that was never enough. Tómas accepted the drink and downed the contents of the glass, the taste smoky and pungent, and he asked for another. Eduardo gladly obliged.

"You truly are Ecuadorian," Eduardo said, smiling with the cigarette still in his mouth. "Even though your hair, your complexion says you are not." He imbibed his whisky, refilled his glass, and then began pacing across the room, his cigarette exhaust funnelling neatly through the open windowpanes.

Putting the bottle down, Eduardo closed and secured the windows. The entrails of his tobacco smoke surrounded him as he sat in his chair peering through the windows, a misty chemical cloud stagnating in front of his desk for a moment before being propelled upward by the ceiling fan, spiralling up like some ancient Chinese dragon.

In the silence, Tómas experienced the same moment of uncertainty as he had when he had first walked into the room. Eduardo seemed to be contemplating something, watching as murky clouds spilled out over the Pacific. He rose and opened one of the windows, sending a brown, congealed mass outdoors and flicking his cigarette after it. Closing the window again, he secured it in place.

"You sent anyone after Juan Carlos?" Tómas asked suddenly.

Eduardo replied, still looking outside. "I am not sure what you mean." He turned around to face Tómas before continuing.

"Now, I will discuss a thing with you," he said, wiping his mouth with his sleeve. "I have a proposal. You will work for me. For the hotel ..." He sat down on the edge of the desk in front of Tómas, uncomfortably close, folding his hands in his lap.

"Supposedly most of the island will work for you," Tómas said. "If the hotel is constructed."

"For certain, the hotel will be constructed. And what you say is true; most of the people on the island will have to work to make it a success. But they will be labourers, and I want you to work for me as an irrigation engineer."

"For a hotel?"

"You will be paid very well. Steady work, with excellent pay: this is what I offer you. Something most people in this country cannot say they have. There are three ancient albarradas on my land, and two modern ones. They will be your research projects. And with this experience you will be able to work on the mainland, if that is what you want, maybe work in other countries like your father, whatever you want."

"I am a student only," Tómas replied.

"Then you know of the problem of the new albarradas here on the island."

"I have studied them, yes."

Eduardo shifted his weight on the desk. "You can help me, then. The modern albarradas on my land have been washed away. The ancient ones have not. This is why I would need you, to help revitalize that land." Eduardo paused for a moment.

"It is very complicated with the need for archaeologists, anthropologists, ecologists, geologists—" Tómas said.

"And many others," Eduardo said, waving his hands as he spoke. "But you will have whoever you need. And I will have, for my hotel, the most magnificent gardens in the country. Full of all the colour and variety this region can give. Gardens that will similar to the Palace of Versailles, and the

Palaces of the Czars your father wrote about and photographed."

"The gardens in Versailles took forty years to build. And we have not made a new albarrada here that can survive."

"These modern albarradas, they did not survive because of the rains of el niño. But the ancient islanders, they knew how to build them, and their albarradas still are working today. Somehow, they knew what to do, and now, with technology and modern experts, we do not? It is a difficult problem, true. But one you can help me to solve."

"Maybe in twenty years, but not at this moment."

Eduardo stood up and walked to the window, gazing out at the sea. Past him, long rows of wave crests were caught by the light of the sun, long, distended, seemingly infinite lines.

"You do not have confidence," he continued. "That is sad. You are of the age; the State has published the military service list. You were on that list. And you do know the importance of getting your military card."

Tómas knew that government officials were exempt from mandatory military service, thanks to having their military card. Feeling brazen from the effects of the whisky, he responded.

"You heard of conscientious objectors," Tómas said. "I am one."

Eduardo turned to face him.

"No, no," Eduardo said, shaking his head. "You are not. Do not let anyone say you are. There is a man, who calls himself that, he is in the courts now fighting our constitution."

"Alejandro Pédro Juarez Jiminez. I know, he cannot work, go to school, or leave the country until the case is done."

"Three years, he has been in court. Three years! I know of other countries where he would be executed, with his family, for being such a coward. I would draft him into permanent service, myself, if I could."

Eduardo waved his hand dismissively. His eyes were swollen, his face red, and the veins in his temples were pronounced.

"No," he continued. "You will need your military card. There are no military cards given to men hiding behind an excuse. Only long and expensive legal battles paid for by our country. I will make certain you get your card from your work on the hotel. Civil service sometimes takes the place of military service. Your father told me to make certain you complete your military term. While I support conscription, in certain cases such as this, there could be an exception. So this is how I will give honour to your father's wishes."

He paused briefly before continuing.

"There is a custom here in Ecuador," he said, "as you know. It says the possession of one person, when openly admired by another, should be given to him. Which," he stopped, pointing around the office at all of the souvenirs hanging from his walls, "is why I have all of these things. In our case this 'possession' is your military card—which I do not have now, but which I have the power to give. Your father has honoured this custom, you see, as I am doing now."

Eduardo sat down in his chair, apparently pleased with himself, turning to peer out at the unpopulated beach below. He lit another cigarette, his flattened hair stiff in the breeze of the ceiling fan.

"I can leave to find my father," Tómas said. "Now I know where he is."

"You cannot go anywhere," Eduardo said, turning back toward him and shifting his weight in his seat. "With your military service to be started so soon, you will not be allowed to leave the country. And then, there is a visa you will need, depending where you will go. For you, your father British and your mother Canadian, that might be an easier step for you than for most but still, it is a step that will take time, much time, nonetheless ..."

"I need to leave."

"You are young. You do not know what you need. All your father dreamed of was to see the hotel built. He knew the island needs it, and he wanted you to help me build it. Your father will return, as he always has. And when he does, he will see that you have helped me to complete this grand hotel, and he will see that it has become a great benefit for everyone here on the island."

He lifted the cigarette to his lips, inhaled, and then exhaled with the words: "You will want to go to the job site not because you have need for money, but because you need to see the hotel built. It will infect you and its workers will infect you. When you are part of the team to see it come to life, then you will see. I was a part of many similar projects before, on the mainland, some of them very successful. Projects like this, but smaller, they have become the most important things in my life. Maybe that is why I did not marry. But you too, you will become infected with this disease."

Eduardo paused for a moment, opening the window and flicking his cigarette outside before adding: "There is a rally tomorrow morning, outside of this building. Come to it. And within two weeks, you will tell me you accept my generous offer."

As Tómas walked through the evening moonlight back to his home, he felt a sense of relief in knowing where his father had gone. A significant research project was before him that could give him credit toward his irrigation engineering degree and his military card. Perhaps Eduardo was right, that the hotel was his father's dream and not Eduardo's, and that Juan Carlos's fight for conscientious objection for him was futile. He could not expect to win such a fight in the next twelve days, anyway, before he was expected to report to the military base in Guayaquil.

Then, as he walked a long route to pass an inlet absent of water at low tide, he had the sudden feeling that this all seemed too easy, as though this offer might suddenly be retracted, or he would awaken suddenly and realize that this had all been a dream.

At the corner of a concrete apartment building, within view across the street, stood Juan Carlos's darkened apartment. And in the bay, several boats lay flat on their sides in the dark mud: all except for Juan Carlos's darkened boat, supported by a wooden cradle to keep it upright. The boat could not travel anywhere, as the hull was bolted firmly to the cradle.

Tómas watched as the sea began to rise and slosh at the cradle's base. He wanted to see what Juan Carlos thought of all this. Juan Carlos was never one to sleep early, though, and the fact that there were no lights on inside the boat indicated that he was with Alfonso, Rodolfo, Hector and others, at a party Tómas knew about at Julio's house; a party that would go on hasta la madrugada—until dawn. Their wives and girlfriends would already be asleep. Tómas knew that if he went he would be greeted by food, music and conversation, and a glass of Caña Manabita would be thrust into his hand.

He didn't feel like that tonight. But still, he was unable to come up with a reason why he shouldn't, the whisky still clouding his head slightly but beginning to lose its effect. And he would have to tell Juan Carlos not to be so foolish, to stay in hiding on his boat instead of going out to parties and allowing himself to be seen. So he turned around and began toward the hillside home of Julio's parents.

The sky was growing darker from the onset of a storm. As Tómas continued walking, he was suddenly bombarded by rain. Each step became more saturated, each one heavier than the last, and he began running.

As he ran, he thought of the new albarradas that were, at that moment, flooding and overflowing with rainwater. His entire life would be spent comparing the flora and fauna still growing in ancient albarradas to the fossilized remains there, thousands of years old—he had known for a long time that he would be doing this. Traditional farmers and their families would seek out his help to document albarrada maintenance programs for future generations. He would learn enough to begin successfully constructing new albarradas. And Eduardo's offer would have been the start of it all.

But if he did not report for military duty and began working for the hotel, would he be forced into service if his unfulfilled obligations were discovered? He would have to do his best to keep his already publicized commitment a secret, a forgotten memory, from those who might seek to send him to the military base at Guayaquil. The year would soon be over, and all of this would be a part of the past. This was the only way.

As he walked through the front door of Julio's house not a spot on him remained dry, and he quickly removed his clothing piece by piece in the bathroom, and wrung them out in the sink before donning them again. Ascending the stairs minutes later, he rubbed his hands together in anticipation of a fiesta hasta la madrugada.

10. The Rally

A RALLY HELD in cooperation with the local government took place at the future site of the hotel, beneath a cloudy sky, in the early afternoon. Eduardo Delgado stood before a crowd of two hundred people, wearing a shimmering grey suit and smoking a cigarette despite the temperature of over forty degrees Celsius. Tómas and Veronica stood steps away from him. The cliff was Eduardo's podium, the sea thunderous behind him.

Tómas yawned and surveyed the crowd to keep from falling asleep. The island's sole grocery store owner was in attendance with four out of his five workers. So were the pharmacy shopkeepers who dispensed single pills without prescriptions and doled out discounted and expired antibiotics, as were the ceviche and encebollado restaurant owners, proprietors of cold and warm fish soup respectively, many of whom dished their fare out of back doors and from the tops of metal pots inlaid within wheeled wooden carts.

The pescadore fishermen had wandered here, after pedalling half-metre long razor-teethed fish on the beach that morning to those who would sell them in soup, or bake the fresh catches for lunch.

Some of Tómas's fellow university students talked with professors from the agronomy department. The island's two police officers and men in military attire hovered behind women with crying babies, the fathers standing a distance away. Padre Pédro and members of the press stood at the front near Eduardo. Juan Carlos was conspicuously absent but perhaps present somewhere among the crowd, in disguise as he said he would be.

Eduardo outlined details of the project. Construction would commence by erecting a series of scaffolds up the cliff's side. After design approval, the foundation would be poured and the walls would be erected with concrete produced in the mainland city of Guayaquil. The roof would then be set in place, complete with a pressure-treated hardwood walking surface on the rooftop. The interior would then be completed in a sea-green tile, with matching carpeting and paint.

"Steel for the walls and ceilings will come from America," Eduardo said, reading from a piece of paper. "The wood for the frame, that will come from Ecuadorian trees; but not from the rainforests. Foreign oil companies are taking care to get the wood out of there."

All other building materials except the wiring, the plumbing and the bathroom fixtures would be manufactured by Ecuadorian hands. Foreign investors—a French holding company, specifically—had made this all possible. An English shipbuilder had been hired to work in an advisory capacity to the architect.

"The architect, he is English too, not Ecuadorian," Eduardo explained. "This will make it easier to talk about the details and make final the design."

Eduardo, after outlining all of the details of the construction, elucidated his vision for the hotel: it was to be an extension of the sea. It would incorporate and personify his love of its vast, seemingly limitless expanses. He moved his hands as if to form the hotel's outline, inviting the crowd to envision the view from 15 metres higher than where they now stood, as if they were all suddenly perched atop the deck of a great ocean liner.

"It will be greater than anything ever built on dry land," Eduardo said, his tone triumphant.

The hotel's roof would represent the upper deck, around which would be metal railings. Masts would support a dance floor with evening dancing and live jazz musicians imported from European capitals. Lights strung around the railing would form the base of the ship, the sea alive below. Angles would be such to minimize views of land from the 'ship'. Portholes would look out from the hotel's edifice resembling the enormity of a steel hull. Water would be pumped to a storage tank disguised as one of the ship's stacks, on the roof. Water would flow down through troughs past each of the rooms, alongside the hull, to remind hotel guests that they were not on an island at all, but out at sea. As the hotel would not actually sway the patrons would, only through their expectation of movement, perceive the slow and methodical motion of a ship. Those who suffered from seasickness would be coached how not to experience the illusion by utilizing techniques such as focusing on immobile elements of dry land: a building, or a section of the island's volcanic rock.

"Tómas Harvey," Eduardo said, pointing him out to the crowd, reviving him from his sleepiness at the mention of his name, "he will be responsible for the water system, and to making certain this happens. Also, he will be responsible for the albarradas on this land, to make them collect rainwater. The gardens growing on and around the albarradas will be fantastic, to match gardens in French and Russian palaces. They will be alive for decades. And Veronica Harvey, Montgomery Harvey's wife, will create the statues, including Jupiter and Triton; lobby statues four metres high."

Tómas looked down the beach and saw the island Centre of Recruitment and Reserves. He could not remove his eyes from the grey brick building as Eduardo discussed how he had contemplated themed events: landings at different ports of call in exotic lands, tying these in somehow to the content of Montgomery Harvey's travel articles. Eduardo described how he would use Montgomery's pieces in Diario Hoy advertisements for upcoming events: "*Cruise* the Caribbean," he said. "Enjoy a Spanish or a Russian Holiday, or pass through Baltic Capitals. Or travel to where no other cruise ship can go, such as through the deserts alongside the great pyramids ..." All of this was to be done through paintings, complicated on-board settings, and stages constructed around the perimeter of the ship.

Veronica suddenly pulled on Tómas's arm to leave. "This is ridiculous," she said, shaking her head. "We will not listen to any of this. We will go."

Instinctively, he consented.

Tómas looked back to see Eduardo and another man with a dark beard in a military uniform, a man he did not recognize, who eyed him carefully as they navigated out through the crowd. Tómas's stomach developed a distinctly sour sensation as they walked back home.

11. Liberation Theology

VERONICA PREPARED LUNCH, plucking feathers from an emaciated chicken. She wore an apron as she often did inside the house, and her long hair was pinned behind her head. All of this woman's features were rotund: the outline of her head, the ringlets of her hair, her plump fingers and her oversized belly. Known to Tómas as his Ecuadorian mother, she had raised him, and did not leave him unprotected, waiting outside the school as everyone was let out when he had a confrontation and stopping the offending boys to scold them and slap their hands. When his grades were not what she thought they should be, she went to the school and didn't return until they had been changed. And when Tómas became a teenager and he no longer confided in her any more, refusing at times to talk or even to listen to her, she would often drag him to someone who would force him to engage in conversation, and who would give him direction and advice: Padre Pédro.

Tómas poured a bag of rice onto the counter. Veronica had purchased the least expensive rice, and so he had to separate the edible grains from the myriad of interspersed tiny sticks and stones.

"Montgomery did not help to prepare the meals," Veronica said, "Or to help with anything else, especially when I asked. But to you, I say nothing, and immediately you know what to do."

Flory's television was now in the kitchen.

There was news of flooding in the mainland campo. An elderly woman told a reporter that the house in which she had lived her entire life had been suddenly and violently swept away in a slide of wet earth. Her child's school was buried almost completely, video footage showing only small sections of green roof visible through the mud. The school officials who routinely surveyed school districts and reported on the state of the rural school system would say nothing about these buried schools. The teachers would still receive their paycheques, and the school officials would receive a percentage of those paycheques. Tómas had never seen this reported in any of the newscasts, though. These pictures of mud led into a news story about the plans to construct a hotel on Isla de la Plata, complete with pictures of the area and a smiling Eduardo Delgado.

"Why did Eduardo, in his speech, say you will work for him?" Veronica asked suddenly.

"I did not say I would," Tómas replied.

"Then why would he say that, in front of so many people?"

"Why would he say that about you, too?"

"You have a wicked tongue." She waved her hand dismissively. "Ah, well. I suppose I gave that to you." She raised her other hand, which contained several feathers, as she continued. "I will never work for him. He knows that. He mocks me by giving me a temporary job, a distraction. It is some comfort, some gift, after leaving me with an absent husband. But you are not thinking of working for him, of course."

"I went to his office, and—" He stopped. She turned the television volume down, and returned to her work before speaking again.

"You met with a man who forced your father out of the country?"

"You do not know that he did."

"Then you are lost," she said, wiping her hands on her apron. "So Eduardo does not know about your military service?"

"Yes, he does."

"Well?" She stared at him for a moment before balking, waving a hand, and then continuing at her work.

The snore wheezing from Flory's bedroom became momentarily louder than the merengue music now radiating from the television.

"Pssst," Veronica uttered, pointing with a nod of her head to a painted statue on the counter beside Tómas. It was a six-inch St. Francis of Assisi, his stigmata hands holding two birds. "Still, he is wet," she said. "I painted him this morning."

"Supposedly to work for the hotel is to finish my military term," Tómas said.

"Yes, and how would that happen?" she asked. "Tell me. Please."

"Civil service. Eduardo said civil service can replace military service."

"Working for a hotel? The maids that will work there, too, cleaning toilets, they will be doing civil service? I am concerned about you, Tómas. People talk, and you listen too much. You need to report to the military in ... how many days?"

"Ten."

"Ten days. And Eduardo and that cursed hotel are the reason Montgomery is not here now, instead wandering about on the mainland somewhere. And," she added, shaking her head, "you went to a friendly meeting with the responsible man."

Tómas did not tell her where Montgomery was, or explain how he knew. She would have too many questions and imputations. His replies would be met with the same distrust and anger she had demonstrated to everyone since Montgomery's departure.

"You think since my father is not here, this is all the fault of the hotel?" Tómas asked.

"Your father leaves, there are some nonsense accusations, and then the hotel is announced. What do you think of that? There is a connection, you must see that too. Eduardo knows, but he tells no one. He is responsible. He has taken my husband and your father from us, when he should not have left again."

Veronica performed a reverse jabbing motion, removing the last of the feathers from the pallid bird. "Ten days," she said, holding the feathers in her fist. "Ten days. Not much time, and then my mother and I will be left here alone. We will miss you, but I will be proud. So, you will go to the mainland ahead of this."

Her insistence that he march off to a premature death in this war suddenly angered him, and made him want to lash out at her, regardless of her recently increased aggressiveness.

"I do not want to die for nothing, except for some oil and uranium," he said.

She threw the feathers onto a pile of them. "Those are the words of a coward, not you," she said, shaking her head as she rinsed the bird in a sink full of dirty water. After placing the carcass on the counter and separating its feet with a hatchet, she removed the entrails and placed them in a pail beneath the sink. She put the feet on a small plate, placed the upright sticks in the freezer for soup, and then wiped her hands on her apron.

"Tomorrow we will go to see Padre Pédro," she said, shaking her head. "He always has sense, when you have none."

Tómas and Veronica ascended the nineteenth century stone steps of the Iglesia Santa Maria, climbing closer to two hexagonal towers crowned with orange domes straddling the entrance. Veronica wore a long dress covered in enormous flowers and Tómas was in one of his father's silk shirts and slacks.

A massive wooden door, elaborately carved, stood open between the towers that each had seventeen paneless windows, lookout points to observe the island. A bell without a hammer was hidden beneath each tower: secrets to all but their operator Padre Pédro, who held dominion over the church.

The same as the majority of the islanders, instead of attending the church service, Veronica would normally listen to a mainland radio preacher at home on Sundays. The sound of the radios would echo through the streets and hillsides at high volume. She would be seated with the neighbour, or Flory, or painting, or cooking lunch alone as she listened. Flory and Tómas would be unseen and in their bedrooms. Tómas had learned out of necessity to focus, despite the noise, on reading Proust, Rousseau, Dostoevsky, Boccaccio or Hemingway, reading the authors from his father's bookshelf who had lived in some of the places where his father too had resided. Tómas would think, as the words from the radio preacher occasionally interrupted the text, that Veronica's piety was different than those who regularly attended the island's only church. Community and togetherness, seeing their children playing in the aisles, and occasional gossip brought those people to Roman Catholicism. But hers was a personal religious devotion apparent only to herself and it made her, and the other radio-listening islanders, seem more devout to Tómas than any of those he now saw in the church before him.

Tómas and Veronica entered the church quietly, slipping past oversized oils on canvas, etched glass and life-sized painted statues of saints. Veronica had created nearly all of these statues, apart from the originals that were still here. She had constructed them in pieces, and Tómas had helped with the assembly by placing the sections over wire frames, before they were plastered in place and painted.

They stopped in an alcove to listen. The pews inside were half full, some people still filtering in through the vestibule as Padre Pédro continued his homily. Padre Pédro uttered each word with care, his hands protruding through the thin sleeves of a long, black robe to recite from a handwritten page, his grey eyes, grey hair and white beard testament to an almost otherworldly quality he possessed.

He breathed heavily between phrases, describing that which, sight unseen, is there. Tiny particles moving through wires to make light. The chemical reactions that were taking place, right now, in everyone's bodies, to allow them to process the information he was projecting with his voice. Rays from the sun that warmed us, and made life on earth possible. Padre Pédro concluded his homily with the statement: "We do not need to see what we know is there. We only need to see the results ..."

Pédro's index finger rose in the air now as he scolded the congregation for its lack of consistent church attendance. "More days than Christmas and Easter should see full pews," he said briskly as he stepped down from the pulpit.

Veronica walked over to a life-sized statue of the Virgin Mary. Padre Pédro stepped near her as she knelt down with clasped hands, holding her rosary beads, before the statue. She thumbed through the rosary, her lips moving, her eyes closed.

Another woman placed tiny roses at the Virgin's feet, just as Veronica rose from her position on the floor. Padre Pédro smiled at Veronica, and invited her to sit down.

They sat in a varnished pew, Tómas between them. Padre Pédro resembled Rasputin, not only in physical appearance, but also in the mannerisms Tómas imagined Rasputin might have had. The same calm, ominous voice. The same intelligence, the same enigmatic demeanour as indemnity against those who might oppose him. The same wintry gaze.

"Tómas must report to the army," Veronica began suddenly. "But he says he will not. He tells me he would die for nothing."

"Really?" Padre Pédro asked Tómas in Spanish. "And Señora Modesta, Señora Palacio, their sons, they also died for nothing?" Padre Pédro's Spanish was quick and cutting.

Tómas was silent.

"No," Padre Pédro continued, his head contorting to one side. "That is only the excuse. If I did not know you, Tómas, I would call you a coward."

"That has been said before," Veronica replied.

Padre Pédro turned toward the front of the church. There was a brief moment before he continued, his attention still focused forward.

"You must serve your country," Padre Pédro said.

"Yes, I will," Tómas replied. "I will do much for my country."

"He will not," Veronica interjected.

"Let the boy speak," Padre Pédro said, raising his hand in her direction and looking over at Tómas.

"He will not ever become an Irrigation Engineer," Veronica continued. "He will not help anyone if he spends time working on luxury hotels and avoiding the army."

Looking over at Veronica, Padre Pédro asked again: "A moment, please, Señora." He turned back toward Tómas and asked: "You will work for Eduardo, as he said at his rally?"

Tómas cleared his throat. "Eduardo wants me to," he said. "The work will be my thesis. And he promised to get me a military card."

Veronica shook her head, closing her eyes. "It will not happen," she said. "It is his father's senselessness, and his father's fear of fighting, coming out of his mouth."

"So Eduardo promised your military card by working for the hotel?" Padre Pédro asked.

"Yes," Tómas replied. "Irrigation engineering work. Civil service, he called it."

"Interesting, and very sensible." Padre Pédro turned his attention back to the front of the church, his gaze transfixed on an array of candles. As he continued staring, the tiny lights now reflecting in his eyes, he said: "Your choice is clear. It involves obligation to the people. The people, they believe Eduardo's election is the beginning of a new movement of liberation theology here on the island. You know what that is."

"Yes," Tómas said. He recalled liberation theology as a movement initiated in part from the understanding that it is against the precepts of religion to be concerned for people's spiritual needs, while ignoring their worldly ones. Padre Pédro had explained it before, at the end of some of his sermons, as being about the elimination of the causes of poverty and injustice; freeing the poor from what limits them; and liberation from selfishness and sin. When Tómas had asked Veronica about it, she commented that God had better ways to liberate the poor and the oppressed than through Marxism—which Tómas knew was probably a reiteration of his father's words.

"The hotel will give the people here employment," Padre Pédro said. "It will give each person tasks according to their skills. That is what Eduardo wants. The effort of many on the island will be required to construct it. You see, I have given this a great deal of thought. You know, I was once a theologian, and I have met with other theologians from other countries: Argentina, Brazil, Chile, Mexico, Colombia and Venezuela. There are many books planned about liberation theology. Fifty-five volumes, a series, in seven languages. Many of the volumes have not been published until now. The island hotel will be a great experiment, and I will document and submit an article for publication. That will be my contribution to that very important work. Think of your work as an obligation to people who will come in the future, and to God. Your responsibility to those you cannot see. Your work will satisfy your military obligations, and, not only that, it will do much more than you realize."

There was a long pause as Padre Pédro began to forage through his grey beard with long, probing fingers.

"You do not know what you say, Padre," Veronica said, rising to leave.

"What I say is best for everyone," he replied, without looking up.

"Something bad has happened to Montgomery because of this hotel. It is an ill omen."

"That, Señora, please pardon me, is superstition."

She raised her voice as if chastising him, as she had over the years with the students who had confronted Tómas. Others lingering around the pews and by the doors glared at them, apparently eager to learn more about the confrontation. "Montgomery is not here," she said. "Do you see him? Eduardo and that hotel are bad for Montgomery and the island and, as you will see, for Tómas."

"I am very sad for you about your husband Montgomery," Padre Pédro said calmly, "But I respectfully, and genuinely disagree with you, Señora."

Tómas descended the stone steps of the church behind Veronica, who was irate. He could not tell her that while he would soon be expected at both the Guayaquil base and at the hotel construction site, he would end up at the latter. He could not explain that he would help construct the hotel as his father requested, or that the hotel might have been Eduardo's dream, and also his father's. Any attempts to console her would only infuriate her more.

12. Comforting in Absentia

THE SIX O'CLOCK sunrise illuminated a sleeping neighbourhood, the bus tossing up dust before slowing to a near stop. Potholes in the dirt roadway caused the bus to lean heavily to one side, then the other, before resuming its previous speed. I saw these wild iguana parks of Guayaquil before, then visible from the bus windows, crowds of tourists watching wild iguanas congregating in trees and munching on lettuce leaves, the feral creatures basking in the sun. A low mountain with homes winding up to its peak overshadowed the road. A woman pounded her laundry against heavy rocks, as a boy hauled his wooden cart shouting through the streets: "Apples! Plantains!" Roosters crowed to the smell of cooking oil and fire-baked fish.

All of this I had seen or heard or smelled so many times before. But never had such sights saddened me so much, knowing that I would be leaving this place forever. And now that my vision was quickly deteriorating, I would soon be able to perceive through only two of these three senses—the other would be replaced by visualizations derived from memories, as though I would be living in a dream.

Traversing the countryside, I saw the remnants of el niño. Roofs of homes buried in mud lay on the ground beside lime-coloured treetops. Mountains of saturated earth waited to slide over on themselves. Statues of the Virgin Mary were scattered in areas without churches. Lit candles were placed on the statues and women prayed before them as men and children removed mud with small buckets from their homes.

As we moved into a more mountainous region, our bus wound around the top of sheer precipices at high speed, the driver motivated by loud salsa music. This scene reminded me of the news stories of buses *that had plummeted down to the valley below, full of people, birds swerving in mid-flight to avoid the screaming metal carcasses. I felt nauseous and began coughing speckles of blood into my handkerchief as we passed through the mountains, and I was relieved as we descended to rock-strewn beaches and boys herding cows, past flooded fields and steel-roofed homes with no visible doors or windows. Farmers boarded the bus with pigs or with chickens bound at the feet, exiting at the next pueblo to sell them. Elderly women and young children stared intently at me.*

We passed through cities with unstable wooden structures next to air-conditioned banks. A bank with its doors closed, both employees and customers waiting outside, had a sign in the window indicating the place was bankrupt. This view took us from Bahia de Caraquez to Portoviejo, and through to Machala where Juan Carlos's family lives. I called his wife, and she invited me to dinner and then to stay overnight. While she said she had read of the allegations against me, she did not seem concerned by them. She looked tired, haggard. Her children have no father, she said. "When is he coming back?" she asked me after they were asleep. I could do nothing but try to comfort her, patting her hand and saying: "Soon, he will be back, soon," which she said Juan Carlos has been telling her for the last year; and she didn't it believe from him, either. She had been told that he was having sex with another woman, a foreigner living on the island. I knew she must have been talking about Colette, but I said nothing. I did not know what to say to console her any more, as though whatever I said would only be hurtful, a false consolation that she would not believe anyway. I began travelling the next evening for Peru.

I can only write now in my journal, by the light of my flashlight. It is my only escape, these words I write. The bus sits motionless and in near darkness at the Ecuadorian-Peruvian border. The border guards, with their semi-automatic weapons, stand beside a tiny wooden shack with dim lights as their constant companion. I wonder if they have read the papers and seen my picture. They are occupied with something. A piece of paperwork has their attention. I wonder what that paperwork says, if it is about me.

I can't look up to see what they're doing. No one is boarding the bus. I would hear and feel the weight of their boots and the side tilting of the vehicle instead of just snores and whispering.

If I don't get past this border, I will be sent back to Quito and ordered to appear in court after waiting in prison some indeterminately long time. I will have to take the blame upon myself, more so than I have already done. Maybe that will become the sole task of my defence, to have my lawyer prove that the responsibility does not extend beyond me, a dying man of no consequence.

The bus has jolted.

I don't know what is happening until I stop writing and turn off my flashlight ... one of the border guards is talking on his radio, and is waving for the bus to proceed ... and combined with my relief is sadness in wondering whether I will ever see my Ecuadorian family again ...

13. Grand Aqueducts

FOREIGN OPINION DIFFERED from local. The Peruvian paper La Verdad called Eduardo's plan a drain on resources and a dead end. The island's Diario Hoy and the mainland's El Comercio were of the same opinion, both of them calling Eduardo a visionary.

The people of the island were divided. Tómas heard them in the streets: elderly men calling Eduardo loco, insane. The island didn't need a hotel, they said, especially one built like a boat that would never float. They described Eduardo loudly as a 'friend to criminals,' citing that Montgomery's articles would be used to advertise, talking of Eduardo and Montgomery's friendship and Montgomery's embezzlement of funds, of which Eduardo was likely a part. They wrote letters to the editor describing Eduardo as a man exploiting the poor workforce for his own benefit, a man whose foreign influences would destroy local tradition. Young men and women wrote letters that were published in retaliation, calling Eduardo the beginning of a new age of prosperity for every one of the islanders.

In Tómas's household Veronica repeated that Montgomery was an old man alone in the world because of Eduardo and his hotel. Flory's television echoed the voices of newsmen and newswomen over concrete walls, all of them asking the same question: *Who will come to a resort here, once it is built?*

Diario Hoy reported that Eduardo considered his rally a success by having garnered the press he needed to attract other potential investors, by earning the support of local business owners and government officials, and by generating a list of one hundred and fifty islanders who were interested in being paid for their labours by helping with the construction of the hotel.

"I went to get the special application form," Juan Carlos said, walking beside Tómas down a desolate highway leading away from the town centre, late in the evening. A hood covered Juan Carlos's head in the chilly air, only a few sodium vapour lamps swarming with insects illuminating some bushes along the roadside. Tómas turned to face him, squinting as they passed beneath one of the lights. "You remember, the article 108 conscientious objection form, from the Centre of Recruitment and Reserves."

"Yes," Tómas replied. "You have that form?"

"No," Juan Carlos said.

They ducked into a bush at a sudden noise and light caused by a taxi honking at them, passing close by at high speed from behind, dust flying, tail lamps flickering.

Returning to the edge of the road, continuing along, Juan Carlos began speaking again.

"There is a problem," he said. "The centre did not have a form, and they could not tell me where to get one. I wrote to some government organizations to see if they might have it, and I have not received a reply. On the telephone a man from the army said he knew nothing about article 108, article 93, conscientious objection, or the special application form. I think the form does not exist."

"So, what now?" Tómas said, suddenly frustrated. "I do not see why the form is so important. A signed letter is good."

"No, unfortunately. You must take my advice on this matter. I have been through this before with Jiminez. I submitted a signed letter to the court and the military, but they would not accept it."

"There is another way, though, for certain."

A light appeared in the distance and they crouched behind a patch of bushes. A red pickup truck flew by on its way to the town centre. A cloud of dust drifted toward them.

"I have discovered the basis for our fight," Juan Carlos continued, coughing and then spitting on the ground beside them. "You know, while sitting in my stifling boat with my books, I have found something in our constitution. It says conscientious objectors 'can be assigned to civilian or community service.' "

"Eduardo said that is how I can get my military card."

"Until two days ago I was not aware, and, I assure you, Eduardo does not know that this is in the constitution. And also it is in Article 108 of the military service law, as you know, which says conscientious objectors, if recognised by the Recruitment Director of the Armed Forces, will be assigned to one of the development units of the Army."

"So?"

"You do not see? I understand now why you are not a lawyer. You see, they are not the same. And that is how we will fight them in court."

The pickup truck stopped nearby, the cloud of dust dissipating. The cab of the truck was loaded with people, some of whom jumped out of the vehicle and headed towards a cluster of houses ahead.

"There is something else I will tell you, so you are not surprised when you see the article in the paper. But you must tell no one. Not Eduardo, especially."

"I will say nothing."

"After the press conference in Quito, I sent letters to the European investors who are funding the hotel's construction. I said the same as I did in that room full of reporters. I also sent news articles explaining how Eduardo's housing plan and his hotel were badly researched, not realistic and invented to *raise* government subsidies on food items everyone needs. All of this, I wrote, was part of Eduardo's plan to get a seat in the government in Quito. Why do you think he had the press conference there, and not here?"

"Maybe to impress some of the politicians there?"

"Yes. You are right to say that. I included, too, the research from French investment companies that have already stopped giving money for other such projects in Ecuador, Peru and Bolivia. And today, in many European newspapers, it was reported that the financial backers will no longer be giving cash for Eduardo's white elephant."

Juan Carlos rose, saying that the driver of the pickup truck was Raphael who would give him a ride home. Removing the hood from his head, he ran toward the open door. After getting into the truck, Juan stuck his head out of the window.

"We will talk later," he said to Tómas. "I need to get the paperwork started for our fight in court."

"Who will we fight in court?" Tómas shouted. The truck did not move.

"The Ecuadorian military."

Tómas suddenly felt uneasy about his conscientious objection being debated in an open forum, even one currently limited to a few drunken observers in the truck, and others on their way back to their homes who were now almost too far distant to hear.

"Our fight has, at this moment, begun," Juan Carlos said, shouting through the open window as the truck swerved and then gathered forward momentum.

Eduardo and Tómas sat on the side of a dirt-filled concrete flowerpot, consuming their lunch in the busy town centre. They cut fried cow tongue on paper plates balanced over their knees and ate unripe, salted mangoes from the market.

"Aqueducts need to be constructed," Eduardo said. "I will need your full time, along with your full attention, to do it."

He would advertise internationally as homage to the great Inca engineers of Machu Picchu, who once produced a city complete with crops on a remote mountaintop for both wet and dry seasons, the only water a river 500 metres below and two springs 800 metres away.

"I have doubts this hotel will be made," Tómas said.

"It will happen," Eduardo replied. "You will see."

They discarded their empty plates and walked past a man holding three inverted chickens bound at the feet. The man asked if they might buy one of them, and Eduardo waved him away. A group of youths in school uniforms dispersed over the square congested with taxis, buses, cars, market stalls, and people. Several of the students held hands, entering bars with sectioned-off and curtained back stalls, padded seats providing the privacy their homes could not: what Tómas recalled from his secondary school days as what was required for kissing, in which he would always sit with a girl he barely knew, feeling awkward, staring at the inside of the red curtains and wondering what to do next.

"During the wet season the aqueducts will lead the rainwater down from open air tanks on the roof of the hotel," Eduardo said as they navigated through the crowded street. "The water will travel down beside each room. It will be sent to splash over the albarrada gardens at the hotel front. In the dry season, a small amount of water from your albarradas will be pumped to the roof tanks in the night when the island is sleeping, when electricity is not being used. It will be not as expensive in the night to work the diesel generators, when electric demand is lower."

A green bus weaved through traffic and came to an abrupt halt beside them. They zigzagged down the sidewalk to avoid a dozen people, most of them students, who had been waiting and who now moved toward the already overcrowded bus.

"The water, when allowed to flow down through the troughs, at certain times during the day," Eduardo continued, his voice escalating as they moved past the crowd, "when it passes the hotel room windows, will give the added sense that you are at sea. Some of the water will splash on the windows as it passes by." Eduardo smiled as he concluded his statements.

After a few minutes of plotting a course through the crowd, Tómas said: "Supposedly, this hotel will not be built because of money."

"No."

"And my father is in Peru at Machu Picchu, I suppose, a known place for tourists. Maybe so he is not found. No plane ticket, and so he is anonymous."

"Perhaps you are right about your father, and certainly wrong about the hotel."

"You think he is not here because of the hotel?"

"Who says that?"

"Veronica. All the time."

"Yes, her thoughts are dangerous. Like a conspiracy against herself, and others."

A shirtless man riding a bicycle hit Eduardo's arm hard, and then continued riding as though he hadn't noticed.

"New leadership," Eduardo said, rubbing his arm. "It is the future of this island. New opportunities. And for the country, myself as president."

"President?"

"You look surprised. I am surprised your father did not tell you. It has always been my goal; the hotel I will build will prove that if this island, one of the most impoverished areas of the country, if this can be made prosperous, then this is a demonstration of possibilities."

"And money for the island, and for yourself."

"A large cash amount will go toward my campaign fund. But more importantly, this hotel will show that there are opportunities for all of the country's people, without regard to where they were born, or what their history is. This type of solution will not work in all areas of the country, of course. Diverse solutions for different areas: that is what is required. But this hotel will become my pilot project. Your father has always supported me in all of my endeavours, and encouraged me along the paths I have chosen. It is because of his encouragement, and yours, that I am on the threshold of greatness today."

They moved into an abandoned street. Eduardo said the consensus of the rally was clear. There was no opposition. One hundred and fifty islanders had agreed to work on the project. Without workers, Eduardo said, all the engineers, architects and construction managers in the country would be powerless to do anything but produce drawings of, and plan for, that which would never exist.

Tómas speculated, asking himself as he stared out at a donkey loaded with plantains and navigating with its owner around a pothole: *who would come to a resort here, if it was built?*

14. The Grand Hotel

AS THE HOTEL Santa Rita de Cascia in Old Quito attracted the socialites of the country—those who gathered to compare gossip and share stories of other socialites—Eduardo Delgado began preparations to construct its sister hotel on the island.

Tómas learned from Eduardo, as rain poured down outside the open window of his office, that a key term for appropriating the property had been that all labour for the project should be found on the island. Promoting a local workforce was a key goal of the government's elected officials, Eduardo said, for any of the island's endeavours. And since there hadn't been any initiatives in several years— the last, a wind turbine power generation plant that had been scrapped before it started because of unfavourable 'cost-to-benefit ratios,' something Tómas did not understand and Eduardo did not care to explain—his fellow officials of the Popular Democracy Party thought the hotel to be an ideal way to stimulate the economy.

"The project, it will create jobs," Eduardo said, standing before an array of continuous, multifaceted trickling as a wall of rainwater poured down behind him, "and it will make tourists come to our beautiful island resort. Also, this will give us the island vote and thousands of mainlander votes in the upcoming election. I have placed an advertisement in El Comercio titled 'A New Future.' "

"You read the international news?" Tómas asked.

"Yes, of course. You refer to the funding issue."

"And that is more than an issue."

"You seem surprised I know. Honestly, I am surprised you are aware about that."

"I heard from a friend."

"Well, I am not worried. I have no cause."

"But the hotel will not be built."

He smiled. "It will, you will see. Everyone will see, very soon. There will be funding. But you, I know you have a more urgent issue. You are to report for military duty—"

"Tomorrow."

"Ah, ya. Tomorrow. As I said, I will get your military card for you. You will go down to the recruitment centre tomorrow and tell them. If they will not believe you, you will have them call me and I, too, will come down."

After leaving Eduardo's office, Tómas walked to the university to inform the Ingeniera that he would be discontinuing his studies for now.

At the top of a narrow stairway, laughter reverberated down the hall from a room adjacent to an empty office. A dark-haired secretary with light freckles invited him into a room full of balloons and various people who worked at the university, most of whom Tómas recognized.

"This is a party for Ivan from the copiadora," she said excitedly, sitting Tómas down and giving him a chunk of white cake. "He does not have malaria any more, and today is his birthday. Two reasons to celebrate."

"You need to take care around water-collecting roof tanks," she continued a moment later as she handed Tómas a styrofoam cup full of dark soda. "Fixing these cylinders did this to him, all that still water and mosquitoes."

Ivan sat barely smiling, his face slightly yellow, with a colourful conical hat on his head.

A short time later Tómas sat in the Ingeniera's office at the end of the hall, behind the closed, frosted door that he had never wanted to see from the inside. He could not explain to this imposing and sturdily built woman about his civil service, nor could he explain that he was in the process of applying as a conscientious objector to the war. So he found himself telling her that he would soon be reporting for military service. The Ingeniera gave him a piece of paper to sign, handing the yellow page to him with corpulent hands.

"Most students who leave the university for the army do not finish their schooling," she said, rubbing her nose vigorously. "You can apply to postpone your military service, for this reason."

"Well—" Tómas said, not knowing what to add.

"Well, that decision is yours. But when you come back you may find your priorities are changed. That you want to work more for the military. Or, you may find studying and examinations difficult after being away for so long. One year does not seem to be such a long time, but now, at this part of your life, it is. You can delay this whole process, if you want. You can apply for a postponement, as I said, and you will sign nothing today."

But his application had already been denied.

"I will sign this now," Tómas replied, without offering an explanation, signing the page quickly and leaving it on the table, before rising to leave. "And I will return to finish my studies."

The Ingeniera took the signed paper back, sighing as she opened the filing cabinet.

Veronica sat painting a small statue of Triton, his unpainted spear high in the air. The waves beneath him were beginning to flow with colour. The neighbour, Señora Modesta, sat examining a white, unpainted statue of Jupiter slightly larger than Triton. She placed it down on the table as Tómas entered the house.

Señora Modesta noticed that a white-grey, fight-mangled cat had followed Tómas inside. She retrieved a broom and immediately chased the cat out the front door.

"Su gatito feo," Veronica said, repeating the phrase in English: "Your ugly little cat."

The Señora placed the broom in the corner as Veronica said: "The tank on the roof, you must clean it. We have no water, as I told you yesterday." She put down her statue and brush, walked over to the sink, and turned the tap handle. No water came out. The cylinder, designed to collect the rainwater that fell faithfully each day in the wet season, for drinking, bathing and dishwashing, before the water trucks began their delivery routes in the dry season, was plugged.

"I came from the university just now," Tómas said. "There was a man named Ivan, and the secretary told me—"

"No stories," Veronica interrupted. "Up to the roof for you."

As Veronica took her brush and resumed her painting, the Señora simply grimaced and sat down.

Tómas entered his room to change into shorts. In the next room, Veronica was conversing with Señora Modesta, blaming the garbage fires for the airborne sediment that had amassed in their water tank.

"He is like his father," Veronica said. "I remember once, asking Montgomery for three days to clean the water tank. He worked hard picking coffee beans and yuccas for money to feed us, when he had no newspaper to pay his way for travel."

"And this coffee and yucca did not give you much money," Señora Modesta added.

"He also talked about buying land for his friend Eduardo, with money he did not have. I told him that. But my opinion, to him, it was not valid. He wanted to start a banana plantation on that same land, years ago. An international organization gave him a letter. 'You cannot have fourteen-year-old children tying the trees together,' they said. Same thing I told him, even though he insisted that boys are lighter than men. He's practical, but he's still a fool."

Tómas, in shorts and shirtless, felt for a moment as if he were a child again, his chest hairless, standing half-naked beneath the troughs at the edges of the buildings in town. These conduits directed rainfall from the roofs where it flowed down the streets and into uncovered holes large enough to fit through. He had stood beneath the troughs at night with neighbourhood children, during the wet season's heavy rainfall. That water that could have been redirected for irrigation was instead wasted for bathing and siphoned into holes and drains, or collected in puddles on the street.

Tómas aimed, retracted his arm, and then threw his sandals up onto the roof. Putting his fingers into the cut-outs in the portico and using a large barrel as a foothold, he climbed up barefoot. Their black guard dog Medianoche, Midnight, was now resting on the corner of the hot roof under the shade of the rooftop cylinder. The dog looked up at him unenthusiastically, his ears flapping, the skin beneath his fur twitching. Tómas pulled himself up and quickly put the sandals back on his feet.

Pausing for a moment to look around at the panorama of mountains, he walked over to the steel cylinder which was overflowing with filth and muck. The dark water was alive with tiny worms swimming just beneath its surface.

Minutes later, the noise of children and dogs, taxis sputtering down the road, and the sounds of salsa and merengue dance music from Flory's television filled the house as Tómas entered. His right arm and his hand were covered to the shoulders in muck, and a foul stench.

"You have not told him, have you?" Señora Modesta asked Veronica. The Señora, still holding the broom, stood up to reveal her full weighty figure and looked on the floor behind him for the gatito feo.

"Told me what?" Tómas asked.

"The hotel will not be built," Veronica said, placing diced peppers in a pan sizzling with oil.

"I heard that," Tómas replied.

"Not enough money," Señora Modesta said, walking to the front door. She stood in the open doorway and picked her teeth, on guard for the gatito feo, staring past the concrete porch stairs leading to the dirt road with the broom still in her hand.

"The companies stopped their funding checks," Veronica said. "Your friend Juan Carlos, he wrote the editorial."

She pointed with her nose in the direction of the newspaper, and Tómas picked it up with blackened hands. There was a short front-page article explaining what had happened. It was exactly as Veronica, and Juan Carlos, had said. He turned to an editorial by Juan Carlos and read through it, leaving black, wet imprints on the page.

"It is awful when a dream is about money," Veronica said as she dumped two handfuls of cooked rice into the oiled pan to fry it and make one of Tómas's favourites, Cocolón. "Those twelve foot high statues of Triton and Jupiter that Eduardo said he wanted me to paint, for his hotel, you remember."

She pointed to the scaled down version of the statues on the table, both of them partially completed. The smell of exhaust smoke from the cars outside mixed with the scent of green pepper and red onions frying in oil, and the combined odour began to fill the house. Tómas had a sudden clear realization of what would happen if this newspaper article and editorial were true. He saw a losing and lengthy court battle, being sent to the war, and an eventual forced, indefinite military service.

"You do not want Eduardo to use your statues for the hotel," Tómas said. "You would not work for him. That is why we left the rally when Eduardo said it."

"No, no. You do not understand. These are small versions of what he wanted me to create, and they too will never be finished."

15. Financial Records

TÓMAS WAS EXPECTED at Guayaquil's military base on the mainland on September 15th. This date came and went, and he did not leave the island. Now a remiso, someone who failed to report for service, he often thought about young Colombian men who were rounded up at random and thrown in the back of pickup trucks as a way of recruiting for military service. Some recruits would be released, but those already identified for conscription that had not honoured their obligations would be forced to do so.

As Tómas walked the streets now, he envisioned himself being forcibly abducted. The sight of trucks made him duck into alleyways or through open doors. He formed theories that various people were conspiring to notify the authorities of his whereabouts. Everything seemed oppressive. The sun was blinding at times, forcing him down pathways he would never normally have taken. The moon was perpetually absent and made the island seem extraordinarily dark at night, so he was not able to walk away his insomnia. The trees seemed to bend easily in the wind, as if trying to point the way for others to subdue him, or preparing to smother and apprehend him.

He understood now what Juan Carlos might be experiencing; and furthermore, what his father must have felt, thinking himself as a known criminal openly defying authority and awaiting restitution and his own dishonour as a result.

Tómas no longer visited the site of the island hotel, fearing the island Centre of Recruitment and Reserves, which was in plain view from anywhere on the work site and which leered at him whenever he was there.

When a rap came at Tómas's window, he awoke with a start. There was a red pickup truck outside. After examining the vehicle, hearing Juan Carlos's voice beckoning him to come out, and seeing that Raphael was in the driver's seat, Tómas emerged and crammed into the front of the cab.

"I was to report for service—" Tómas said, addressing Juan Carlos.

"It seems you have no faith in me," Juan Carlos interrupted. "Our court case is moving ahead. You see, I have already applied. I'll show you the letter." He produced a piece of paper and, holding the wrinkled sheet and a flashlight, he began reading. As he did, Tómas became increasingly nauseated.

"*The petitioner, Mr. Tómas Montgomery Dixon Harvey,*" Juan Carlos began, "*alleges that conscientious objection indicated in Article 188 of the Political Constitution of Ecuador, and the 1984 Law of Obligatory Military Service in the Armed Forces Article 108, are contradictory. The same Law of Obligatory Military Service states that conscientious objectors, if recognised by the Director of Recruitment of the Armed Forces, will be assigned to one of the Development Units of the Ecuadorian Armed Forces.*"

"So I will be sent to another place to work, if I am in a Development Unit."

Juan Carlos looked up from the page, no longer reading the words. "There, as I read in the research Raphael helped me get from the university, you would have to build roads, bridges, and help excavate when floods and mudslides happen. That would not be a problem, really. You would have the same training as your pre-military course in secondary school, except you would not be taught to use weapons."

"Development Units. I will apply then."

Juan Carlos looked at him quizzically. "However, as I was reading," he continued, focusing again on the page: "*The constitution states conscientious objectors 'can be assigned to a civilian or community service,' which is not consistent with the Law of Obligatory Military Service.*" Juan Carlos looked up from the paper, into Tómas's eyes. "Chile also has a case, almost the same, in the courts. But theirs is not as strong as ours."

"Yes, but to me, that means nothing," Tómas said.

"That means I will continue to fight for you, and we will win."

This was all too complicated, and there were too many unknowns. The court case had to be kept secret, just as the fact that he was a remiso working for the island hotel.

"You have paperwork about my father," Tómas said.

"Tomorrow," he said. "I will be here, at your house, to show you. In the night, I think. The police, I see them sometimes near my old apartment, through my boat's porthole, always in the day."

Tómas told Juan Carlos that he should look after Veronica and Flory if, one day, Tómas was suddenly gone, to which Juan Carlos immediately consented.

"But to where will you go?" Juan Carlos asked.

Tómas looked away and did not answer, departing the truck, saying goodbye to Raphael and Juan Carlos, and closing the door behind him as though he had not heard.

The sound of roosters and children shouting in the streets, accompanied by the smell of plantains frying in oil and baked mandango con mani, cow intestines in peanut sauce, ushered in a dark and damp Tuesday morning. Tómas, Veronica and Flory watched Eduardo Delgado in a television interview as he explained that there was alternative funding for the hotel, that this would be detailed in upcoming radio broadcasts and newspaper articles in El Comercio, and a brief statement, apparently part of a longer dissertation, that Diario Hoy was now prone to printing fabrications and lies. Tómas stopped eating the chewy, tasteless fare served that morning with naranjilla juice, as Eduardo appeared on the concrete porch before the open door. He rose and walked over to the open door to greet their visitor.

Eduardo shook his hand before offering him an envelope. Inside was an invitation to a festival in the town centre, celebrating the inauguration of the hotel's construction. The Diario Hoy article declaring that French investors were no longer interested in the project was unimportant. Funding had now been secured.

"Who is giving money?" Tómas asked.

"Our own government has given the money," Eduardo answered, pointing to the envelope. "That invitation is a special pass, for my employees. For you and a guest."

Eduardo inched forward to peer through the door. "Good morning, Señora," he said. Veronica simply glared at him. Eduardo turned around. "Do you still see Juan Carlos?" he asked.

Tómas was silent.

"Well," Eduardo continued. "I hear he is still on the island, but his apartment is abandoned. I will need you to tell me where he is, if you know. Or discover where he is, for me."

Unsure of what to say, Tómas responded: "I will."

He returned to his room, experiencing the same sense of relief as he had when he first left Eduardo's office after the initial offer to work for the hotel. But unlike then, this path seemed right now, somehow. Less of an easy course of action, and therefore intrinsically more valuable. Placing the invitation carefully on his desk, beside the journal he had found in his father's mainland office, Tómas sat down on his bed and re-read the page of the book he had marked: *Violet told me last night, as we sat in front of a fire on the beach, that I think too much, as she does. She said that this is the source of our unhappiness, that we are too much alike.* This entry led into the events of the next days and weeks and months. He continued reading, more closely than he had before:

Her resolve to leave seems to be growing along with the child inside her. I want her to stay; I want her and our child to be with me. Yet she seems to want nothing else, other than to leave. Whenever I ask of her plans she says that, in her mind, she is already gone. I say that I will marry her. She will not concede to my request, saying that I am already married. And besides, she says, she already feels far away from here, as though she is now in Canada.

She no longer talks about the reasons that brought her here. Now, she only says she stayed longer than she had ever intended, and she is ready to return to her previous life in Canada. I cannot hold her back, even though I want nothing more than to do so. I rationalize that even if I convinced her to stay, she might feel as though I was keeping her from the life she truly wanted, and leave anyway. I must let her go.

It will be the most difficult silence I will ever have to endure, saying nothing as I watch her board a plane with the only child I will likely ever have. I will travel to see them in Canada, one day. Once I learn about where she and my child live, that they are comfortable and happy and safe, when I meet their friends and comprehend enough of their daily life there to be able to visualize what I would be doing if I was there beside them, only then will I be able to leave, to let them go once again.

Or perhaps I will be unable to leave, and will have to stay there with them.

Along the side of the margins, written in different coloured ink, were the vertically written words: "*I convinced her to stay until Tómas was born. She talked of giving him for adoption back in Canada. She was not a mother, she said. I told her to leave him with me. She agreed. I have never seen Veronica so happy, or Violet so sad.*"

Tómas wondered if he would ever be able to ask Montgomery about all this. He had not thought that his father was already married to Veronica while impregnating Violet, although when he considered the timelines now, this made sense. And what might have happened if his father had not taken him, and if he had been adopted somewhere in Canada? He would have longed to know the island of his birth, to know his father and his birth mother, and the causes of their early rejection of him. If he was unable to find them, he would have spent a lifetime wondering.

"Reading too much means you think too much," Veronica said with a grin, a box in her hands as she peered through the open doorway of Tómas's bedroom.

She placed the box on his dresser, and Tómas quickly closed the journal.

"Here are your father's things," she continued. "You can have them. I do not want to see them anymore. And also, Juan Carlos is at the door."

Veronica disappeared into the light emanating from the kitchen, and Juan Carlos moved in to fill the doorway, hobbling, his bruises glimmering. He was dressed in a silk shirt, sunglasses, and an unzipped jacket with a hood covering his head; his shiny belly seemed to exude impropriety here, in one of the country's most impoverished areas. He carried a slender manila envelope under his arm.

"I almost ran into Eduardo at the bottom of the street," he said quickly, removing his sunglasses and lowering his hood. "I thought I saw him coming from this house."

"He knows you remain on the island, and not in your apartment. He wants me to tell him where you are. I am certain he wants to talk to you."

"I am certain he does. Why did he come here? And why does he want you to tell him about me?"

Tómas shifted his position on the bed.

"He invited me to a party celebrating his hotel. And apart from that, you said you would be here tonight, not this morning. You want Eduardo to see you?"

"I must tell you, I am quite bored with sitting in that boat all day, every day, in the heat. Besides that, I am suffocating. And I cannot drink enough water."

"You should go back to the mainland, be with your family."

Juan Carlos was silent for a moment before moving in to the room, sitting down on the end of the bed, the bed frame creaking in response.

"You are not to work for Eduardo anymore," Juan Carlos said. "There is no project."

"The government gave the money," Tómas replied. "He told me."

"He has accused my paper of lies, but he is the one committing them."

"I will work for him, now there is money. Civil service. My father wanted me to. And apart from that, where is that paperwork about my father?"

Juan Carlos looked around the room at the walls where Montgomery's paintings once were, at the Ecuadorian flag, the tin roof visible above, and he seemed ready to leave before finally answering.

"You are not listening to me," he continued. "I found this in your father's office on the mainland. Here." Removing the manila envelope from under his arm, he tossed it onto the bed. "Before we went to Quito together, when you and your father were still here on the island, I went to Quito alone. I had suspicions about your father, and about Eduardo. I had to destroy your father's office, almost, to find what I wanted. The place had no working lights. I found the details of some cash exchanges. Your father's name was on them, and so was Eduardo's. There they are." He pointed at the envelope. "But be warned, this will make you think differently of your father."

"It is okay," Tómas said. "I do not think of him, as I once did."

"Really? I suppose you are maturing, then, moving beyond simple family loyalty."

Tómas rose from his bed and sat down in his desk chair, dumping and then leafing through the contents of the envelope. "What about these exchanges?"

Juan Carlos sighed. He paused for a long time before answering. "Between the funds for the housing plan and the funds for the hotel," he said.

"I do not understand."

"Your father is guilty, Eduardo too. They used money from the housing plan. It is all in the records. The money was still there after the housing plan was abandoned, and Eduardo must have known that. He must have told this to your father, and that is how he knew as well."

There were pages and pages of numbers, a few of them highlighted to indicate the amounts, where the money was derived, and where the funds were allocated. The records all seemed to corroborate what Juan Carlos was saying.

"So Eduardo used money for the housing plan to pay for the hotel," Tómas said. "And my father took blame, protecting his friend."

"Why do you think it does not matter about the French investors? Because there is enough money there already."

"But you already printed in the paper that the funding—"

"I wrote," Juan Carlos interrupted, "all the investors removed their funding for the hotel, which is true. Also, I said the hotel is a white elephant of self-glorification which needs to be replaced with a cheap hotel for people of the mainland, so they can stay there, so the hotel can be a success, which also is true. But one day I will print the truth of Eduardo's involvement in the scandal, and I will provide all this evidence. For this reason, I want to know why you insist to work for Eduardo. When he is accused, if you are working for him—"

"Many on the island will be working for him also," Tómas interrupted.

"Yes, but they will not be the same relation to him. He mentioned you, by name, in the rally for the hotel. You are very close to him now, as your father was. The relation between you, your father and Eduardo will become very important to the people when they are against him. You are closer to Eduardo than you have ever been, will you not admit this? This is why I became so angry with you before, when you sent those letters to El Comercio and Diario Hoy:

because you know, I have tried to protect your father, just as I am trying to protect you now, my friend."

Tómas said nothing, contemplating instead that Montgomery had safeguarded others by selflessly leaving the country to protect his friend, a self-sacrifice he had also shown when taking Tómas as a baby and agreeing to care for him. Two acts of profound altruism Tómas had not previously known.

"So what will you do with these papers?" Tómas asked, slipping them back into the envelope. Juan Carlos reached for the envelope, and Tómas held onto it.

"Nothing yet. El Comercio will build up Eduardo's reputation, before I crush him in the people's minds. The blow will be more powerful that way. For now, I will continue to ruin Eduardo's credibility with the islanders, but without damaging, even more, that of your father's. Eventually, though, these papers will be published."

"I will destroy these papers."

"You can, if you wish. Those are copies. I have the originals hidden. I am afraid I cannot destroy those. I want to return to my wife and children one day, to work for El Comercio. The editor there, he does not like me now partly because of his politics, but when I show him my investigation skills, he will not deny me a job there."

"True, that you need to return to your wife and children. So, go ahead. You do not need El Comercio. There are other places you can work. Set fire to the originals, I will do the same to the copies. I want freedom to stay here now, to return as I choose."

"Your father's name is already stained. And you can find work on the mainland, in Machala, with me. You may have troubles finding work here. You are right; there are many places to work there, but for you, not for me as a newspaper editor. And about Eduardo, you cannot say with all he has done and never told you about, that you still are faithful to him."

Tómas opened the envelope and removed the paperwork.

"Keep those," Juan Carlos said, pointing to the papers. "And do not burn them or throw them in with the garbage. There may be a time when I need you to mail these to Diario Hoy, if Eduardo or anyone else ever gets the originals—and also, you must not tell Eduardo you have these."

Veronica appeared suddenly behind Juan Carlos.

"Hola Señora," Juan Carlos said, smiling and turning around quickly. "I am just now leaving. Are you going to the celebration tonight?"

"I did not plan to go," she said softly. "But yes, I will be there."

"I will return at seven," he said. "It will be dark. I will walk there with you on the back roads, and watch from a distance. I need to see this celebration for myself."

"I will be your guest tonight," she said, turning toward Tómas.

"For certain," Tómas replied, putting the paperwork copy in the drawer of his desk.

16. Newfound Freedom

THAT EVENING, VERONICA'S mother Flory would be the sole occupant of the house. She would celebrate her newfound freedom by stepping out on to the porch beneath the light of the stars. Tómas had explained to her once before that the light we see is not what is actually there, but the illumination of stars that might have burned out hundreds or thousands of years ago, and the panorama is therefore a representation of what was there at one time. Flory would perhaps remain there for an hour or so, looking up at the points of light, contemplating this, and wondering if and when each of them had died. She would step into the backyard to see Medianoche on the roof, barking at her. The television would remain off tonight.

Tómas and Juan Carlos treaded slowly beside Veronica on a mud road, just before sunset, on their way to the town centre. Juan Carlos wore the same red silk shirt and hooded jacket he had worn earlier that day, his hood raised to cover his face. Veronica was in a dress outlining her potbelly and carrying a loaded cloth bag as her heels sank into the mud. Tómas was dressed in a thin grey sweater and cotton pants.

They passed the university grounds, past taxis honking through flooded streets, and past men with machetes hacking at the grass, continuing toward the Place San Cristobal at the town's centre.

"Tonight is a mock celebration," Veronica said, placing the bag and its contents over one shoulder. "A fiesta for nothing."

Tómas and Juan Carlos were silent.

"Did you know your father and I had a child?" Veronica asked suddenly.

"Montgomery told me that one time," Tómas replied.

"The baby died before it was born. I, too, almost died. I was forty-six."

"You were an old mother," Juan Carlos said.

"It was a surprise; I thought I could not become pregnant. Now, it is of no importance. You were the only child we ever had, Tómas, though you were another woman's baby and not mine. Now, I am almost sixty. No more chances for me now. This is why Montgomery traveled so much, to forget about our baby. And he had other things to feel guilty about, other reasons to escape." She had said these last sentences to Tómas many times before, but never with such sorrow.

Tómas was reminded of what Juan Carlos had said about Montgomery's guilt, but he said nothing. He felt a slight dizziness as they continued walking, Veronica flashing the submissive look of a woman powerless against the effects of nature and age. Juan Carlos, it seemed, was listening to none of this, focusing instead on avoiding the mud, sticks, puddles of water, fallen trees, and other obstacles in their way.

Tómas had not heard anyone talk about his biological mother since just before Montgomery left the island. Montgomery and Tómas had been on their last trip together, at the beach just down the coastline from San Cristobal. Montgomery asked, as they sat eating cold shrimp soup at a cevicheria while Veronica and their neighbour Señora Modesta swam nearby, if Tómas ever thought of her. Tómas added rice to his soup and then watched the shrimp fishermen on the beach with their long poles and their buckets, trawling for larvae not far from where Veronica and the Señora were swimming. He replied that he only thought of her on his birthday, or when his father would tell him of the auburn-blonde shade of her hair, or how she loved her town in Canada, or that she once said she had to go back where she belonged. His father said nothing else, but finished his soup. Montgomery went swimming alone on the beach, and Tómas watched him swim far away from the shrimp fishermen until he couldn't see him anymore. He had not considered asking Montgomery if he ever thought of her, at least not until now.

As they walked along the path, Tómas felt the billfold in his pocket with his mother's photograph. He had examined it often, and at length. It was a snapshot taken for a graduation of some sort. Her fingers were curled over themselves in a neat pile, a puffed wrap around her neck as white as her young smile. She had brilliant teeth and eyes of which Tómas could not discern the meaning. He had always feared asking Montgomery or Veronica about her, afraid that their answers would make him want to learn more. So he simply never asked anything.

"You know anything about my mother Violet?" Tómas asked suddenly, stepping around a fallen tree.

Veronica's face turned sour. There was a long pause before she responded. "*I* am your mother, who took care for you, your whole life. She knows nothing of being a mother. But what do you want to know about *her*?"

"Anything."

"Well, I will tell you this. She left you and never came back. You should think of people who accepted you and loved you, and not a person who threw you away like garbage to the street. You should try to think about your father, and me, and appreciate us in place of thinking about someone like that."

"I do."

"No, not enough. Your father is not perfect; he cheated on me many times. You were the result. Your father was so accustomed for travel his whole life, and he finally told me he would quit traveling, forever."

"He told me he would quit also."

"And then, all this nonsense about money and a hotel, and now he is gone. Seems you do not care, but I do, yes. I thought God would finally give us our time together. Now it is all very clear. Your father maybe knew about some missing money, maybe not. Juan Carlos wrote an article saying he knew. Now the names Montgomery Harvey and Eduardo Delgado are connected, from articles in the paper." She turned toward Juan Carlos. "Why did you print the article starting all this?"

"I don't know, Señora," Juan Carlos replied nervously.

"How could you not know? You are not so innocent as you seem." Veronica shook her head. "You must have shame. You are as guilty as Eduardo for Montgomery leaving his family. You can say you are protecting him; but the cause is Eduardo, and you, that he is not here with me in this moment."

Juan Carlos was silent, looking ahead now to the pathway. Veronica walked around a large stone surrounded by water, which blocked their way.

After a while, he said: "You are right, Señora. Even though Montgomery wanted it, I should not have written the article. And Eduardo is now as much my enemy as he is yours."

She scrunched her face up, and shook her head. "What garbage comes from your mouth. Eduardo is my enemy. I think all is very clear now. Eduardo knew all this and said nothing. Dishonesty comes in many forms. And you, Tómas, if you say nothing and work for him, if you stay away from the army, you are not better than them."

Tómas tried to think of something that would dissipate her anger. No words came to mind. And what Juan Carlos said next was apparently intended to provoke her.

"Tómas has applied for conscientious objection," he said. "So he will not have to go to the war. I will be helping him."

Tómas took a deep breath, and then sighed, feeling lightheaded. Veronica scoffed, and said nothing.

"I met your mother many times," she said finally. "Let me tell you about her. She was very beautiful, and lived very much for herself. She left you alone. Why, I cannot imagine. I did not ever give birth, but I cannot imagine leaving my only child with strangers. Something is wrong with her. A woman in the countryside here on the island, a woman named Colette—"

Juan Carlos turned his head suddenly toward her. "I know her," he interrupted. "I know her well. She still lives here."

"Your father knew her too," Veronica continued. "She lived in Canadá with your mother."

She paused, and then sighed. "You are ungrateful," she said, turning her gaze toward Tómas. "Ungrateful like your ugly little cat that follows you inside when you come in the house. If you push that animal outside with a broom or if you feed it, still it will come back. And it will return with no gratitude. It appreciates nothing, and keeps coming back, wanting more. Just like you."

There was silence for the remainder of their walk which, to Tómas, seemed a great distance.

Over a hundred people stood beneath coloured streamers and torch lighting in the Place San Cristobal for an outdoor concert in the heart of the island. Some were there for the celebration of the hotel, others present for a love of celebration in any form. Groups of men stood around making comments to the women passing by, the women disregarding the men whose remarks were fuelled by bottles of Caña Manabita and aguar diente.

The hexagonal, orange-topped spires of the Iglesia Santa Maria loomed overhead. Just below, a band brought their guitars to a stage, a collection of planks set over top of the mud, as people mingled about the square. For a moment, as Veronica surveyed the crowd, the noises of the group and the band's instruments squealed and seemed to merge into one voice.

There were too many people, people who could throw him into the back of a pickup truck at a moment's notice, or in an instant notify the authorities that a remiso was wandering freely about the island. The lights overhead were too bright. His head was pounding. Tómas thought he heard the words "Payaso, clown," and some laughing from a man's voice in the crowd. He heard the voice notifying the military police of his presence here, the voice echoing the words over the phone: *"El payaso asustado, the cowardly clown remiso, he is not in Guayaquil's military base where he should be ... his father, he is a coward and a thief who runs from responsibility, too ... if you have read the papers, you will know all this ..."*

Padre Pédro suddenly appeared, startling him. Juan Carlos adjusted the hood covering his head, and departed for an area to the side of the stage. Veronica, seeing Padre Pédro and clutching on to her bag, departed into the crowd.

"Your work for the hotel will be very important," Padre Pédro said, smiling and shaking his hand. "Eduardo told me what you will do for him."

"I have not agreed to work for him, yet," Tómas replied.

"That is not what he told me," he said. "And please choose, not for yourself, but for the others." He began walking away, before turning back toward Tómas. "Have you any letters from your father recently?"

Tómas looked over to see Eduardo Delgado, alone, wearing an immaculately cut red suit beside the Place San Cristobal's central fountain. He had a drink in his hand, and his thin face, his suit, and his greased hair gleamed brightly beneath the plethora of torchlight and overhanging light strands. The dormant fountain was filled with rainwater and overgrowth. He appeared content, his eyes and his expression glinting optimism. Tómas wanted to speak with him, without others around. Now was the time.

"No," Tómas said, starting toward Eduardo. "And I do not know much."

"I will pray for your father to find his way home," Padre Pédro said. "And for you to take the decision you must. I will tell others, too, and they will pray."

The band's guitars made a series of noises as they were being tuned. As he approached Eduardo, Tómas thought of what Juan Carlos had said earlier that evening. When Eduardo smiled, offering his hand in a greeting, Tómas shook his hand and then immediately began to speak.

"Some paperwork from my father's Quito office," Tómas said, "it showed money moved between a housing plan and the new hotel."

"Your father, always he has been a very good friend to me," Eduardo said, still smiling. "The best of friends."

"My father's name was on the paperwork. Your name too. I suppose my father left Ecuador to protect you, to take the blame himself."

"Really? So you have seen such papers, if they do exist."

"I have."

Tómas looked up to see Juan Carlos in the distance now, his face hidden in shadows and fog, away from the lights reflecting off the streamers, the torchlights, the band, and the swirling crowd. He was smoking and sharing a bottle of Caña Manabita with several others. They drank quickly and passed the small bottle between them. Tómas moved to ensure Eduardo's focus was away from Juan Carlos's direction.

"I hear files were stolen from your father's office in Quito," Eduardo said. "Those are the papers you talk about. So you know who stole them, and where they are now?"

"I cannot say."

"Well, I could assume you took them. But I know you did not. So I assume Juan Carlos has them. You have been talking to him. You two have been friends for some time."

"I have not talked to him."

"You lie! People have seen you together. And you will need to tell me where he is. I heard, only minutes ago, that he lives on a boat. Do you know about that?"

"I cannot say."

"But know that talking to him, it is dangerous. He has a harmful pen that spreads wicked lies. Those lies will ruin him, and will stain anyone else around him."

Eduardo coughed, his expression turning sanguine and sombre. He put his arm around Tómas. "Feel it," he continued. "This is what I always wanted, and what you can share. My dream, your father's dream, finished."

Eduardo retracted his arm, pausing for a moment to light a cigarette. He placed his drink on the fountain's edge. Alfonso, a man with a shaved head and acne-pocked skin standing beside Juan Carlos, moved on to the stage. He took the microphone and said they would begin with ballenato, then salsa, then merengue, before moving into rock music from America. The band would continue to play through the night, from a slow to a fast pace, before moving to the beach to lead the crowd from late evening into early morning.

Tómas noticed that Veronica was now standing several metres away. She had a frantic look in her eyes, and was visibly agitated.

"Tómas, move to the side," she said in a stern voice.

Tómas was standing between her and Eduardo, and he turned his body to face her. Her head was shaking strangely, and the odd look on her face possessed a sort of frenzied determination he had never seen. As she produced a partially painted statue from her bag and drew her arm back, clutching onto the small figurine, he wondered what she might do.

"Tómas," she repeated again.

He stepped away not only from instinctive obedience, but from an instinct of self-preservation combined with a desire to escape her stare, her anger. He tried to pull Eduardo with him, but Eduardo resisted the grip, raising his arm enough that Tómas stumbled backward.

"Good evening, Señora," Eduardo said, still resisting as Tómas pulled on his arm again.

"Your statues," she replied.

She threw one of the objects toward Eduardo. It missed him completely, and smashed on the side of the fountain. Eduardo glanced back to see where it had hit. A few people yelled and some jumped to avoid being hit by several pieces that flew into the crowd. A small head hit the ground, a scaled down version of Triton. Looking up, Tómas saw another statue bouncing neatly off Eduardo's face. A bloody Jupiter landed with a thud on the dirt beside him. Eduardo covered his face with his hands, blood now visible on his fingers as people rushed to his side. Veronica stood there with a blank expression.

At that moment the song Tierra Mala, or "Bad Earth," prompted a throng of dancing islanders who had not noticed this commotion to begin removing their shoes, tracing the outline of their body rhythms into the wet soil.

Tómas felt his dizziness returning, stronger now, almost overpowering, as though he was ready to fall to the ground. His vision was blurred. Maybe he, too, had been hit by part of a statue. But he looked on the ground around him, and felt for blood on his face. He wasn't bleeding. Juan Carlos's voice came from behind him.

"You do not look well," he said, drawing Tómas away from the melee. "You are pale. Are you drunk already?"

"I want to get Eduardo to the doctor," Tómas said. "And to see Veronica ..."

"Someone will see to them," Juan Carlos said, holding Tómas upright. "For now, I will see to you."

17.Cuszco

I HAVE FINALLY arrived in Cuszco, the ancient capital of the Inca Empire. I step from the bus into the cool, early evening air and find myself surrounded by mountains teeming with homes. My vision makes my environment increasingly blurred. There are rusty ancient cathedrals with huge open doors, cathedrals ornate with gold interiors. It is a blend of tarnished Spanish and Inca architecture. All the buildings around the Plaza De Armas, Cuszco's central square, are the obscured colour of rust and baked clay.

I've been to this mystical city before, and I've written about it for foreign journals. The details of which I cannot see, I can remember. The city now lies between archaeological museums and houses of religious art, cathedrals and temples with beautiful examples of elaborate ancient irrigation and drainage systems. Porticos lead into rooms with holes carved into stone, holes where jewels and artefacts once proudly stood.

If viewed from the air, this Plaza de Armas represents the heart of a giant puma, an Inca sacred beast. The puma's head is a nearby fortress, Saksayhuaman, and two rivers outline its torso and merge to form its tail as homage to their ancient gods, the gods they believed looked down on them from above.

The yellow spotlights casting light on the buildings around the plaza make me wonder what the designers and stonemasons might have said about this new technology being applied to their antiquated structures. Perhaps it would drive them to destroy the lights, and insist on sacrificial rituals to the sun god Inti, in atonement for this supernatural evil.

I wander into an outdoor market with vendors sitting on wool blankets pedalling their goods: a blur of knitted caps, bright blankets, llama sweaters, silver jewellery, Inca statues, bongo drums, masks, pottery. They are all modern artefacts, pieces of modern history. The techniques and products derived from them have not changed in a thousand years.

I drink pisco sours in a dimly lit bar before walking down the Avenida El Sol, where I am given passes to African and Irish pubs, and other passes advertising e-mail, dance music, cable television, games, movies, and pizza delivery. I often think now about Tómas. He has never travelled, and the foreign influences here would perturb him. I often wonder about others, too, about Veronica, Eduardo and Juan Carlos. They must be getting along fine without me, as they always have. But still, I wish to see them again, to spend my last days with all of them.

I have instructed Eduardo to tell no one of my whereabouts. I believe he will abide by his word that he will not, especially to the press. But perhaps Tómas will insist on knowing, and will come in search of me. And even though I do not wish that, still, I would welcome his company in my final days.

Eduardo is responsible for me being here now, but I cannot fault him. I made the decision myself. I would like to have someone apart from myself as culpable, to shift my anger and blame toward someone who is not a lifelong friend. I freely offered him these gifts of money that belonged to neither one of us, to provide a new hope and future for the island and for him. Perhaps this was my most altruistic act. I should feel contented about my sacrifice, regret nothing of my decision, and think ill of no one because of it.

But my mind keeps drifting toward the time, just before I left the island, when I first proposed leaving and having the article printed that would place all blame and suspicion on myself while leaving Eduardo's name unsullied, and out of it altogether. Eduardo was very quick to accept, as he only did normally with ideas he had thought of himself. This made me think that perhaps he had thought of it before. In the days that followed, as I began my preparations to leave, Eduardo had started his own arrangements for the press forum at the Hotel Santa Rita de Cascia. He barely talked to me as we drove together, after that forum, from the Hotel Santa Rita to the bus station. He spoke with the same sense of detachment as someone engrossed in thoughts and plans. But still, even then, he never told me not to go, that I had a family to consider, or that we should confess responsibility for our scheme.

I am reminded of an article I once wrote about the controversial wedding of a Royal couple in Oslo, Norway. The woman who became princess, of common birth, who had already rendered a child out of wedlock to a man jailed on drug charges, had a lust for power and a desire for prominence that was more important to her than the Royal Family's reputation. She still sits in the seat of princess, one she has perhaps always wanted as have so many other little girls. Maybe she will one day realize that to have what you've always wanted at the expense of others is worse than having nothing at all. I can do nothing about her realization of this, any more that I can help Eduardo to comprehend this sooner than he would otherwise.

I slept well last night, one of the deepest sleeps in recent memory. It must be the cool mountain air, and the elevation of three and a half kilometres above the sea.

I awoke to the morning light sifting in through the blinds. For now, I have no signs of altitude sickness, except for dizziness, which could also be from my weakened condition. I cough some blood into my handkerchief. My vision is mostly blurry, as it is every morning. I am becoming more and more ill each day. I wonder how much time I have left, but I think it is really not much.

When looking out the window, I have a passing feeling that while my body has been dynamic, travelling the globe, my mind has become static. I cannot think of anything when I see the hazy structures outside, except how to describe them for people to visualize. I need to have interacted with people more, instead of preferring the company of other foreigners or my precious solitude. I should have examined the lives of local people, apart from what they can offer tourists. That would have been something of worth.

Locals with tiny, coffee-skinned babies protruding from their backpacks direct me to the local guides who can, in turn, direct me to the Machu Picchu trail leading to Aguas Calientes.

"I can take us there," a small woman with dark hair and dark skin, one of the guides in a local business, says. *"I have been there many times."*

I am ready to say that I can find it myself, and that I only need a map. Instead, I find myself saying that since there are over a thousand Inca trails leading from this city, I want her to escort me there. But in my exhaustion, following the exertion of going around in search of a guide, I know I do not have the strength to hike four days on any trail. I will need to take the train. After I have some time, simply to rest.

18. A Cyclical Disease

IN TÓMAS'S FEVER-INDUCED dreams that fleshed into waking thought, he could see Montgomery in the remotest areas of the earth. He could see him beneath a sprawling tent in the silent heat of the Mojave Desert, under the sultry seduction of a belly dancer and a feast before him; or on a harrowing journey to the centre of the dark continent by water, reliving Conrad's tale; or traversing the Neva River's moonlit night, past shadowed and unlit buildings to the Mariinsky theatre where Tchaikovsky, Mahler, and Wagner once performed. Tómas saw him living in seclusion and then envisioned him amidst a sea of faces, conceiving that he despised where he was, and then that he loved the familiarity of these places.

But what he realized as he saw Veronica's mother Flory beside his bed—his only seeming connection to reality—was that these were not visions of where Montgomery was, recalling now that he was in Peru, but instead these were visualizations of where Montgomery had been and what he had already seen and written about.

Flory stood by the mosquito netting that hung over the bed, reading a letter aloud, holding the paper at arm's length. Months had passed since Tómas had last heard her speak, and her voice was now scratched and throaty, and her Spanish was slurred. She seemed to be ignoring whether he was asleep or awake as she read, unmindful of what was happening around her, the same as when she had entered the bathroom and washed her hands at times when Tómas stood naked beside her under a trickling shower, nothing but her obliviousness between them.

Tómas began to drop off into sleep again, watching her hand tremble and listening to her shaking voice: "*I hear you are sick, and I hear also from your doctor that you have malaria. Take care. Rest. Malaria can be a serious disease if it is not benign. Please, if you need help—another doctor, or anything else—please ask. We are like family, you and I. I often feel like that when we are together. You know you can ask anything of me. As for myself, I am fine. Recovering. The Señora Harvey you live with, she is wicked, spiteful and misguided.*"

Flory stopped reading for a moment, scanning through the document, muttering something and then flipping the page before continuing.

"*... Montgomery left here because he wanted to leave, but I think Señora Harvey is blaming me. I hear she is still at the island's Office of Police. I need your support in one thing—I have sent an article to my friend, the editor of El Comercio, and signed your name to the letter. It will be published in the next edition, to deflect what opinions Juan Carlos has about my hotel. Read it. I will need you to write other articles that are similar. I will give you whatever information, whatever ideas you need. Recover soon.*"

Flory concluded, no longer reading, and dropping the letter on his desk. At the bottom, it was signed by Eduardo Delgado, Mayor of San Cristobal.

Tómas awoke abruptly, hours later, as Flory removed his blanket and quickly rubbed a strong-smelling ointment that burned on contact into his chest, his neck, and then his entire body. She did this just as she had when he had suffered through his intestinal infection ten years ago. Thirty-six hours of sleep were required to recover, and he only awakened when rubbed with ointment or to take one of his four sets of antibiotics. Veronica told him afterward that encebollado, warm fish soup, should never be eaten cold the next day after it has been served warm. Flory said nothing, giving him no advice or admonishment, but only giving him what his body needed to recover.

When he awoke later, the blanket was no longer over his face. Flory must have returned to his room to lift the blanket after its warmth, combined with the odour of his own body and that of the ointment, had put him to sleep. The mosquito netting was down for the night.

"Take it," a voice said to Tómas in English, the room consumed by near darkness. A shadow seated at Tómas's side handed him a small, yellow pill through the opening in his mosquito netting. "Your father had malaria once, too," the voice continued.

Tómas recognized the voice now as that of Cristobal, a mainland doctor who had only visited the house a few times, whenever anyone was very ill. "He had amoebic dysentery one time. He's had many illnesses. You may be having alucinaciónes like he did, and problems of the stomach."

"What are alucinaciónes?" Tómas asked, taking the pill and swallowing it with a glass of water from his bedside table.

The doctor began speaking in Spanish. "When you see things that do not exist," he said. "But you must be thankful you do not have cholera. There was an outbreak of cholera on the mainland, you know. I was working there, in Manta. Terrible disease. Some people die in hours."

"Cholera, it is from the water. We have not had that in our house."

"I know, be thankful. Some cases happen from not boiling their water.. There was another outbreak too, in Guayaquil, where I worked. Groups of children live in the sewers there. They go under the ground because they have nowhere else to live. But, I am sure you do not want to hear any of this ... only you must know there are worse diseases you could have ... and so, with that, I will be leaving you now."

The doctor rose. As though accustomed to one-sided conversation, he continued without waiting for any reaction or response. "Now I will visit Eduardo Delgado again. Then, unfortunately, I will have to go back to Manta."

Tómas put his hand on his own sweaty head, able to feel his fever. "What is the problem with Manta?" he asked.

"My wife and I, we will have a baby. We want to raise the child on this island. I talked about this before to Eduardo. There are not enough people, no need for more doctors here, he says. Only room for more pharmacists selling expired medicine, I suppose, one pill at a time. So I grew tired of asking."

"How is Eduardo?" Tómas asked. "Have you seen him?"

"His face has been bruised, and there are cuts, but he will be better. You, however, will not. You will always have this disease in your blood."

He held up two bottles of yellow pills, setting them by the bed. "One is for now; the other is for next time your disease returns. Just know that while other diseases may be worse, your disease will come back, probably many times in your life."

He walked out the door without closing it behind him.

Tómas closed his eyes and listened to the doctor, talking with Flory, as he began to fall into sleep.

"There's a water cylinder on the roof," Cristobal said. "Is it working?"

"Yes, for the last many days," Flory said. "Tómas unplugged it."

Then: "It's where mosquitoes breed," and "stagnant water."

Tómas wondered suddenly why there was no Artesian well in the house in place of the water cylinder. In fact, he wondered why all the houses on the island were not fitted with Artesian wells. He knew then that he was feverish, that his mind was not right, as there were no Artesian wells anywhere in Ecuador at all, as the soft rock was not there for them.

Tómas heard the voice of the doctor again, sporadically now. "A few days, with treatment ... do not miss any doses ... you will need to treat the mosquito netting with a spray insecticide ..."

Tómas awoke, hours later, sweating profusely in near darkness. The eyes of a Lilliputian gecko flashed at him, its fingers as fine as thread and holding it tight to the wall. The spindly tail resembled a snake chasing after its prey. Then, he wasn't quite sure if he had seen it at all. One of Vivaldi's violin concertos was echoing through the room, as though his father was home and was playing the record as he often did. But his father was not home, nor was Vivaldi on the record player. The noise was just that of Flory's television, his delirious mind having constructed what he wanted to hear.

Staring at the top of the mosquito netting, which hung down from the ceiling over his bed, he noticed that the knot at the top was not tight. There was a small hole that could allow insects inside. He wanted it tightened, but could not rise out of bed.

After the television was turned off for the night, his hearing became more acute. The continuous, high-pitched squeal that accompanied any silence, the tinnitus that constantly rang in his ears, also seemed more pronounced. The intermittent buzzing of insects was followed closely by the distinctive hum of the mosquito. The tiny, winged vampires had flown in, unimpeded, through the ventilation openings, and into the interior of his mosquito netting. He lay there listening to the whining of their tiny wings intermittently buzzing next to his ears and the ringing of his own eardrums, clapping at the air as he felt himself falling into the world of dreams.

19. Opponents with Nothing to Say

El Comercio, March 29, 1988
Tómas Harvey, Guest Contributor

EDUARDO ANDRE BRIONES Delgado has started to construct his grand hotel. It is something most people never thought would happen. Since the 1978 revolution changed military dictatorship to democracy, this gives opportunities for entrepreneurs such as Eduardo Delgado. He has not realized his vision to bring low-cost milk to island markets, or to build low-cost housing here, or to give more government subsidies on rice, cooking fuel and gasoline that keeps the prices of these items low. Until now, what he has wanted, and what he has achieved, have been two different things.

I walked by the west end of the island on my way home yesterday. I saw that there were machines digging holes in the ground for the hotel. Another was lowering a concrete pilaster into place. There were many island workers there, maybe two dozen or so, every one of whom I recognized. It is true, as was promised: the workforce for the hotel is from the island. It is true too that the people are beginning to be behind him. Maybe he has vision that others have not.

Many people say this hotel will become his triumph: the grand event, the pinnacle of his career, an accomplishment that will bring tourists here and will allow the island to rise above its poverty, and will let all of us profit from the island's beauty and the filling of its empty beaches.

And after all this has happened, after what Eduardo Delgado has wanted and what he has achieved are the same, his detractors will have nothing more to say.

20. La Mandarina

TÓMAS'S MALARIA FADED quickly as the rain-collecting cylinders began to dry up. As he recovered, he looked through the old wooden box of his father's articles that Veronica had left him. Inside was a collection of writings, travel articles and photographs, most of which he had already seen. Near the bottom of the box was an oval locket, as big as his thumb, engraved with floral imprints and made of silver.

Inside the locket was a picture of two women, their heads crammed together, both of them smiling widely. Looking closely, he could see that one of the women was his mother Violet. The other was a woman he recognized, perhaps the woman Veronica had spoken of, Colette, whom he had seen on the island before. He clasped the small lid shut and put his new possession into the pocket of his pants, beside his wallet with the picture of his mother.

When his illness had fully dissipated, Tómas went outdoors, walking past the university, past mules carrying wares and taxis dodging potholes, to the west coast of the island. In the heat of the sun, his shirt clung to his back with sweat as he arrived at the bay housing Juan Carlos's upright boat.

Three boats lay flat on their sides at low tide, their hulls submerged a foot deep in dark mud. Tómas's feet sank into the saturated earth as he started toward Juan Carlos's boat. Unable to remove his shoes from the mud, he extracted his feet from them, recovered the two sodden clumps and promptly tossed them ashore. He continued on, the mud halfway up to his knees.

Juan Carlos, lighting a cigarette in the cabin, was sitting at a small, fold-out table that extended out over one of the beds. Upon seeing Tómas in the boat's cockpit with his legs and arms covered in mud, his eyes widened.

"Please," he said, dropping his cigarette on the floor and quickly retrieving it. "Please, tell me when you are coming. A signal. Shout something before you approach. Anything. When I looked up and saw you standing there, I nearly died."

"Sorry," Tómas said.

"You know," he said, drawing on his cigarette and exhaling, "the same men that assaulted me, the police officers, they came here the day before yesterday, at high tide, in a small boat."

"I told you not to go out during the day. People have seen you."

"I dove into the water before the police saw me. I almost did not come back. When I did, I found they had left with most of my things, including all of my important papers. But for now, you need to come here, inside. I do not want you to be seen talking to a man who is supposedly not here, on a boat that is supposedly empty."

Juan Carlos provided a towel, which Tómas quickly dirtied on his limbs before taking Juan's hand to help him inside. As he sat, Tómas's feet dipped into a few centimetres of stinking water in the bottom of what was meant to be the only living area.

"Bilge water," Juan Carlos said. "I will empty it now."

Juan Carlos took a black handle at the head of one of the beds, and began moving it back and forth. The water began to ripple as he pumped.

"Eduardo knows files were stolen from my father's office in Quito," Tómas said, coughing with the cigarette smoke. "I told him about the papers showing money changed from the housing plan to the hotel. He wants the paperwork."

"Well, he has my originals now." His face was overly sombre. "And you still have the copies."

"I do."

"You should have said nothing to Eduardo," Juan Carlos said. "Why would you do that? I told you that in trust, and you should have told no one. Especially him. What else did you tell him? Did you say where I was living?"

"For certain, no. I was angry and had to confront him. I had to ask him why, to see if he knew of what I was talking, when I told him of the paperwork."

"He admitted to no involvement in any scandal, of course."

"For certain, no."

"When he does, you must tell me. You will." Juan Carlos stopped pumping as the last dregs of water drained out. He looked expectantly at Tómas.

There was a moment before Tómas responded. Juan Carlos stepped back from the bilge pump and sat down on the bench seat, peering into his friend's eyes once more.

"I will tell you," Tómas replied.

"Good." Juan Carlos nodded his head approvingly. "Anyway, I must get away from here. I have seen Eduardo staring at this boat, walking around my old apartment. He looks out from my old balcony. I think he must have heard my voice when I came up to help you, when you were sick at the party."

"He could not hear, or see. He was covered in blood. Someone for certain told him you live on a boat, though."

"Not you?"

"Not me."

"I will stay with Raphael," Juan Carlos said, distracted with his own thoughts. "Or Alfonso."

After a few minutes he offered Tómas a glass of bitter sugar cane alcohol. Tómas noted the smell of the boat's rotting wood and Juan Carlos's ripe body odour as tobacco filled the boat's hold. Tómas shifted his position down to the table.

"The poor man's drink," Juan Carlos said, placing the glass in front of Tómas.

After drinking for a time, Tómas reached into his pocket. He opened the silver locket and handed it to Juan Carlos, who was rubbing his eye.

"Do you know this woman?" Tómas asked.

"Colette," he said, taking the locket and blinking quickly. "The other woman, who is very beautiful, I don't know. Why?"

Setting the jewellery down on the table, Juan Carlos opened one of the windows. A flock of rowdy tijera birds flew across the opening.

"That is my mother," Tómas said.

Juan Carlos looked at the tiny picture again, this time more closely. "Your mother has a very beautiful face," he said. "Your father was right."

"What do you know of Colette?"

"She lives in the campo. I can take you there, if you want. Now, it seems, is a very good time."

He offered a cigarette to Tómas, who accepted. Picking up his glass, Juan Carlos took a mouthful of alcohol and swallowed it quickly.

"My wife is very angry with me about Colette," he said. "She returns my letters unopened, and hangs up the phone when I call. Someone told her how I once saw Colette. I think she figured the other parts herself. That we had sex together, and all that."

"When will you go back to your wife and children?" Tómas asked. Without receiving a response, he lit his cigarette and rolled the filter between two fingers, crushing the tiny charcoal rocks.

"My wife, she does not really love me anymore. My children, they will never forgive me for leaving, and they will not care about the reasons, even though they are valid. I almost do not know my children. That is the ultimate sadness of my life. But I will stay here for now, anyway, to work for the newspaper. Here I have power. At my home on the mainland, with my wife, I have no power. You know, what is a mandarina?"

"A woman who controls a man."

"Yes, just like the drug from the coca plant. She who controls. But for now, my wife has no power, and I will do nothing to give her power. But you must come to the hotel worksite tomorrow, in the morning. I will be there."

"You will? And you will be safe here tonight?"

"For tonight, I do not think they will return. Tomorrow may be different. See Raphael in the morning. He will be there, and he will know where I am. We will go to the campo together, you and me."

21. Prosperity

CONSTRUCTION OF THE island's only hotel brought a general feeling of prosperity to Isla de la Plata, the island newspaper Diario Hoy printing phrases such as: 'a much-needed stimulant to awaken a sleepy island,' and 'a new future in prosperity'. The island's general sense of elation came about as fishermen, after their morning fishing runs, arrived at the construction site ready to work. They talked about it in the streets with salsa music thundering behind them, in their cement and caña homes, and on the beaches with bellies flopping onto the waves. The Peruvian papers asked why such an elaborate resort is needed on an island with no history of tourism, and no infrastructure to support it.

The only opposition on the island came from a group of elderly men, who mounted a campaign with the goal of halting the building's construction. They sent an editorial letter to Diario Hoy and El Comercio citing an end to traditional island values. The printed letter in Diario Hoy, the rebuttal in El Comercio, and the campaign involving protests at the worksite, went unnoticed. Realizing the futility of fighting the newly hired island workers and other islanders who did not help but still endorsed the project—a significant portion of the island—the elderly men let their protests die in Diario Hoy's back issue. Recognizing the general state of excitement surrounding the project, these elders even began contributing that which was most precious to them: their time.

The fishermen and the elders met with university students who arrived after classes, the pharmacists and restaurant workers closing their shops early to go to work there, and the taxi drivers drove them all to the worksite, over pothole laden roads, sometimes for free, sometimes leaving their taxis behind to earn a better wage in construction. The sight of children watching the building being erected and playing around the workers where there was once desolation, the dogs foraging for leftovers and chasing competing cats away, the naked concrete and wooden frame of a building beside the sea salt air of the ocean, all breathed into the workers a sense of vigour and anticipation.

Tómas walked down the beach, watching as fishermen removed plastic tarpaulins covering the wooden beams. Egrets, tijeras and seagulls fluttered by as the tarpaulins were folded away. The workers sweated in the sun, lifting beams and digging and pouring concrete as the island's elderly men and women collected garbage from the ground in the shade of palm trees and newly formed concrete walls. Tómas was careful to avoid looking at the island Centre of Recruitment and Reserves, but caught sight of the building and saw that the metal roof was glaring back at him in the sunlight, blinding him and leaving an imprint in his mind after he closed his eyes. Going to the campo, away from that reminder, would be a welcome relief.

Tómas walked over to Raphael as he approached the worksite.

"I am pulling the beams up," Raphael said, lifting his arm in the air to imitate how he might perform the task. He had been assigned to pull the wooden beams to their full upright position as they were set in place and reinforced, just as he pulled in the nets full of picudo fish. The farmers worked on the landscaping of the gardens near the entrance. Men stood guard to permit only workers, and none of the idle curious, to enter the construction site that had now been cordoned off with orange fencing. These guards did not seem to notice the children, nor care that they were there, but busied themselves checking the identity cards of those entering the site. The restaurant owners had set up gas stoves beside them, to prepare food for the workers.

"The grave diggers, farmers and grocery workers, they are digging a hole for one of the pools," Raphael explained, pointing in the direction of half-covered wooden support beams in the distance.

"Ah, ya," Tómas said.

Glancing around, seeing no one else nearby, Tómas said quietly: "So where is he?"

Raphael stopped, and looked around suspiciously. "Who?"

"Juan Carlos."

"Oh, him," he said, nodding in the direction of a nearby palm tree. "He is over there. In the hut, not far from here. He is hiding. Doing the same as always. Being lazy."

Tómas ambled over to the hut overshadowed by two palm trees, carefully observing all those at the worksite. Enrique, a man with a lightly rusted machete, was striking the tops off unripe coconuts next to the hut. He stopped to smile at Tómas before handing the topless fruit to Señora Modesta's daughter. She inserted a straw into the white, watery fluid and offered one to Tómas, who took the green half-coconut and thanked them both.

Tómas walked over to see Juan Carlos sitting at a table inside the hut, writing in a notebook. Juan Carlos stopped writing, and stood up upon seeing Tómas approach.

"Good morning, compadré." Juan Carlos lumbered toward Tómas with a coconut in his hand. He barely avoided tripping over a pile of caña sticks before reaching out, embracing Tómas, and then letting go.

"A construction management company and an architectural engineer are hired now," Juan Carlos said, sipping from his straw.

The wooden window was open wide enough to see past Enrique and take a limited visual survey of the site. Looking through the opening, Juan Carlos nodded in the direction of a man Tómas did not know, a man who stood in front of a group, in the distance, waving his arm. "He is the engineer, showing what is to be removed."

The engineer drew a line through the rocks of the cliff with his hand: a quick, sweeping motion showing what part of the overhang was to be cleared.

The wind rose, blowing at a white tarpaulin covering a mound of building materials. The canvas slipped away to reveal the beautifully crafted bow of a boat. At the front was a painted mermaid, looking remarkably lifelike, sweeping in to the beginning of a polished cherry wood deck. Two workers chased the tarpaulin, becoming wrapped up in the plastic sheet before trying to fold it again.

"More workers are coming from the mainland," Juan Carlos said, shaking his head. "Better workers. Machines, too. But still, it will not be a success."

"I read your articles. Eduardo sent one to El Comercio, with my name as the writer. It said the hotel will be his triumph."

"I saw. I knew you were not truly the writer of that. Unfortunate for you, having your name printed as author of such nonsense. Everyone knows there will never be tourists here. Even the whale watchers, they will go on to stay in the Galapagos Islands, or on the mainland. Never to the Poor Man's Galapagos. Eduardo is only thinking of his politics. And I am thinking of mine."

The men chasing the tarpaulin finally caught the fluttering material, running into each other as they tried to subdue the edges of the canvas. Juan Carlos threw his coconut aside.

"Come," he said, placing an oversized Panama hat on his head, and donning sunglasses. "We must go. We have seen enough here."

22. Monte Cristo

NO ROADS LED into the campo town of Monte Cristo. Nothing except for dirty footpaths. Bushes encircled by moths, butterflies and birds crowded the path. Juan Carlos looked over at Tómas repeatedly, as though waiting for him to speak. But Tómas did not feel the need to say anything. As Juan Carlos navigated around a sunken patch of earth, he began speaking.

"Colette and I are not in love, any more," he said. "We fought. She said she would not see me again. Now, she does not know yet, but she will."

Another period of silence followed, where the sun pounded upon them and they listened to the soft grinding of their feet into the dirt, the birds screeching and the insects buzzing in their ears. They approached a colony of leaf-cutting ants that Tómas had studied in entomology, a line of the creatures carrying tiny leaf fragments. They would chew the leaves into mulch, spit out and add the mass to fecal matter and fungus to harvest for food.

Tómas stopped on the trail beside the expertly balanced, bobbing leaf morsels to wipe his forehead in the heat of the sun. Juan Carlos stopped beside him, his face glistening with sweat, his shirt moist.

"Where did you meet Colette?" Tómas asked.

"At the Cinco de Mayo festival," Juan Carlos said. "We were drunk. Eduardo sent her to Monte Cristo to become their doctor, she told me then, because she had medical training. She wanted to leave Monte Cristo. The last time I talked with her, she wanted to go back to Canadá. But still, she had no one to replace her."

"She should stay in Monte Cristo if no other doctor is there, for taking her place," Tómas said.

Juan Carlos shook his head. "No. Eduardo, too, he thinks as you do. He said she has an obligation to stay until someone else with medical training can be found. A doctor would be best, of course. But she is Canadian. I asked her why she does not go back to Canadá, she can go back any time. She said she will go nowhere until a doctor is found. I cannot understand that woman, any more than I understand your or Eduardo's views on the subject."

"Maybe she feels in debt to those people. Maybe she does not want to leave them without help."

"In debt? She's been waiting for years and years. Any debt was paid long ago. Others could say that you need to fight in the military instead of fighting the draft in court. And I say Eduardo should build low-cost housing or a low-cost hotel for the people, so they will not have to live as they do in Monte Cristo. Instead, he builds a luxury hotel that will be good only for a few rich foreigners. And maybe, too, I should return to my wife and children. What people perhaps should do, and what they actually do, is often very different."

They resumed their walk into Monte Cristo, the dirt path winding to provide vistas of trees, dust, and insects. Hours later, they arrived at a log bridge. They crossed the unsteady tree carefully to find dozens of homes spread out on a vast expanse of land. The homes looked abandoned except for occasional plumes of smoke rising into the area that was enclosed on three sides by rows of leafless trees. This community had been originally located here, Tómas understood, because of its proximity to electrical lines and the river used for bathing and irrigation.

They walked over to an embankment of the river. Tómas stepped down to examine some of the irrigation routes the community had created. They were the same style of canal banks as those of ancient Mesopotamia, made of mud like their Mesopotamian counterparts but, unlike them, these were not strengthened with timber or stone or cane reeds. And the angles were not right. Some of the banks were too steep and had eroded completely. Some were not steep enough and were overgrown with vegetation. He could easily help them with this.

A family milled outside a caña house as a cooking fire glowed outside its walls. A small girl in unsullied clothes stared at him, her dark hair wet, her dress clinging to her lean frame.

"Alo, Señor," Juan Carlos said in a hoarse tone to the father of the family. "Do you know where is Colette?" The man was busy gathering up sticks and paid little attention to them.

"She will be back, soon," the man replied, without looking up. He placed his sticks by the fire and continued with his task. The mother, flattening the edge of an empanada, slapped it into a pan of hot oil over the fire.

Juan Carlos sat down. Tómas rose up from the riverbank and looked over at the girl, who was still staring at him. She may never have seen red hair, or his particular shade of pale skin, or freckles. Looking away, he sat down in the dirt beside Juan Carlos to wait.

Tómas recalled his father's article about the girl who ran through the crowds in Quito, begging for money to please her toothless grandmother. This girl here was likely still staring at him, even though he no longer returned her gaze. He wondered which of the two girls was happier, and why. One had little money and lost it; the other had none. Both had no need for it. One was dressed in filthy rags; the other was cleansed by river water. Both might live to see their children morphing into their own younger selves. Neither of them would attend school, and both would spend their lives caring for family.

Tómas lay back and fell into sleep, awakening an hour later to see that the same little girl was busy chasing a bronzed pig. She skipped away, following the pig behind the caña stick house.

Rising from the ground, he dusted off his pants. Juan Carlos was nowhere around.

After waiting for a few minutes, the girl reappeared with an empanada and handed the clump of fried dough to him. Thanking her, he bit into a hot, oily lump of rubbery Ecuadorian cheese and dough as she watched.

Tómas looked around for any vegetable plants, but saw none. The mud canal banks for irrigation leading into the areas where there should be plants held only dirt and overgrowth. Instead of lying down as he wanted to, he resolved to restructure the canal banks.

He began by digging up some of the banks with a rusty shovel. A few families gathered around him. Padre Pédro was here among them, and he helped to shovel as Tómas showed them how to place fresh mud along the sides and reinforce the base and the sides with banana tree leaves. Imagining that he was digging banks for new albarradas he had designed himself, he showed them the importance of the channel slopes.

"When I return here," he said to them, "I expect I will see the Egyptian Delta." They did not understand the reference to the ancient controlled irrigation from a predictable floodplain, but thanked him and fed him pescado estufado made with the giant ocean fish picudo, a fish that one of the men proudly exclaimed he had caught a half kilometre off shore that morning.

Tómas smiled as he ate, and the men laughed and poured him glasses of Caña Manabita as the women encouraged him to eat more. He felt that these people truly appreciated what little he had showed them and, wishing he had the time to show them more of what he knew, he vowed to return.

23. The Foreign Trained Midwife

THE SUN HAD set, and Tómas walked beneath a dotted night sky laced with leafless trees, still unable to locate Juan Carlos. He passed through the beginnings of a fiesta. A spitting grill with a small blue marlin, picudo blanco, its sword more of an elongated dagger, was being roasted over a wood and brush fire. Periodic plumes of smoke reeled into the air. Several pairs of running shoes and high-heels, removed as if to liberate the people's spirits, lined an impromptu dance floor. It was a shedding of physical impediments to set the dancers into the warmth of a torch lit night.

Moonlight came and went with the clouds. The smell of cervezas, unconsumed fish, and warm bodies writhing on dirt accompanied the pulsating rhythms and beats of guitars and drums, greeting the river as it rolled gently against huge rocks at its edge. Tómas walked down to a barren area covered with stones beside the flowing brown river, an area resembling the tributaries near his home. He sat down on a patch of dry dirt.

A lone shadow danced to the music, observing the stars that could be seen in the moonlight's lustre. A woman holding a lit cigarette danced toward him, the vague light of moonbeams frolicking on her curves.

"Cigarillo?" she asked, extending a cigarette toward him. Tómas accepted, the carbon filter crushing between his fingers.

"You were not enjoying the party?" Tómas asked.

"I could ask you the same question." She spoke in English, but with a foreign accent. She handed him her cigarette to light his own, and was still dancing when she retrieved it.

She smelled faintly of jasmine and sugar cane alcohol, her moonlight skin the colour of faded lapis. As she continued dancing, moving with the flame of her cigarette, he recalled the fire dancers of Borneo. His father had photographed them over twenty years ago. Montgomery had captured the dancers in different time-lapsed speeds, each photograph giving an entirely different picture of the same event: two torches on the end of chains, the fire stiff and rigid, a Bornean aboriginal in sandals practicing his ancient art in the midst of his rainforest home. The pictures in lapsed time showed perfectly concentric circles: a hazy, fogged silhouette of fire that ended where it began; each burning ember ignited fingers that exerted a hush on their dark surroundings, as though the flames were guarding some age-old secret.

"I know one person here," Tómas said, talking to her dancing figure. "And I do not find him."

Looking down at him, she smiled. "I don't speak much English these days," she said. She stopped dancing, and stood there. "It's nice. I am Colette. And you are Tómas."

"Yes."

"Your friend Juan Carlos is sulking in my room. I had to leave. He was asking me too many questions about my plans. I told him he needs to forget about my plans, and think about his own. He needs to go back to his wife and children."

"I told him many times, also."

"I didn't want to see him again," she continued. "But here he is. I shouldn't have become involved with him. He makes too many demands on me, like the people of Monte Cristo. But tonight, I will listen to no requests."

She began dancing again and, observing her movements, Tómas had the sudden urge to make love there on the beach. He had never made love to a woman before, he would tell her, without divulging the reason: that he had refused, on his traditional first time, in the whorehouse covered in wood panelling with sad women seated on folding chairs next to wooden rooms. Juan Carlos had taken him there and had been disappointed with his refusal to succumb to what he might have supposed to be Tómas's desires.

His new sexual urge quickly faded into the realm of rejected thought as the music stopped, and she ceased dancing. As she sat down Tómas saw that she was much older than he had originally thought.

"I've never met an Ecuadorian who doesn't dance," she said, smiling. "Until now."

He produced the silver locket, the wide floral imprints twinkling silver in the faded light, and gave it to her. Seeming to immediately recognize the piece, she opened the clasp and examined the picture.

"This was mine," she said, staring at the photograph. "I haven't seen it in forever. I gave it to your mother a long time ago." She paused for a while, her attention focused on the diminutive picture, before she finally looked out at the dark river water. Her face was wide, her lips taut. Tómas imagined that, in her younger days, this woman must have been quite beautiful. He thought of the reasons he was there as loud merengue music suddenly erupted to fill the silence.

"About my mother," he said. "The Señora Harvey, my Ecuadorian mother, she told to me that you knew her well."

"I knew your mother, Violet, a long time ago," she said. "She lives in Canada. That's where I lived with her, before you were born."

"I thought maybe she died. She sent me no letters, or letters to anyone in my family. Not for all of my life."

"She sent me letters over the years. I still have some of them. One of them is addressed to you. I'll fish them out, and give them to you when we meet again. She sent letters to your father too, but she stopped sending them after Señora Harvey—your Ecuadorian mother—put a stop to it."

"Some things I wonder about Violet. Like why she came to this island from Canada."

"She talked me into coming here with her, a sort of extended vacation, on a year-long program for midwives with an international aid agency."

"She was a midwife?"

"She still is, so far as I know. But it was the most adventurous thing I have ever done in my life, the first time either of us had ever left Canada. I thought this place was so exotic, so wonderful when I first arrived, but now it's only depressing."

"You have been here since a long time ago."

"Yes. And in that time I've grown to love the people here but still, more than anything, I want to leave. I've been here in Monte Cristo far too long, with far too much responsibility. I want to go somewhere where people don't need anything from me. Where I can just exist, and survive. No demands, no responsibilities."

Colette buried her unfinished cigarette in the sand. The noise of laughter and a smashing bottle reverberated over the heavy bass of the party. It was the time of day the islanders basked in: a time of freedom, selfish abandon, recklessness and a time to engage in celebration of the evening air. It was a time that the island's social animals lusted after.

"We delivered many babies in San Cristobal," she continued, "Violet and I. You were the first baby I ever delivered without her help ..." She paused. "Well, you know what I mean."

"Why did you and my mother come here?"

"Because we had medical training, your mother and I were asked to come here to Monte Cristo after their last doctor died of old age. I accepted, and your mother went back to Canada. She was the smart one. I realized I made a mistake when they wanted solutions to their heart problems, breathing problems, and other pains."

"I do not understand why you stayed."

"There was no one else here with any medical training, so I learned what I needed to do to help them. With the medicine I had, I could fix wounds, burns, some sprains and fractures. I could help with nausea or heat exhaustion, the men working in the fields nine or ten hours a day. I worked with women having babies, some as young as fourteen. The women told me of other midwives they had heard about who went through suffering and intense dreams, saying that God talked to them, telling them to become midwives. They seemed surprised to hear me say that my calling was not so dramatic, that there simply wasn't anything else I could see myself doing."

She paused to light another cigarette.

"I wonder why my mother left this place," Tómas said, looking into her eyes.

"Her departure coincided with your birth. I never thought she would leave without you, though. But then again, I thought I would never leave this place, either, and now here I am. Very soon, perhaps."

Tómas heard footsteps behind them. The voice of Juan Carlos rose over the rapidly increased rumblings of music and laughter.

"I am ready to go back to San Cristobal," he said, placing his hand on Tómas's shoulder.

"Tómas isn't," Colette said. "You shouldn't go, either. It's too dark."

"The moon is out," he replied. "We can find our way."

"You're drunk."

"We should stay," Tómas said. "I will go back with you in the morning."

"All good, I will stay," Juan Carlos said, removing his hand and stepping back. "But only because you want me to, Tómas, and not for the reason that she does."

His footsteps faded into the noise of the party, and the water splashed against the rocks for a moment before the party flared up again with blaring music.

"Sorry for that interruption," Colette said, smiling. She began speaking again a minute later. "When your mother said she didn't want to stay, I tried to convince her to. Life here is easy, and life in Canada is difficult. I remember saying that to her, and I recall your father trying to convince her, too. She said she didn't know what to do, and so she did what was easiest. She left. And she hoped, one day, you would understand and forgive her."

"It is not easy, to forgive such selfishness."

"Everyone is selfish, though, really, when you think of it."

"She was unhappy here, too, from what I've read."

"You wouldn't know it to see her. If she was here now, she'd be in the middle of that party back there. But during the day she said very confusing things, like she needed to 'embrace her autonomy' by leaving—that's how she put it—and when I asked her what that meant, she said she was living her life according to her own free will, and she didn't want to be what others expected her to be. I think she was very confused at the time she was here, the same as I am now. Only my confusion has to do with morality, hers had to do with justification of her actions ... but I suppose, now that I think of it, our dilemma is the same."

"I do not understand your words," Tómas said. "But to where will you go?"

"To the mainland," she replied. "I have good friends in Portoviejo. All of my family is in Canada, but I haven't seen them in so long, I'd hardly recognize them."

"And the people here, after you leave, they will not have a doctor."

"This place will find a real doctor that can actually help these people. The only reason no one has, I think, is because I've been here doing the job."

"You cannot leave them alone, with no medical help. That is not right."

She contorted her face into an odd grimace. "Do you talk like this to everyone?"

"No."

"Well, I've tried to get a replacement here for years. I wrote to hospitals on the mainland, to doctors and politicians, and to Eduardo Delgado, who told me he had a doctor that wanted to work here. But that was a very long time ago, and I have heard nothing since."

"The doctor's name was Cristobal."

"Cristobal, yes. You know him, then."

Tómas looked up. In the moon's absence, he could see the constellations and a sea of stars. Looking upward for a time, he suddenly thought of what Eduardo had said in the letter Flory had read to him as he lay ill with malaria. Tómas could ask anything of him. They were like family.

"I will talk to Eduardo for you," Tómas said. "I will have Cristobal here, before you leave."

She grinned, picked up a small stone, and used it to extinguish her cigarette that had turned into a long cylinder of ash. "Very nice of you, but people have promised me this so many times before. I won't believe it until I see him standing here."

She tossed the stone in the river, followed by another, and then another.

"So you lived with my mother back in Canadá," Tómas said.

"My family is from a town called Deux Rivieres, in the province of Ontario. I lived with your mother in an apartment there, over a general store that sold everything to do with hunting and fishing. There are bears, fox, moose and deer everywhere there, and endless forests. It's on the border of a national park, and the town is near the capital of the country."

Tómas said nothing for a few minutes, listening to the sounds of the party behind, and the water lapping against the rocks before him.

"One day, I will go back there," she said.

"I would like to go there, too. My father, he applied for a visa for me almost ten years ago. My Ecuadorian mother Veronica did not like it. Not at all. I have not heard about the visa."

"Why? Are you thinking of visiting your mother in Canada?"

"Yes," he said quickly, without thought, as though he had been considering this possibility recently.

"She will probably be there in Deux Rivieres. But if not, you could find out where she went." She paused, and then added: "If you really want to, that is."

"I do. But I do not know what I would say to her."

"I don't think you would have to say anything," Colette said. "I think you could simply listen."

Colette opened the locket again and smiled, staring at the picture of her and Violet together.

"I've heard your father has left the island," she said, still examining the picture.

"He is in Peru, near Machu Picchu," he said.

"I've been there many times." She snapped the locket shut, and handed it back to him. "There are over a thousand Inca trails that lead from Cuszco. You can get a guide there, but sometimes they will lead you down the wrong path and rob you. I know from experience."

"I want to see my father there. I want someone to go with me, then to come to Canada. Maybe you know someone interested."

She paused and then, looking surprised, she asked: "What makes you think I would want to do that?"

"I will get you out of here, and get a doctor. I have saved money over many years. My father gave it to me. I can pay our way. I have almost three hundred American dollars."

She smirked. "That won't even pay your way," she said.

He was silent for a moment, looking up at the sky, before adding: "This might be the only chance I have to meet my mother, and see my father again. If you leave—"

"Yes," she answered. "And I promised your mother I would look after you. But sadly, your father and his Señora have always done that."

"Perhaps this is your chance to look after me. I have seen pickup trucks on the island. Military men collecting recruits. I am a remiso. If I am picked up there might be no escape for me. I need your help. You might be able to help me get a visa, too, at the Canadian Consulate in Peru. We can say we will be married. Tell them I applied for a visa almost ten years ago. I need your help, same as you could use mine."

He gave her the silver locket back, and closed her hands over it. She smiled.

"I have some money," she said. "I didn't spend any of it living here. If you find my replacement, I'll take you. You see, the people here in Monte Cristo, they've taught me many things. Such as caring for people, without knowing them ..."

"They are compassionate," he said in Spanish.

"Yes," she said, smiling. "And giving. The same as I strive to be."

24. The Red Page

TÓMAS AND JUAN Carlos carefully traversed the log bridge over the river, in the early afternoon. A woman collected water in a large pot below, her eyes fixed on the riverbed. She did not seem to notice as their feet hit the dusty footpath leading toward San Cristobal.

Thinking of what Colette had said about Juan Carlos and his family, Tómas began contemplating how to start a conversation that really, they had never had. After a few minutes of hiking in the silent, dusty heat he began: "How are your wife and children?"

Juan Carlos explained that his family was still living in the mainland town of Machala, where a banana queen is chosen each year, crowned and paraded through town on a float of bananas. His wife was chosen as second in line to the throne several years ago.

"Everyone in their life is known for something," he said, smiling. "And that was *her* moment." His expression became more solemn. "I miss her. I miss my boys, too."

"You can return."

"Soon, I will write to Edgar Rodriguez, the editor of the mainland newspaper El Comercio. I have known Edgar for very long. He will help me return to my old job, and to be closer to my children. I fought with Edgar many years ago, but now I am talking to him on the phone often. You know the mainland newspaper, El Comercio. It is everywhere. Diario Hoy is not. You buy a cigarette, candy, and El

Comercio for five hundred sucres in the candy stands. The back page, where all the printing is in red ink, has stories of people who died that week."

"The Red Page."

Juan Carlos stopped to pick berries from the side of the pathway, plucking the coffee beans from the branch one by one and eating them as he spoke. The noise of birds flared up and then died down again, as if in protest. Tómas stopped beside him.

"That is it," Juan Carlos said. "And you know that beside the columns are pictures of the deceased. Not as they looked when they were alive, which any decent and moral paper would do, but as they looked when they were dead. Last week I saw the picture of a gringo, who hiked where no foreigner should hike, in the mountains near the Colombian border. They found him after a week, in the river. No one even knows what country he was from, because he had no identification. The photographers from El Comercio were there, as the body was lifted from the river, taking their photographs. Disgusting."

"And you want to work there."

"No, not really," he said, shaking his head and tossing another small, bright red berry into his mouth. "But I should."

Producing a small bottle of sugarcane alcohol from his pocket, he uncapped it, took a drink, and gave it to Tómas who swiftly returned it. They continued walking.

"When I was living on the mainland," Juan Carlos said, "working for El Comercio, I fought with Edgar about an article I wrote against Eduardo Delgado's housing plan. When Edgar went to a conference, I was put in the charge of the newspaper, and I printed it. Front page. I also printed an article condemning his friends, Eduardo, the president, and the Pichincha Eighth Civil judge for their actions in that conscientious objector case with Alejandro Pédro Juarez Jiminez that forced me out of practicing law."

"Edgar fired you for that?"

"No. He returned from the conference and said he could not stand to see these articles in his paper. He accused me of prejudice. After that, he moved me to work with the editor of the Red Page, who I tell you, was truly a pig. The articles I had to write had nothing about the people's lives, only their deaths. I would guess how they died, how long ago, and what they were doing right before the moment when their souls left their bodies. I have thought, since I was a child, that my own death will be an early one, that I will not live a full life, and my job made me think and talk about that too often. I was disgusted with my articles and with myself, and my wife, too, she was sick of this. I quit to make her happy, and for myself for certain, but I could not find another job."

Juan Carlos took another drink from his narrow, glass bottle, and offered the alcohol to Tómas, who tipped the bottle into his mouth before returning it.

"And then you moved here," Tómas said, wiping his mouth with the back of his hand.

"That is when I moved here to the island, yes, to work for the only other newspaper in the country. My wife refused to move away from her mother, who accused me of trying to end our marriage. Even though she doesn't love me at this moment, I still love her. My wife, I mean, not her mother ... I said to you before, a man here on the island phoned to tell my wife about Colette. I think it was Eduardo. Now, I am not with Colette anymore."

"You must go back to your wife," Tómas said. "And your children."

"You repeat yourself. I should, but I will not. I cannot live with my wife. Being close enough to my children to visit them often; that would be better for everyone."

"You need do what is right. You said you still love her, and I know you love your children. If I had family waiting for me somewhere, I would do anything to be with them. In fact, I am."

"The editor of El Comercio is a supporter of Eduardo's, but when Eduardo is ruined, he will not support him anymore. That is why he will talk to me and give me work, and how I will move back to be near my children."

"Do not move close to your family, move back into your house. Think of what I said. Think of what your family, Padre Pédro and God wants. Your wife can forgive you. So will your children. I am certain all they want in the world is to be with you."

They moved into an area thick with bushes. Juan Carlos coughed in the dust, and continued a moment later. He nodded as he began speaking. "I will think about that," he said. "You should be a lawyer, maybe a politician. It is true. I have lived apart from them for too long. But my own success will come from Eduardo's failure."

They hiked for two more hours before they reached the Place San Cristobal, passing a mule heaped with caña and its boy conductor, both of whom strode listlessly down the street as the sun began to hang its tired head.

"So," Juan Carlos said, finally. "You extracted my story from me."

They paused to look over the empty square, garbage lining its sides. Merchants packed their goods away on the street, and shut the metal doors of their shops. Tómas had walked these same streets with his father at this time of the day, with nothing to buy, watching the steel folding doors unfurling to the ground and being latched in place. His father would say that it reminded him of watching the marketers in Whitechapel where he grew up, as they secured their wares or transported them elsewhere by horse and wagon until another day.

"We have a thing in common," Tómas said, looking out over the town square nearly devoid of people.

"What is that?" Juan Carlos asked, turning toward him.

"A need to be with our family. An obligation to those we cannot see."

Juan Carlos smiled. "We will have to talk more about your court case soon," he said. "The people talk about renewed fighting in the border war. They will need men. It may not be safe soon for me or you or any remisos, conscientious objection or not."

Tómas's smile disappeared as tires squealing on the pavement nearby broke the silence in the square. As they parted, Señor Olivos closed the metal door of his pharmacy. Tómas turned away quickly, and began walking in the direction from which he had come. Señora Modesta de la Nieve suddenly excused herself as she blocked his way with a cart of unripe mangos. He had to turn away, darting down an alleyway that stank of fish.

No longer isolated in the campo, his fear of being captured and forced into military service had returned.

A loud shout echoed through the empty streets "Drunks," Tómas said quietly, to himself. "All they are. Only a bunch of borrachos."

As he rounded a corner, a pickup truck with several men in the back, on seeing Tómas, braked and swung around. Tómas turned to run, but as if in a dream, his feet felt heavy. His breathing was laboured. The noise of the approaching vehicle increased. His motions became slower. Then, suddenly, they were upon him, the truck at his side.

He was flying into the air now, lifted from the ground by three sets of hands that pulled him into the cab of the truck. He could no longer move. In a moment, one of the men's knees was on his neck, and Tómas was lying face down on the dirty metal with the smells of earth, sweat, and rust: what he would remember as his own scent of subdued panic and fear. He wondered at that moment where Juan Carlos was, if he was in the back of another pickup truck, or whether he had seen none of this and was on his way home, or if he had viewed this entire abduction and had quickly absconded, fearing for himself.

25. El Remiso

TÓMAS RECOGNIZED THIS building, recalling the last time he had walked through this white, painted door. During his pre-military course in Secondary School, he had visited this island Centre of Recruitment and Reserves nearly every day for a year. The entrance was guarded by military personnel. Several of his classmates from the university were here. Closing his eyes for a moment, stopping to stand in a line-up, a guard's boots shuffled on the wooden floor. A clock ticked in the near-silence. If there was a diversion outside to draw the guards, he could escape through the doorway and run away from this island, the same as his father had done. And as his father, his humiliation and disgrace would not matter, except to his own conscience and to those he had left behind.

Someone shook his shoulder. Opening his eyes, an Ecuadorian military officer in a grey uniform with a pressed white shirt, solid black tie, and silver stars overlaid atop red and yellow shoulder stripes appeared before him. Thin tufts of black hair lined this man's head, his hair nearly cut to the scalp. One eye was brown, the other green. His beard gave him away as the officer beside Eduardo at the hotel inauguration who had eyed him suspiciously as Veronica pulled on Tómas's arm to leave; and Tómas's stomach became sour with the same sensation now as when they had navigated through the crowd.

"Come," the man ordered.

Tómas followed the officer into a small, dimly lit workspace with a desk, two chairs, and a window that looked out onto a concrete wall. An electrical panel hummed nearby. A wall clock ticked away.

"Sit," he said in Spanish, indicating one of the chairs and closing the door.

Tómas sat down, and rubbed his arms. A heated draft from an overhead vent descended and pierced his thin cotton shirt.

"Your record says that supposedly, you were to report to Guayaquil military base on the date of March the third, and yet you did not go. Why, no?"

Tómas sat without answering. No words that might satisfy this man's question came to mind.

"You are a remiso, and you will be fined. More men are needed at the border at Twinitiza. You will be among the next to be sent."

Tómas said nothing as the man sat down and began completing paperwork on the desk. He asked for Tómas's postal box number, the street he lived on, information on the location of various relatives and friends, and what course of study he was taking in university. Tómas claimed he knew nothing about his father's whereabouts, despite the man's repeated question.

"I am a conscientious objector to this war," Tómas said suddenly. "I perform civil service instead of military service."

The officer said nothing but stared hard into Tómas's eyes, remaining motionless for a time. Tómas tried to look away, staring at the silver stars on his shoulders and examining their lustre and small imperfections, his gaze returning repeatedly to the officer, whose focus remained steady.

"You are misguided," he said, looking down at the pages on his desk. Pausing for a moment, he added: "Your words sound rehearsed. You have held a rifle of course. You have learned to clean one and take it apart."

"For certain," Tómas replied.

"Well then ..." He left the comment suspended and exited to the other room. Returning a minute later, he held what Tómas knew to be a standard infantry weapon.

"Your file says you applied for conscientious objection as you said," the officer continued. "There is nothing about civil service. Your lawyer who no longer practices law, but who writes slander and lies in our island newspaper, he has filed your application for conscientious objection. But we have not reached him by phone. Take this." He handed the weapon to Tómas, who set it on the arms of the chair. "A Belgian 7.62 mm rifle. You will need to become accustomed to holding one. You will hold onto it until he gets here; if ever he does."

The officer closed the door, talking with guards in the next room, their voices barely audible. Some of the men opened the door to look in on Tómas, who turned his head away. Envisioning escape and checking the rifle, he found that the chamber was unloaded; and he was relieved that he did not have a decision to make.

When the door opened again, Tómas was asleep, the rifle still resting on the arms of his chair. Hours might have passed.

Juan Carlos appeared at the entranceway, sweating heavily and carrying a collection of files. "I heard the pickup truck, then I saw you in it. I chased after you until my legs and lungs stopped working," he said. " I knew where they were taking you. Before coming here, first, I had to go to my newspaper office. No one except Inés saw me there, and she asked me many questions I refused to answer. I have a plan to get you out of here. First, these government round-ups are illegal. And second, you are a conscientious objector. You cannot be sent to Twinitiza, or anywhere else."

Juan Carlos stared at the rifle on his chair. "What is this?" he asked, touching the muzzle with his finger.

"I cannot fight in public," Tómas replied, undecided. "Maybe I should perform a year of military service. Maybe I will not be hurt."

"You will not be hurt; you will be killed. Twinitiza is especially dangerous, now there is talk of renewed fighting there. You must fight, only not at the border, but in court. We have already started. You know of the Second Law of Thermodynamics, you are an engineer."

"Yes. But not an engineer yet. That law is about chaos and randomness."

"No, I'm thinking of another one, then. What is the one about ... how do you say ... motion that does not stop?"

"Newton's first law of motion, about inertia."

"Yes, that is the one. My point, now weakened because I did not know the laws of motion, is that once this fight has started, it must continue."

"Perhaps you are right."

Juan Carlos sat down behind the desk, and tossed his files on the desktop. The papers fanned out. He retrieved them, and shuffled the papers together again.

"What did you say to that company officer?" Juan Carlos asked.

"Nothing."

"You must have said something. You were in here with him for a while, from what the other officers said."

"Ten minutes, maybe fifteen."

"Then?"

"He asked where I lived. He knew about my conscription. He said I will be sent to the front. Then I told him I was a conscientious objector to this war."

"You said that?" he asked. "Now, think carefully. You said you object to *this* war?"

"Yes."

Juan Carlos sighed, and said nothing. Tómas peered out the window at the concrete wall as sounds invaded him: the nearby electrical panel humming, the wall clock clicking, boots shuffling on the wooden floor in the next room. He looked up at Juan Carlos, who was staring at him.

"What?" Tómas asked, shifting in his seat and putting his hands on the rifle so the old weapon would not fall to the floor.

"You must say you object to *any* war, not just to *this* war. But, maybe it will not be talked about in court. Please, say nothing more to anyone without consulting me first. Either that, or answer any questions with a simple yes or a no." He sorted through the papers on the desk, to produce a yellow file folder.

"We have received a response to our petition," he continued, opening the folder and producing a letter. "The letter says that the Law of Obligatory Military Service supersedes the other articles we have mentioned. It says that if the petition is accepted, you are to carry out service in the development unit of the Armed Forces. If you refuse to do that, then you will be punished by law."

"The development unit is probably best for me," Tómas said.

"No," Juan Carlos replied, shaking his head, his green eyes opalescent in the vague lighting. "There is a contradiction here, one they do not admit. The Constitution and this law are not compatible. This is the basis for our fight, and this is what they have not acknowledged. They have not accepted your status as a conscientious objector. Even though there has never been a single acceptance of conscientious objection, there must be a first in everything. We will fight in court tomorrow, in the morning. Manuel Fernando Ortega Ramirez, he will be the lawyer for the Armed Forces. With him, you must take care what you say. For now, you will have to stay incarcerated here for the night. And I must prepare you for the morning."

After several hours Juan Carlos left the room, and Tómas was escorted out by a moustached officer. The man led him to a group of cots in an adjacent area. As Tómas lay down he felt a man's knee on the back of his neck, the man's illusory knee, only a crossbar on the cot. Feeling lighter, he fell asleep.

26. Selective Conscientious Objector

THE NEXT MORNING, fear set in. Veronica had always told Tómas to prepare for the worst. His father had always told him to be the best at whatever he chose to do. So he merged this guidance by carefully contemplating the worst possible outcome. Now, apart from being sent to Twinitiza and indefinite military service, the most terrible conclusion would be for everyone to discover that he was a conscientious objector. Or was that the worst? Perhaps that would be his insignia of honour. Otherwise, he would only be a coward hiding behind an excuse; still, after all these years, el payaso asustado, the cowardly clown.

His father once said he wanted to help document the Second World War, to show people who wouldn't otherwise know what was happening in Europe; to document the truth through his writings, but more importantly through the dispassionate objectivity of the camera lens. Tómas could justify his own absence from the war, and his conscientious objection, by showing the truth and reality not only of the war, but also of forced conscription and the seeming impossibility of winning a claim of Conscientious Objection. Perhaps, in addition to acting as Tómas's lawyer in the court case, Juan Carlos could also write a news story about the closed session where no press would be allowed. By going to court Tómas would have an opportunity to voice his opinion to the people in the courtroom and, through Juan Carlos, to extend that voice to the people of the island and the country.

Entering the room escorted by the moustached officer, Tómas scrutinized an oversized map of the country above the red, blue and yellow flag of Ecuador. Isla de la Plata was represented by a small dot just off the coast, the island unlabelled. Sitting down in a row of black chairs and waiting as people slowly began entering the room, recognizing none of them, his heart beat faster as the room began to fill and he saw, among those entering was the dark-bearded Ecuadorian military officer who had handed him the Belgian rifle at the island recruitment centre. Juan Carlos was here, and he invited Tómas to sit beside him.

These aged men wore suits, and sat in seats arranged around him. Everyone stood up, one by one, and introduced themselves before being seated again. All of the ten or so gathered there were from the mainland, all lawyers presiding either in Ecuadorian Superior Court, or in the National Court. Johnny Galo Delgado Gonzembach introduced himself as the judge, a man much younger than Tómas had expected, in a loosely cut grey suit with long hair tied back, hanging over one shoulder and still wet from a shower. Flicking the tail of his hair back behind his large ears, he sat down.

Manuel Fernando Ortega Ramirez introduced himself as the State Lawyer. He wore a gold tie, and a crisp white shirt. A chain dangled between his back pocket and belt loop. He had neatly cropped black hair, large lips, and a large nose, and remained standing after announcing his name, extending both hands forward to lean on the table as he talked.

Looking at Tómas, he began: "You have not answered repeated letters, summoning you to come here. Once we found you were in custody, we have quickly arranged for this special meeting to take place." Turning to Juan Carlos, he added: "Your petition alleges conscientious objection as indicated in Article 188 of the Political Constitution of Ecuador, and the 1984 Law of Obligatory Military Service in the Armed Forces, indicated in Article 108, are contradictory. Is this your contention?"

A mural behind Manuel depicted a woman in a green and purple dress. She stood in a swamp bearing a slight smile and holding a scale with a bird in her left hand, a sword with the blade extending downward in her right. Even though the question had not been addressed to him, Tómas still carefully considered a response while perusing this mural, slowly recalling all of these article numbers and names from what he had been told the night before.

"Yes," Juan Carlos replied. "They are. And this should be resolved by recognizing the supremacy of the constitution, Article 272, in this instance."

"And the defendant is engaged in, and has not yet completed a year of, as you call it, 'civil service.' "

Juan Carlos took a moment before answering: "No."

Tómas, not intending to contradict Juan Carlos, still answered: "I am."

Manuel leafed through his papers for a moment before sitting down. Taking a pen in his hand, he opened his notebook and began to write. Looking up after a short time, addressing Tómas, he asked: "So, what are the reasons, morality and philosophy, for your objection to military service?"

This is one of the questions he and Juan Carlos had carefully rehearsed. "I prefer my lawyer to answer that," Tómas replied.

"I wish to hear your response," Manuel said.

Even though Veronica, Eduardo, his father and Padre Pédro were not there, Tómas could still feel their gaze penetrating into his, as though they sat among the shadows between the collection of lawyers now in the room. Suddenly flushed, Tómas's heart rate began to rise as his gaze moved from the bearded military officer to Manuel, and then over to Juan Carlos.

When Juan Carlos began to speak, he was immediately interrupted by Manuel, who was looking directly into Tómas's eyes.

"You must answer the question," Manuel said. "Are you afraid to fight?"

"Again," Tómas said. "I prefer my lawyer to answer."

His face at once flushed, his tone impudent, Manuel interrupted. "He cannot speak for you about this, you understand. You must answer."

Tómas wanted to say nothing. They had not practised what to do if Juan Carlos was not permitted to respond.

"Well," Juan Carlos began, taking a deep breath. "Let me begin. Tómas will answer, but I will begin. Tómas Harvey is a peaceful young man, an atheist who reads Nietzsche and Sartre, who believes that all we have in this life is what we accomplish on this earth. His conscience will not allow him to participate in any war, for he is a young man who, until now, has accomplished nothing. He will now tell you about his objection to the conscription system." He turned toward Tómas, handing him a piece of paper.

Tómas stumbled over the words as he read from the page: "*The conscription system enables war to take place, and it also propagates war. I cannot refuse to register for conscription. And at registration, conscientious objection is not acknowledged by the government.*"

"In the Second World War," Ramirez said, "five thousand people in the United States went to prison for fighting 'the draft.' What would have happened, if they had fought instead in the war? How much earlier would the war have ended? How many lives would those five thousand have saved?"

Juan Carlos stood up. "That is speculation, we cannot say. We cannot suppose what might have happened. We can only look to the future. We are here to discuss conscientious objection in Article 188 of the Constitution, and the Law of Obligatory Military Service, Article 108, and their contradiction."

Manuel eyed Tómas. "Please," he said, "Continue with your statement."

But Tómas had already divulged his entire written statement. Together he and Juan Carlos had discussed additional assertions he could make, though, contemplating what the law said and how the law would view such declarations.

Tómas took a deep breath, wiped his hair back with his hand, and began by stating all he could remember.

"War objectors, they are well-studied in their beliefs," he said calmly, his heartbeat rapid, "and in their philosophies; and some include their philosophies in their religion, or the reverse. But sometimes, too, our ideas are simple. I know beliefs can be religious, apart from traditional religion. I know members of the Catholic Church are not all Catholic, or Christians. For war objectors, our religion is pacifism. But at the same time I do not say I have a love of peace. This is a complicated problem, like the albarradas I study, that you have for certain heard about."

Juan Carlos attempted to interrupt, but Tómas did not let him, instead clearing his throat before continuing. Tómas's heartbeat was steady, his voice and demeanour more tranquil now. He had the attention of all those in the room.

"How do I show what I learned from my family," Tómas continued, "my objection to war, is part of my personality? That is what you might ask. I have not fought in any wars. I have not fought against the government, or the military. In a protest against the government, I once held a Molotov cocktail waiting for a military vehicle. I thought about throwing it, but I could not be a part of such violence. I threw it later, when I was near the edge of the cliff. There were only a few crabs on the rocks below. I read books, the Red Badge of Courage, The Wars, and war spy novels. I read a book about Canadians executed during the First World War for deserting. These books made me think of fighting in a war. And they made me understand I cannot."

"You have always been a pacifist because of books you read?" Manuel asked. Juan Carlos was slumped down in his seat.

"Yes."

"And yet you took a Molotov cocktail thinking to use it against a government vehicle."

"You might say I did not have courage. But I know if a boat sank, I would try to save others in place of myself. That is not lack of courage ..." He paused, cleared his throat, and then continued. "My Ecuadorian mother told me to think and prepare for the worst. The worst, for me, would be forced military service and I would not be allowed to leave the country again. I had teachers, I will not say their names, and they taught me war, not only this war, is wrong. I have seen movies, my father brought them from other countries, and they showed me why it is wrong. I was never part of any rallies against war here on the island, because there have been none."

Tómas stopped, hoping he had not said too much. From the look on Juan Carlos's face, he had. The room remained silent for a moment.

"And the Second World War," Manuel said hoarsely, before clearing his throat. "Your father left England as the war was being fought, for reasons I do not know. Would you have done the same? You could let someone such as Hitler rule all of Europe?"

Tómas did not recall this line of questioning from his preparation with Juan Carlos.

"Again, he cannot speculate on what he might have done in any past war," Juan Carlos said, sitting up, suddenly flustered. "We are talking about the present, and this war he has been called to fight in."

"But you talk of an objection to any war," Manuel said forcefully, "and others can always fight for those who are afraid to go themselves. But that is an act of treason. Your client said himself that he has a book of Canadians executed during the First World War for such cowardice. Perhaps his father, too, has read this book, understood the contents and sympathized with the deserters."

Tómas, his head spinning now, suddenly began speaking, despite Juan Carlos's apparent opposition. "The problems in this war are land, uranium, oil, and the government wanting the war to continue, even after fifty years—"

"So," Manuel interrupted, addressing Tómas now. "You admit you object only to this war?"

Tómas was no longer being careful with his words, as Juan Carlos had instructed him to do.

"No," Juan Carlos said. "Me, or him, we do not say that."

"That is what you both imply," Manuel said, his firm gaze returning to Juan Carlos. "And he would be labelled as a selective conscientious objector because of this."

"No, he is not," Juan Carlos replied.

"And his claim will be denied."

"And the denial will be appealed."

"And ... he said that one of his fears is never leaving the country. Many people look for Montgomery Harvey." Turning to Tómas, he added: "Is that why you wish to leave? Do you know where he is? What do you know of these accusations that he has taken millions of dollars from our government? If your military service is now inconvenient for a reason such as visiting your father, or you have more knowledge than the rest of us here about a crime against our government, you understand, you must tell us. There is more than your military term to think of. Think of prison."

Tómas did not answer immediately, not having anticipated any of these questions. But then, he thought of a response. "We are not here to talk about my father," he said.

The door to the room suddenly swung open, and Tómas had the notion that his father was there. Eduardo entered instead, wearing a blue suit, with several stitches in his nose that had not yet been removed, his face bruised from Veronica's fit at the hotel's inauguration. Tómas, sweating now, shuddered when he grasped that Eduardo somehow knew about these proceedings; following that came an instantaneous relief at the understanding that Eduardo might be able to help at a time when Juan Carlos was apparently unable.

"Please, excuse me," Eduardo said, staring at Juan Carlos as he took an empty seat next to the judge. After a moment, Eduardo, still eyeing Juan Carlos, began whispering into the judge's ear.

Standing up to address Juan Carlos, Manuel said: "Tómas Harvey began by calling his beliefs a 'religion of pacifism.' He told us about some of the books he has read, movies he has seen, teachers he has had, and he said all this made him know he could not fight in this war. I think he is afraid. He fears being forced to the front or indefinite military service so he could not leave the country again and visit his father. He fears death, and killing. He objects to this war against land, and resources. Specifically to this war, as he and his lawyer said."

Juan Carlos shook his head slowly, defeated, staring back at Eduardo. There was silence before the door opened again, a thin woman in an apron entering with a jar of instant coffee and a few steaming mugs, making cups of hot coffee for some of the lawyers. Stifled conversation began as Manuel continued, addressing Tómas now.

"You are a 'selective conscientious objector,' " he said. "I wish to petition the court to deny your claim on this basis. It seems your military service is inconvenient to you for reasons I have already outlined, and perhaps for other reasons we will not explore."

Juan Carlos gazed over at Tómas, and then back at Eduardo, as the conversation in the courtroom grew louder.

Tómas waited in the hallway with an armed guard until Juan Carlos emerged from the courtroom a while later.

"Eduardo has guaranteed the judge that he will get you a military card," Juan Carlos said. "But he cannot, as I told you many times before. You will be released for now, on Eduardo's word, but he only has two weeks. When he fails to get it for you, you will be brought in again. And their decision is already made, so we will have to appeal the decision on your status as a conscientious objector."

"I will tell Eduardo to get me what he promised," Tómas said. "There is no choice."

"He will do nothing for you. You have done this to yourself. As with any of the struggles you will face in your life, you have faced this one alone; ignoring my advice to you the same as Jiminez did to me before. But even so, when you are defeated, your friends can help to pick you up. Before we appeal, I will write to the Director of Mobilization of the Ecuadorian Army, who is responsible for obligatory military service, and—"

Tómas interrupted. "No. I thank you for trying, and for your concern. But with respect, I refuse. It is a hopeless case. The fight ends here."

"You will be forced into service, if you do not listen to me. Maybe never see your father again. You are being foolish."

The guard coughed, and Tómas looked over to see that the elderly man was listening to their conversation. Taking Juan Carlos by the arm, Tómas led him into a corner, out of earshot of the guard.

"Please," Tómas said quietly. "Do one thing for me. Print an article about all this in Diario Hoy. You are not a practicing lawyer, you can do that. Maybe that will help others to begin their own fights, so my case will not end so hopeless."

"You are right," Juan Carlos said, his voice subdued. "About the article, at least. We will wait for the decision of the court to be final to appeal, but we can print an article now. I, too, had this same idea, and after this I am on my way to—" He stopped. The judge, lanky in his grey suit with his long hair still wet, had suddenly appeared in the hallway accompanied by Eduardo and one of the lawyers.

"The same result as your last case," Eduardo said to Juan Carlos, who turned toward him. "Only now, I am here to save your client."

"You do not know of what you speak," Juan Carlos said. "You do not know the law; you know only how to talk. To be a lawyer you need both."

"You know neither. And you are to be arrested, by order of the court."

"On what reasons?" Juan Carlos said.

"Conspiracy, and other charges."

The judge turned toward Tómas. "You are free," he said. "You are released for now."

Before he was led away, Juan Carlos suddenly stopped, discretely putting a cupped hand with a sheet of folded paper into Tómas's palm.

Once outside and alone, Tómas opened his hand to find a letter with the words "Diario Hoy" written in black letters on the outside.

27. The Beginnings of a Departure

TÓMAS WALKED ALONE the following morning, past the university gates and down to the future site of the hotel. The dry season had again brought aridity to Isla de la Plata. Shop, bar and restaurant owners wetted their storefront dirt roads with water to stifle the dust from passing vehicles, even when their toilets and their sinks had none. Taxis, cars, bicycles, motorcycles, and mules drove through the puddles produced in front of the businesses in the increasing heat of the afternoon.

Groups of students sat around plastic tables and chairs drinking cervezas at the table's centre, filling a single glass with a shot of beer that was downed quickly before being passed to the next around the table. Salud, a toast to others. To your health. For others, por arriba, por abajo, por el centro, por el dentro as they raised their glass, then lowered it, then placed it in an imaginary centre, and then let it wash over their teeth and down their throats as salsa music played in the background. Tómas longed for a time when he could relax and enjoy a lazy afternoon, with nothing but drink and conversation on his mind.

Eduardo was facing away, standing and observing the worksite. Looking down at the island Centre of Recruitment and Reserves, Tómas said: "I cannot wait for my military card. And Juan Carlos must be released."

Eduardo turned around. Upon seeing Tómas, he said: "I was very disappointed to hear you were working with Juan

Carlos on a legal case I knew nothing about. Johnny Gonzembach told me. If he had not, I would not have known you were in court. You knew Juan Carlos's home as well, where he lived. You said nothing, even though I asked you to, and I told you where your father was when you came to me looking for answers."

"Juan Carlos was helping me. He says you cannot get me a military card."

"And still, you take his word, but not mine," Eduardo said, shaking his head. "Juan Carlos will be incarcerated for three weeks, to teach him lessons he needs to know. Then he will be released to the mainland."

"And my military card."

"I will get you your card before he is released, but you must begin working for me. I have assembled a team, one you will lead to repair the damaged albarradas or construct new ones. Also, I need updates on the construction. Articles need to be printed; not in El Comercio, but in Diario Hoy, now that Juan Carlos is not able to print his lies and slander. I will convince the editor. Soon, Juan Carlos will be on the mainland, without a pen, and you will be here to help me."

Tómas obliged Eduardo's request to obtain updates on the construction by going to the tienda and buying eight Pilseners, and bringing them to the construction manager responsible for building the hotel, who promptly hid them under a nearby tree for later consumption. The manager was a talcum powdered and musked man named Antonio from Argentina, who was in the middle years of his life, and he wore expensive clothing and carefully eyed all the women as they listened to him complain of his divorce. The man gave a quick update that Tómas wrote down.

The weekly columns in Diario Hoy explained how the construction workers were planning to start working fifteen-hour days, with the introduction of paid overtime. The projected timing was too short, and longer hours were required as a result. Other menial details followed, such as the completion of the east foundation, and the beams on the north east facing wall.

What was not printed in the paper, and what Tómas wrote separately to Eduardo, was how the supervisors varied shifts to have work performed day and night to achieve production targets; that most of the workers were not from the island as it was promised they would be; that there were different workers at the hotel worksite almost every day; and that some of the workers drank small amounts of aguar diente and caña manabita—both variations on fermented sugarcane—to help them sleep during breaks, or other times, under the shade of palm trees, and to promote an atmosphere of unparalleled camaraderie as they worked through the night under lights attached to loud diesel generators projecting noise out over the sea.

Tómas also wrote to Eduardo that the construction manager wouldn't accept the idea of building canals alongside the windows to create the illusion of being cast out at sea. Antonio said to Tómas that the canals would have no purpose and, if anything, they would allow water to leak into the rooms which wouldn't be sealed. The gardens weren't being landscaped as Tómas had wanted them, and the suggestions he made to the construction manager were now being ignored.

The team Eduardo had assembled for Tómas was comprised of sixteen students from the island and mainland universities. Tómas walked before them one day under the hot noonday sun as an empowered novice, Eduardo beside him. Antonio, at Eduardo's request, stood among the young men and women who were students of botany, ecology, irrigation engineering and geology. Archaeologists and anthropologists were still needed, but with time, patience and dedication, and by enlisting the help of experts in various fields, Eduardo assured them, they could construct new and durable albarradas. And canals would be built alongside the windows to transport water from tanks on the roof, the hotel windows would be sealed, and the gardens would be landscaped exactly as Tómas wanted. Or else all of them would be looking for work elsewhere, he said.

"These embankments, they will be shaped like horseshoes. They will trap rainwater to refill the aquifer water table," Tómas began. "We will dig small pools and wells beneath, too. That will give water for the flowers around it. Any extra will go to farms. These new embankments, you know, they are easy to destroy with even small changes in wind or rainfall."

Tómas explained that he had already spent time poring over aerial photographs in a large hut at the north end of the island, mapping the ancient albarradas, digging up fossilized fauna and gathering samples of what was currently there. All to discover the reasons why the ancient albarradas survived the weather fluctuations of el niño, while recently constructed embankments were destroyed by those same rains. Now, he said, they only had a very short time to complete the task.

"The rainwater from the wet season will be collected, pumped from the albarradas to large tanks on the roof," Tómas continued. "In the dry season, some of the water will go daily to the gardens."

Tómas instructed the team to first empty the seawater out of the damaged albarradas. They would clear the embankments and empty the stagnant seawater. Next, they would quickly study the optimal locations, researching papers and consulting with experts from Mexico, Colombia and Peru. They would build new embankments parallel with the shore, as was done in ancient times.

Tómas approached the group one sultry afternoon as the students were busy digging. The most brazen of the students asked why Tómas had not yet reported for military duty, as his name was on the list in Diario Hoy so long ago.

"Someone else will lead this group," Tómas explained, nominating that same student, who quickly accepted. Tómas then informed them that he would be leaving soon for the country of Peru, before embarking for Canada.

28. Forever a Foreign Man in a Foreign Land

I HAVE TAKEN the train on what I was told would be a four and a half hour trip from Cuszco to Aguas Calientes. The train stopped so many times I ceased counting, and the trip took longer than I care to recall. The workers onboard spoke of mechanical problems, and problems with switching of the tracks.

As I step down from the platform, two young Peruvian boys with hair the colour of midnight stoop over like pack animals with their large backpacks and fly up the trail toward Machu Picchu amidst a frenzy of activity before me. I recognize the smell of orchids and bromeliads, and see panoramas of misted mountains all around. A tour guide who stops to escort me to the main town area along the length of the railway, a woman introducing herself as Yolanda who says she is ready to escort me to Machu Picchu, stops at the edge of a nearby precipice. I stand beside her, seeing only faint outlines and distorted colours.

"On the trail," she says, "looking at the peaks of the mountains, only when you are still can you see the daydream of their movement."

In the strange iridescence of this Inca air, dizzy with my fear of heights and my insufficient sight, I stand motionless on my imagined mountainside leading down to a sheer face, peering over the horizon at the illusory weight of immense green mountains rolling across the plains. I have not experienced this before, as I have previously only passed by as I strode up the Inca trail, eager to reach and describe my destination.

I tell her how I have described the ancient Peruvian holy city of Machu Picchu in the past: rediscovered in 1911, the archaic city comes as a thunderbolt. Suddenly, while navigating around a winding stone pathway under the light of the afternoon sun, the antiquated stone city appears, standing ominous, majestically hovering atop one and shadowed by another intensely verdant mountain. All under a cloudless rooftop.

A hundred tiny people traversed through the stonework and temples. I observed the place from a vantage point through two hills, on a cliff overlooking what has so often been referred to as the "cradle of Andean civilization," once abandoned by the Inca so the Conquistadors would not discover it.

Then, I imagined the original appearance, hardly different except for the green grass carried from Spain, the absent thatched roofs once made of straw, the grain storage buildings, the smoke rising from its fires, the mules, llamas, ancient rituals, and the treasures that its discoverer claimed were not there.

"I think now of my family," I say to Yolanda. "And how they are accustomed to my absence. Tómas has had a lifetime without me, and Veronica has endured without me for all the decades of our married life. Now in Aguas Calientes, I will not contact them. They would not expect it. To them, I am already dead, deceased in the same solitude in which I have spent my life selling worthless descriptions to pay for further travel to do more of the same."

She stands there and smiles, saying she is heading to Machu Picchu today and asking if I am interested in going, I am sure because she is uncertain of what else to say.

I ask at the hotel about the man who helps people seeking political asylum, after Yolanda escorts me there and then departs. No one at the hotel admits to knowing anything about him; but I know he exists, the same as I know I will somehow find him, and that I will spend the remainder of my life here in this town at the edge of this ancient city, alone.

29. Uncertainty

"EDUARDO WANTS US in his office," Veronica said as Tómas entered the kitchen for breakfast. "To talk of your father. I knew he had some information he would not tell. And I know what happened to you, and what you said in court."

"What?" Tómas asked. "How?"

"From others, in the market, who talk about it. Juan Carlos and Eduardo, they are poisoning your mind. You will not see either of them, any more, after today."

Her voice when making this demand was shaky and uncertain, an intonation Tómas did not remember ever hearing from her.

After eating, and without further discussion, they walked together to the government building. Veronica stood with him at the entranceway into Eduardo's office.

"Tómas, please take a seat," Eduardo said, shaking his hand while standing behind the desk. "Good day, Señora," he added, his face solemn as he continued: "It is unfortunate, what I need to tell you."

In this light, the whiteness of the thread in the stitches across his nose contrasted with the purple skin beneath. Tómas noticed that his father's gifts of paintings and masks, and the framed excerpts from his travel articles, had all been removed from the walls.

"You have news of my father?" Tómas asked without being seated, partially disregarding the pleasantries that Eduardo was still carefully observing. Veronica moved in front of Tómas.

"What is unfortunate?" Veronica asked Eduardo, as though Tómas had not spoken. Sensing her impatience, Eduardo opened the window and began speaking.

"I have called to the Colombia embassy here, to have them contact the Colombia embassy in Peru," Eduardo said, fighting with the window latch. "We are at war with Peru; it is not easy to get answers. Even though the United States, Argentina and Chile, and Brazil too, are making paperwork for us to sign to end this border war we have been fighting since two hundred years."

"You mean since fifty years," Tómas said.

"Two hundred years ago, these wars started, but we have been fighting since the last fifty years, continuously, you are right."

Veronica gave him a frowning look. "And what do you know from the Colombia embassy?" she asked.

The window opened violently, crashing against the wall, somehow without damaging a pane. Eduardo secured the latch and sat down.

Settling back into his chair, he brushed aside a few long strings of greased black hair that had fallen over his face.

"One of the Colombia ambassadors, he reported your father was in the area of Cuszco," he continued. "There is a report, too, that he has died."

"I do not believe it," Veronica said.

"Died? How?" Tómas asked.

"I am not certain. The reports are not certain. The air there is thin. As he was seen near Cuszco, he could have been going on the trail to Machu Picchu. Too long a hike for a man so old. Unless, maybe he had a donkey. If he found Aguas Calientes, he might go anywhere afterwards. There are trains there. Tourists. But your father is a very old man. I do not see why he would attempt that. He should have stayed here, in Ecuador." He looked down at his desk.

"Why do you think he left?" Veronica asked.

"You will not hit me again?"

"Perhaps, no."

"Well, he may have left for many reasons I do not know."

Veronica frowned. "You do not know."

"No."

"What else did that ambassador tell you?" Tómas asked.

"All, what I have told you. All this has been reported to Peruvian authorities. But never in the news. And it was reported, too, that he was the victim of theft. But that is common in the mountains there, if he did not have a guide."

"What else?" Veronica asked.

He paused, sighing. "There is nothing more I can tell you now. I grieve for my friend Montgomery, as you both do."

Veronica walked out of the office, through the door and started down the road.

"But we are not grieving," Tómas said. "Nothing is official."

"It may not be, now. But over time, please believe that it will be. Allow yourself to grieve. It will hurt less when you see it in the Ecuadorian news."

Tómas ascended the hilltop near the office building as Veronica headed home. The morning sounds of equipment roaring, and the sounds of construction overburdened by mechanization were accompanied by the sweat of bodies and the sweat of the sea, the raw lumber, the fresh concrete, the instant coffee and the fried fish, all in anticipation of what would be. Amidst the treetops and the tops of bulldozers a giant claw rose, then dropped like some unnatural hand sifting through the earth below. The hydraulic actuation of the cylinders providing the machine's motion groaned in his feet, through to his knees. The construction taking place there was only the movement of earth from one location to another, he thought, the same as the concrete was only a conglomeration of different portions of cement, mixed with water and aggregate from different areas of the mainland. One set of earth placed over another, as with irrigation. Just as easily, his life's direction could be changed.

Veronica had said, not long ago, that Tómas had forgotten about his father as he was accustomed to doing. His father wanted the hotel to succeed, and for Tómas to help with its construction, perhaps envisioning Tómas in front of these machines, day after day, until they were shipped back to the mainland under a sky littered with seabirds. Montgomery might have pictured his son overseeing the ploughing of earth, with no other concern than how its carefully sculpted flowerbeds would be irrigated. Tómas wondered now what he had done to honour his father's wishes. By not reporting to the newspapers about Eduardo's guilt, on behalf of Juan Carlos, he concluded that he had allowed the hotel's construction to progress and had therefore respected what his father wanted. But now was the time to act, for Tómas to do what he wanted and needed to.

After reaching the top of the hill, he stopped, found a patch of grass and sat down. The bow of Eduardo's hotel-boat, attached to two steel cables, was naked without its tarpaulin. Antonio directed the workers, who took the bow of the ship and lifted its bulk with a small crane attached to the cables. As the fore section was lifted in the air, the polished dark wood breasts of its mermaid shone against the morning sun. As it rose, a hook, attached to one of the beam's fore sections, slipped. The workers beneath started scrambling out of the way as the entire weight had shifted, but the cables were still attached. The crane moved toward the cliff's edge, inching forward, the section again slipping under its own weight on the cables and readjusting to a new position as other workers quickly moved away from its path.

The crane inched forward again, stopping as the bow began to swing and find its new resting place. As the bow was ready to be set in place near the cliff's edge, a cable snapped, whipping upward and sending workers running in all directions. The cable whipped against nearby rocks, coming to rest behind the crane's cab as the fore section of the ship's hull began slowly slipping from its weight along the length of the beams. The one remaining hook skimmed along the hull's length, snapping the cross braces until it finally slipped free from the end of its supports.

Everyone watched as the hull fell 30 metres to the bottom of the cliff in increments, plummeting from one crag to another, the hull smashing once, twice, again and again, before rolling over and coming to rest in a heap of dust and debris partially consumed by the incoming tide.

Tómas moved to the cliff's edge along with several other workers to witness the mass of finely finished lumber that had smashed violently on the rocks at the cliff's bottom. The remnants of the hulking vessel's fore section resembled a shipwreck, a vessel that had been washed ashore. A roar of shock turning to anger and then sadness rang out among those gathered.

After arriving home shortly afterward, tired and confused by what he had witnessed, Tómas found a handwritten message from Flory. Eduardo had phoned, and he wanted to meet Tómas on the beach tomorrow morning, this time without Veronica.

30. Fear

POISED ABOVE THE island's horizon, its only volcano
thought dormant, Mount Pichincha trickled smoke from its
belly, more than they had seen in recent times. Tómas
approached Eduardo, who was sitting upright with a handful
of papers watching the volcano smouldering in the distance,
his back against a tree between the sand of the beach and the
cover of a palm leaf-covered roof. Eduardo was dressed in
shorts, a floral print shirt, and sunglasses. The empty beach
widened out where he sat, sand extending before him five
hundred yards to the sea dotted with fishing boats.

Before Eduardo had a chance to speak, Tómas began:
"I told you there are different workers at the hotel almost
every day," he said. "They do not know what they do. A
construction project cannot work like that. The accident
yesterday is proof."

Eduardo combed his black moustache with his fingers,
scrutinizing Tómas's auburn hair as he pulled a cigar from a
walnut-coloured case. He placed his paperwork in a yellow
file folder on the sand, a small tape recorder beside him
falling over on its side. The flame of his lighter met the cigar
and illuminated his greased hair.

"Do not talk to me like that," Eduardo replied, his
voice loud yet more strained than Tómas had ever heard.
"And do not talk to me about that catastrophe. There will be
another crew next week. They will start by getting the
mermaid out of the sea, if it can be salvaged, and she will be

placed in the front of the hotel's hull. And how do you know how a construction project is to work? You know no more than the people there yesterday. I fired all of them, the construction manager included."

"... Who was checking the new albarradas. So that is why no one is there today."

"You and your students were nowhere around, otherwise I would have fired all of you, too."

"I am quitting anyway. I am leaving for Peru. With my military card, or no."

Eduardo's back slumped down against the tree. He looked away briefly, puffing on his cigar, the spicy wooden smell of the smoke dispersing quickly in the wind. His gaze fixed on Tómas again. "You will not be allowed out of this country without it," Eduardo said. "And you will, for certain, not be allowed into a country with whom we are at war."

"If my father left for Peru, why can I not?"

"That is different. He has a British passport, you do not. And I was talking just now out of anger. I could not fire you."

"I will go with Colette. She needs a doctor to replace her in the campo. She is a midwife. She has been the only doctor there, for many years."

"Yes, yes, I know about her."

Eduardo turned toward the volcano in the distance, the palm-leaf roof rustling in the wind, the distant fishing boats reflecting in his sunglasses.

"And Cristobal, the doctor from Manta," Tómas continued. "He wants to work there. He said you promised to him a job."

"I do not know if I did. And I do not know why we are talking of this."

"Please, I need your help. I need to get him here to the island. If I do, Colette agrees to come with me to see my father, then my mother."

Eduardo sighed, and then began digging in the sand with his fingers.

"It would be a great mistake for you, to go away. I have told you what happened to your father. Maybe you cannot accept this. But there is no reason for you to go."

"I must know about my mother, too. She waits for me in Canada."

"You expect to get to Canada? You must realize she might never want to see you. You need to face that. She left you here so long ago, and she has never once returned. Why is that, do you think? Have you thought about that?"

"I do not know."

"In Diario Hoy, you reported you have started constructing one of the new albarradas. I sense that really, you never gave all you could, as though my faith in you was not sensible. I thought you had the ability to finish what you started, and to do what your father wanted of you."

Eduardo puffed on his cigar, peering out at the ocean, awaiting a response. The sun went away, hidden by clouds, and then returned. Tómas's long shadow fell back onto the beach.

After a moment, Tómas replied: "I do."

"You say so. But maybe, instead of serving the hotel, if the albarradas could be used also by some of the local farmers, maybe then you would become motivated. Is that what you want, to help the people? Maybe you think the hotel will help no one, as you have been so interested recently in what Juan Carlos has to say? Or, is it Veronica you have been listening to, because of how she feels about me, is that why?"

"The albarrada the students are digging, it will not last long."

"So you admit the construction is poor, your efforts puny."

"Always, I have been truthful about that. I told you it is impossible, with such little time and people. I will dedicate my whole life to this project, but not now. For now, it is too late for that."

"Why? You will not go anywhere," he waved his hand wearily as he continued. "Still, I will get your military card, only because I told the court I would. You have done nothing to deserve it, and you have not finished your year of service to me. I will get Cristobal to come here, to work in Monte Cristo, if you want that done for some reason. I will need you to do a thing for me in return, though ..." He paused before continuing. "And I tell you again, forget about Peru, or Canada, or anywhere else you will not be allowed in to those places. You would regret leaving."

The sun subsided behind the clouds again, the volcano's distant white plume becoming momentarily grey.

"Do you have regret that my father left?" Tómas asked.

"Yes, of course, why do you ask that?"

"Then, why have you done nothing?"

"And what you would you have me do?"

Eduardo's face was flushed, his expression irritated.

"Tell your guilt to the public," Tómas said. "Accept your responsibility. Juan Carlos showed me evidence against you, and against my father. There is only a short time before this comes out in the news. You will be ruined, the construction halted."

"You are not only stubborn, but insensitive," Eduardo said. "I knew about this. I spoke to Juan Carlos for many hours. The papers were found on his boat. There were no copies made, he promised that to me, which for certain I cannot trust, so I had his office searched too. But those papers, which I destroyed, they put blame on your father more than me. So I have done another favour for you, and for your family. And I had to release Juan Carlos at the order of the courts."

"He is free?"

"Packing up the few things he owns. But even though he is free, he has no proof of anything. Just his own words. And he told me he wants a job at El Comercio, but I have talked to the editor there, and Juan Carlos will have no such opportunity. He was fired, too, from Diario Hoy as he was in jail. In his last ridiculous article he tried to defend conscientious objection, saying that women will be conscripted next. I am surprised he did not suggest that some of them would be pregnant and others would have children, left alone, crying in the streets for their mothers. Now, Juan Carlos will have to become a taxi driver, a fisherman perhaps, to have money for his family."

Tómas said nothing. In reply, Eduardo stood up and continued speaking. "The people of the island, including you, are beginning to be against me. Your father left me so much, and for you, and for the island. I thought you might work for me. I thought your new future would be for the good of the island, payment to Montgomery for the sacrifice he made for me. You are like your father in your dislike for politics. I can see this now. And I can also see you are like your father because you have been so fearful."

"Fearful of what?" Tómas asked.

"Your actions in the courtroom, working with Juan Carlos without telling me, are shameful. Maybe because your parents were never here, your father was always away, I do not know, I am no psychologist, but you seem afraid to make a decision for yourself; as though you are fearful of the bad opinion of others as a result. Juan Carlos must have pushed you, to get you into that courtroom."

"I was put in a pickup truck and brought to the recruitment centre. For that reason, I was in court."

"Juan Carlos's previous Conscientious Objector case was like a mule. His performance in the court demonstrates he does not know the law, or how to argue. Now is not a time, however, for you to be afraid or incapable. Now, I need you to do one thing for me. I need you to trust me."

"I told you, I will be leaving."

"Then one last thing before you go. Nothing else. Just one thing. That is why I asked you to come here, but you have not let me talk until now. You will do this one thing for me, and I will do what I have said."

Eduardo looked out at the sea and the fishing boats along the skyline, sucking on his cigar. Tómas paused before answering, trying to contemplate any other options he might have. When he came up with nothing, he asked: "What is it you need?"

"You know the Retired Generals Club?" Eduardo asked, looking over at him.

"I hear it does not exist."

"It was reported like that in El Comercio, you are right. *An anarchist military organization rumoured to have started at the end of military rule, and the beginnings of democracy, almost twenty years ago.* But I tell you, it does exist. The group sometimes waits for protests, that I hear are ready to start on the island, to hide their movements. It is strange, no? The first time they have met here. I hear they will meet at a remote hut at the north end of the island to talk of the border war, and the hotel. There will soon be more fighting in the war because of nonsense talk of peace that will not happen. I think they may be planning to sabotage the hotel."

"Why the hotel?"

"Because your friend Juan Carlos, working in secret, he has already done more damage than you think. He put nothing about it in his newspaper, but the secretary in his office gave me copies of letters he wrote addressed to the head of the Ecuadorian Armed Forces about me and your father. In the letters, he talked about the money for the hotel, and how it came from funds for the cancelled housing project. And most damaging of all, he claimed this money was supposed to go to the military. He continued by saying I am a pacifist who gave your father the way to take the money, and your father took it because he wanted no military funding as he is a pacifist too, which is why he quit reporting on war stories, and how the hotel will be a protest, a monument to peace in a time when we are still at war, and so on and so on ... lies, all lies ..."

Tómas thought about, but said nothing of the paperwork Juan Carlos had given him, now in the dresser of his room. Those pages might be a final strike at Eduardo.

"I did not know if Juan Carlos sent any of the letters to the Ecuadorian Army," Eduardo continued. "But now, with this Retired Generals Club meeting here on the island, I know that he must have sent them." He took a puff of his cigar, and moved into the shade as the sunlight intensified over the palm roof. "You must know that for your father's sacrifice, and for the good of everyone here," Eduardo continued, "that any revolt cannot happen."

"I do not know what you expect of me."

"The group will meet tomorrow, in a hut on the east of the island. I want to know what they say, what they plan. That is all. You can write it on a piece of paper, and let me read it. That is all I need. That way, I will be prepared. That way, my hotel, your father's hotel, will not be a failure."

"I cannot attend a meeting like that."

"Yes, that is true. I could not, either. But you have been to that hut before, the one the university uses for studying ancient albarradas."

"I stayed at a hut on the northeast end of the island, before. I am not certain the hut would be the same one, though."

"You know how to get there, so you can leave this tape recorder running in the hut, or somewhere outside, then go back and get it after." He handed Tómas the small recorder that had been sitting on the sand. "I know the exact time of the meeting from the police here, who helped arrange it. You will have two hours of conversation recorded." Looking up at the volcano's smoke on the horizon, he then produced the file folder that he had placed on the sand. "For now, I have to go to Diario Hoy. I have my own articles to be printed."

On the road leading back to the town of San Cristobal, after descending the hill and passing through the nearly empty San Cristobal Square and the church overshadowing it in the light of the cloud-covered sun, Tómas passed the Chinchila lagoon and trees full of birds to arrive at the bay housing Juan Carlos's permanently docked boat 10 metres from the shore. Stopping in front of the boat house, the wooden stilts now hidden by water, he had the sudden thought that perhaps Eduardo was right. Maybe Tómas didn't even trust himself and his own decisions. But Eduardo may have said that, and promised what he had, in an attempt to use Tómas for his own purposes.

Now, Tómas wasn't sure whom to trust, or who to help.

31. The Retired Generals Club

JUAN CARLOS'S BOAT was the only one in the bay. The tide had risen up to the level of the red hull and the craft appeared to be floating, bobbing up and down in the water. The motion of the waves normally had no effect on the dry-docked vessel, the water lapping against what might have been a piece of land or a rock pier. But the boat was actually moving now, and a rope extended into the bay showing that an anchor had been dropped.

At first there was no response to shouting his name. A minute later Juan Carlos's thick head appeared, first through the porthole window, and then from the top of the boat's hold.

"I am here," Juan Carlos shouted. "I will soon be with my wife and my children, but I am here now."

He disappeared into the interior of the vessel. Several minutes later, an inflatable raft covered with dark tape was thrown out. Catching on the end of a rope, it landed upright in the water with a splash. Juan Carlos emerged, labouring to get into the dinghy.

Juan Carlos embraced Tómas before they pulled the raft ashore, which was filled with water. They pushed the raft on the side, emptying the contents, and stepped under the shade of a tree.

"Your boat can go in the ocean now?" Tómas asked, pointing out at the bay.

Juan Carlos did not answer immediately but stood, staring at him.

"No, no," he responded, shaking his head. "The motor, I do not know if it works. Raphael has been working to fix it. The boat, she is named El Coche, she suffers from neglect, mostly, but I have removed the wood supports and patched the hull with fibreglass. Now, she floats and the bottom no longer has 20 centimetres of water; although she still smells of bad wood."

"There must be sails."

"The sails are there but torn, and I started sewing them together with coarse thread. I have not sewn since pre-military training but still, I remember how. El Coche, she will be ready in a day or two."

"I need your help," Tómas said. "I need to get off the island."

Juan Carlos grinned with yellowed teeth, an expression which faded as he spoke. "I must get off the island, too. Already, I have received many threatening letters because of the article I wrote about you. You may be threatened as well. I agree we should leave for a time; at least, until the people forget. I will go back home, you will come with me."

A green and white bus passed nearby.

"Now you will be together again, with your wife," Tómas said.

"Yes, but more important, I will be with my boys." He smiled. "I want to thank you for keeping my wife and children in my mind. Maybe now I can take back some of my mandarina wife's control. I have been away for so long, and she knows about my girlfriend Colette. My threats will go far, now. I like to think it is because you always questioned me about them, that I am going home to live. You have been a wonderful friend to me."

"I am happy for you, and for your family, Juan Carlos," Tómas replied as water sloshed at the opaque, sun-aged plexiglass windows, the boat rolling in the increasing waves. "But Eduardo said you sent letters to the army, letters about him and my father, with accusations that were untrue."

"I sent a few letters, yes, but none contained untruths. I am certain the head of the Ecuadorian Army was very upset to learn how much funding he is missing. And I told Inés to shred those copies. She has failed me."

"But when we get to the mainland, promise you will write the story about my father and Eduardo; about their involvement with embezzling government funds in El Comercio. I must go home to get copies of the paperwork for you, to say goodbye to Veronica and Flory also. Eduardo said he talked to the editor of El Comercio, who supposedly is his friend. He said you would not get a job there, but you can still write the article."

"Eduardo threatened that when I was in prison. Once Edgar sees the article, though, I think I can convince him to print it, and maybe to hire me despite Eduardo."

"I also want to go back to the decision about my conscientious objection."

"To appeal."

"To appeal, when the decision becomes official. I do not trust Eduardo to get my military card."

"You can always have confidence in me, compadré," Juan Carlos said, seemingly pleased, patting Tómas's shoulder.

"There is another news article I want you to write. One that will need more work from you. It involves something you need to do, before you leave."

"What?" he asked, smiling. "Anything. You say it."

Tómas produced Eduardo's tape recorder from his pocket, the black case gleaming in the sun.

"Here," Tómas said, offering the device to Juan Carlos.

"What is this?" Juan Carlos asked.

"Eduardo wants me to go to a meeting of the Retired Generals Club today. I know the location and the time. But I want you to go, to report on what is happening there."

Juan Carlos examined the tape recorder before contorting his back, cracking his neck with hands pushing from each direction in turn.

"The Retired Generals Club you talk about, that is a fabrication of El Comercio," Juan Carlos said. "That club does not exist." He smiled.

"Why do you smile?"

"Because for now, that is what the people think. Though I knew about the meeting, until now I could not discover where and when the meeting will take place."

"How did you know about the meeting?"

"I heard from a member of the group, because of the letters I sent to the military. I was invited to attend, the first time for a reporter; to see the results of what I have started, he said. But still, he has not told me when or where. I promised not to report on it, but I will record their conversation and write the article. It will be an important story. One that will declare that the Retired Generals Club does exist."

"They will discuss the protests in the country. They are against the hotel and plan an end to it."

Juan Carlos raised his eyebrows. "Interesting," he said. "Let us go." He directed Tómas away from the bay, producing a pen and small pad of paper as they walked toward the town. "Will you tell me more?"

"What there is to tell."

"Beers," he said. "I will buy. Now is my turn to extract a story from you."

32. Protests

THE FAINT SMELL of shrimp and lime was overpowered here by the chalky-sharp smell of oil paint. Veronica was gathering her statues as Tómas approached her market stand alone, the stench of beer on his breath. Their neighbour Señora Modesta, who owned the cevicheria, sat close by eating her lunch from a bowl outside her empty restaurant. Veronica looked up momentarily.

"It is the statue of a Patron Saint," she told Tómas, holding the nearly completed statue in the air and then wiping some paint on her apron. "Saint Jude of desperate causes."

Tómas recognized another statue as that of Saint Bartholomew, an unpainted and disembodied head in his hand with his eyes toward heaven. There were others he did not recognize. She wrapped two of them in newspaper and then placed them in a brown paper sack.

"Why is everything closed, in this time of the day?" Tómas asked.

"I have heard people will protest the hotel," Veronica said as she placed Saint Bartholomew into the bag. "Everyone has left from here, like I am doing now. Same as Señora Modesta is doing, after she eats the last of the ceviche. There is much there, if you have hunger, go eat. We will stay inside for the next week."

"I wonder what happened to change the people's attitude toward the hotel."

"The military, I hear they are starting this, saying Eduardo took their money. I knew he was guilty. A part of the hotel was destroyed, too, thrown off the cliff. Some important part that cannot be replaced. Eduardo is from Vilcabamba; that is why protests start there. The people now fight against the military and the police."

Señora Modesta disappeared into the restaurant, shaking her head. She dropped her bowl into the sink and increased the volume on her television set that was visible to the street. The newscast blared news of a group of protesters in Vilcabamba, where Veronica's mother Flory had lived for so many years. The television showed a small group of protestors throwing stones at police with Plexiglas body and face shields and wide-mouthed tear gas guns.

"The people lose confidence in Eduardo," Veronica said.

"I did not trust Eduardo since Juan Carlos showed me paperwork of money changed from a housing plan to the hotel. Montgomery took the blame. Eduardo is quiet about what he knows. I have the proof."

She paused, seemingly uncertain what to say. This surprised Tómas, in this woman not easily brought to silence. "You will give it to the newspapers. Listen to your mother. I read Juan Carlos's article, about the court case. If what he wrote is true, or no, you have been shamed to the people like your father. You have fear to fight in the border war with Peru, like your father had fear to fight for his country in the world war. I think you have fear to trust in me, and to fight Eduardo and Juan Carlos for the honour of your father."

"My father is not innocent of the charges against him."

"You do nothing I ask, and you listen only to those you want. You fight only for what you should not. I am sad with you, Tómas, very sad. You can help the country, and the island. Show Eduardo as a coward and a thief and a liar. Juan Carlos, too, he helps no one. You cannot trust what he will write."

She paused, a look of concerted disappointment he had never seen. "Promise one thing, Tómas."

What?"

"Before you think to go anywhere, or to trust Juan Carlos, talk to Padre Pédro. You will not listen to me, so listen to him. Most times, he has sense where you have none. Promise me."

He was silent.

"Promise me," she repeated, placing the remaining statues in her bag while waiting for the response she knew would come.

"I promise," he said.

Tómas walked down the road leading to the hotel worksite. Veronica's words were on his mind as a taxi motored by, sputtering and kicking up dust and exhaust fumes. There was no one washing down the streets here to keep the dirt from becoming airborne. There were no students, no cars, and no bicycles on the main road ahead that led out of the town. The rolling steel doors of the patio bars were closed, the plastic tables and chairs hidden away behind them. Much like the market of San Cristobal Square, there was no music of any kind; only a conspicuous silence.

There was a noxious scent here, one he recognized. Its memory intensified in his mind as its odour did, the stench scratching slightly at his eyes, his nose, and his throat with tiny claws. He knew what was happening on the road ahead. It was the smell of tear gas.

He ducked sideways through an open gate, an iron side entrance to the university that was not normally open. Swinging the gate shut, he had inadvertently locked himself inside the concrete-walled fortress of the university grounds, recalling that protesters often did the same.

A bow-tied professor led a group of students out of the business building. The professor pushed the students into the group to keep them moving. They marched to the front entrance, now populated by only a few students. As they were shepherded into this area, a gunshot rang out nearby. Tómas had run from this sound before. This time, he would not be afraid.

The group began moving frantically toward the back exit of the university. Several students broke away from the rest of the group and moved toward Tómas, as though he might be able to provide them direction. Past the agronomy building, toward the entranceway of the university, was a gate that might provide a way out. It was closed and secured with a padlock. There was another gate, used for automobile traffic. The only other exit at the back of the university was secured shut, locked, and had boards nailing the route closed.

The noxious odours invaded his nostrils again. The scent was stronger, overpowering. And as he closed his eyes to rub them, he found himself unable to reopen them. The moisture from his eyes was replaced with a stinging sensation.

As dryness invaded his nose and throat, his vision returned briefly. Some of his newfound followers were still beside him. A lone man, wearing his shirt over his head like a bandana, ran from the chained gate toward the automobile entrance carrying something in his hand. The bandana was a flag of sorts; worn by those his father had once photographed, protesting an oil company's deforestation to reclaim their native land. Tómas, seeing a few of them in a pile, donned a bandana himself, a blue cloth covering his forehead.

Another gunshot sounded in the distance. He could not move, and the others beside him looked around frantically. The powder-burn of the shells mixed with the smell of burning rubber, a combination of smells he so acutely remembered from the last time. Over the concrete walls of the university, thick, black smoke from burning tires blocked the main road into the town and stifled the air.

Several protestors, many of them in bandanas, stood inside the university grounds by a bush at the automobile entrance. The protestors stood there, some shirtless and others wearing black makeup, looking out onto the street.

This was the only exit that was not locked and secured shut, this one guarded by two military vehicles firing periodic bombs of tear gas over the wall.

Those beside him began to run toward the blocked back exit of the university, and the corner of Tómas's eye caught the flash of a lit Molotov cocktail, waiting to be thrown.

His mind flashed to the last time he was here crouching in the bushes with other student protestors, thinking about his anger over his father, and the government that had allowed his conscription. Then, he had believed his father innocent. Now, none of that mattered.

Tómas ran over toward the protestor, everyone staring at him in disbelief as he snatched the bottle and threw the flaming mass through the bars of the gate. The aperitif blasted violently against the military vehicle's side producing a small explosion, but still leaving the vehicle unchanged, its tires bouncing over the uneven dirt road. A man stared back from the other side of the gate with one brown and one green eye, a dark-bearded Ecuadorian military officer in a grey uniform, a man Tómas recognized but could not take the time to place from where, as there was the *thwump* of the tear gas cannon a second later, and he scrambled away.

Running through the gate, past the military officer whose gaze was still fixed, his heart thumped in his chest. Tómas was exhilarated, with a sense of triumph. A group of students followed him, and they all rushed out through the same opening. Passing a group of cheering protestors who stood around burning tires lined across the road, he parted from the other students and headed for home. A promise had been made to Veronica, one that he would have to honour before he left.

The smoke of flaming rubber lined the town's main street, effectively preventing traffic from leaving the town or entering it. Providing the protests were carried out in unison, this would disrupt the island's transportation. Smoke would carry the message to other demonstrators, paying homage to the sanctity of their ideals, to a unity of purpose acknowledged by the winds that swept up each message and blended it together with the next.

Tómas now recalled the identity of the dark-bearded Ecuadorian military officer who had been staring at him. The officer had been at the hotel inauguration, and then at the island Centre of Recruitment and Reserves, and once again in the courtroom where Tómas had claimed conscientious objection.

This was a protest against the military in which Tómas had taken an active part. And by causing that small explosion, participating in this demonstration without covering his identity and having been observed by the military officer who had certainly recognized him, Tómas had shown his hand. He would have to flee, through the back roads, as soon as he could.

Walking quickly through the streets, with clouds gathering above, passing by the ocean's waves crashing powerfully against grey rocks 30 metres below the protestor fires, with the island hotel's destroyed fore-section laying as a shipwreck rotting away in the splashing seawater, and then knocking on Raphael's door where he would stay the night, all he could think of was the military officer's stare.

33. Liberation Theology, Revisited

THE FOLLOWING MORNING, Tómas slunk into his house like a thief, through the backyard fence, as Medianoche barked from the rooftop. Inside, there was a pervasive silence only interrupted by snoring from Flory's room. Veronica was not there. Dirty dishes had been left on the table, evidence that she had already eaten breakfast and departed, having said they needed to stay inside for the remainder of the week yet not doing so herself.

Retrieving the copied paperwork Juan Carlos had given him, folding the pages and placing them in his pocket, the snoring became louder as he walked out the back door. Señora Modesta, over the fence next door, asked him where he had been, said her daughter had been looking for him, and informed him that Veronica had gone to church.

Walking carefully through the empty streets of the town, wearing a hat and dark sunglasses, watching carefully and pulling his hat down tight over his head, he ascended the wooden back steps of the church. A few farmers and hotel labourers stood outside, eyeing him suspiciously.

The church was nearly empty, only a few people seated in the pews with their families or lingering around the painted statues. The morning service had not yet begun. Veronica was there, on her knees and throwing flowers at the Virgin Mary's feet. Her skin tone was unusually pale when she looked up and saw him.

"Where did you go?" she asked. "Men from the army were at the house yesterday for you. Señora Modesta's daughter went out yesterday, in the afternoon, and again this morning. She walked all through town asking for you."

"I was at Raphael's house," Tómas said. "I will return, to see you, before I leave the island."

He began to walk away, and stopped when she started speaking again.

"You will go no place. The ferry does not run. Some fishermen took their boats to the mainland to protest, the others will not go there."

"I will be going with Juan Carlos, on his boat," Tómas said, rotating to face her. Veronica turned away and threw another flower at the virgin's statue, looking into the plaster eyes with a deprecated sadness.

"Ungrateful like the cat," she said quietly, rhythmically, as he walked away. At her words, Tómas comprehended that he had never experienced such severe disapproval from her, or from anyone else.

He approached an altar boy, who pointed to a wooden ladder rising up to a square cut-out in the ceiling. Padre Pédro was in the bell tower above, and Tómas ascended the ladder quickly.

The wooden floor was only partially visible beneath Padre Pédro's black robe. The bell hovered just above their heads in this hexagonal tower with seventeen paneless windows looking out over all points of the island. The thick tire smoke of protestor fires were visible, as was the island volcano ejecting smoke over the horizon.

"Many people say you left the island," Padre Pédro said, his greyish eyes reflecting the sunlight. "There are rumours of your father being in Peru, also. But still, you remain here."

"I will go to Peru," Tómas said. "Then to Canadá, to meet my mother for the first time."

"What of working for Eduardo? These protests will not last. And what of your military service, which I see from the newspaper you have not done? You can do both, easily, and at the same time. Otherwise this is a great dishonour for you, your father, and your family."

"There are reasons for which I must go. Eduardo is guilty of embezzlement to fund his hotel. He does not want anyone to know. But I have the proof. My mother wants it printed in the newspapers."

"Your mother?"

"Veronica. My Ecuadorian mother."

"Well. You must print nothing in the newspaper. You must not leave the island, too. I do not understand why you want that. You have thought of this recently?"

"Yes."

Through the opening beneath them, they watched Veronica explaining something to a young boy in the middle of a small group of people that had entered the church. Tómas knew this boy, five years old, who stood beside Veronica as she pointed to the tiered levels of votive candles lit with a prayer to make that prayer come true.

"Your father does not need you," Padre Pédro said. "And you will not get to Canadá without a visa. You will need to apply, and wait. One day, perhaps, you can go."

"I need to go now. My father applied almost ten years ago, and still I wait. I have a plan to get a visa in Peru."

"And really, you do not want the trouble that might cause for her, and for Eduardo."

Tómas had not contemplated what might happen to Veronica.

"Stay here, and keep her from trouble," Padre Pédro said. "Protect her. Protect Eduardo. Finish your work on the hotel. Your father made his choice. He does not need you. People here now, and in the future need you. Think of Liberation Theology, and what God wants. Because you should never fight God's will."

"I have to go."

Padre Pédro stopped and scratched his eyebrow. "Eduardo has brought Liberation Theology back to the minds of those on the island. A priest must ensure his congregation is aware that Christ is the only way to heaven. But people won't listen when they're hungry. I thought you knew this too, but I suppose you do not ..."

"I have simple solutions for the irrigation problems here. I will return to the island one day to help with simple solutions and the more complicated albarradas, Padre. I will."

Looking down at the crowds below, Padre Pédro added: "I do not believe you will, not if you leave. Like your father, you may never come back except for visiting. But I hope I have given you something to think about. And now, you must excuse me. I am late to deliver my sermon."

Padre Pédro shouted at the children to back away as he began descending the ladder.

Tómas went down over an hour later, after everyone had cleared out of the church. There was a momentary pause before he decided to leave the place, watching as Padre Pédro, the only one left, stood in front of the pew with the crackling noise of the candles illuminating his face as he lit one candle, and then another.

As Tómas descended the steps of the Iglésia Santa Maria and walked out into the empty city square of San Cristobal, the seabirds hovering overhead, rain pouring down on his hat and glasses on his way to Juan Carlos's boat El Coche, he knew that he would not be doing what Veronica, Eduardo, or Padre Pédro wanted, any more. The paperwork was heavy in his pocket and he was grateful that soon he would be relieved of the pages.

34. Leaving the Island

MOUNT PICHINCHA CONTINUED to trickle angry smoke from its belly. A Diario Hoy news article had forecast a new eruption, the first full one since the time of the conquistadors, when a spectacular explosion of liquid rock, smoke and ash reportedly vomited its protest against the occupying army. The NASA seismologists stationed at the base of the volcano had not yet confirmed the findings of the newspaper, but the smoke was undeniable, billowing over the horizon to be seen up to five kilometres away.

Veronica was startled to see Tómas, who had appeared in the back doorway without a sound, under cover of cricket song and evening darkness, wearing a backpack.

"I do not know where you roam," Veronica said. "But men from the army, they are here every day for you. Maybe it is better I do not know. I would drag you home by your ear and give you to them."

"I have been staying with Juan Carlos and Raphael," Tómas said. "I have to go back to meet Juan. We leave at sunrise. I came to say goodbye, to leave you with better feelings. Everyone says my father does not need me, and I need to stay here. I am disappointing everyone except myself."

"Well, that is right."

Veronica pointed at the kitchen table, which contained two newspapers and a plate of rice, beans and Ecuadorian cheese.

"They say the volcano will erupt," she continued, visibly agitated. "And the island will be evacuated. It is all a distraction of the government from the protests, but they did not say that. They did not say the police and military will control the island. But they will never make me leave my home."

"You should come with me," he said, to which she scowled.

Colette stood in the hallway, ballooning sheets onto a cot. "Hello," she said, smiling. "I arrived last night, very late, and very wet, from Monte Cristo. Cristobal and his wife are there now. Thank you. Thank you. A thousand times, thank you. I had the feeling, even though I had planned to, that I would never actually leave that place ..." She paused, obtaining a bundle from beneath the cot. "Here. I want you to have this."

She handed him the package, which was wrapped tightly in white plastic. Opening the bag, he was startled to find letters inside that were signed by his mother. They were all addressed to Colette, with the exception of one of the notes which was addressed to him. He would read all of these at once, sequentially according to the dates they were written, when he had the time. But for now, wrapping them up again and placing them carefully in his backpack, thanking Colette, he returned to Veronica's gaze.

"Diario Hoy no longer talks about the hotel today," Veronica said. "Today they only try to give fear to the people of the island."

Tómas looked through the paper closely after Veronica left the room. The cover, and all the pages within, was peppered with photographs, drawings and stories of past eruptions from ancient Pompeii to those of present-day Italy viewed by satellite, to those volcanoes on Jupiter's moon Io, where more than one hundred volcanoes can erupt at once. Between oversized crimson photographs of mountains spitting their venom were the charred bones of Vesuvius, the same colour as grey ash, an ash spread over one of the buried cities of the past, its former occupants petrified in place, huddled together, mothers frozen with children still locked in their arms.

Today's edition of El Comercio was also on the table, which had a front page article written by Juan Carlos about the Retired Generals Club. In the article, Juan admitted to thinking this organization only rumours; but a meeting of the group had been convened at the north end of Isla de la Plata, and he had attended. The meeting had discussed the island's hotel, and how the group wanted construction halted immediately because of Montgomery Harvey and Eduardo Delgado's reallocation of funds from a cancelled housing plan to the new hotel, money which was slated for the armed forces. The same paperwork that Tómas had recently retrieved from his desk and had given to Juan Carlos was now reproduced in the pages of the newspaper. The Ecuadorian military would be sending more troops to the island to put an end to the construction of the hotel, and to evacuate and maintain order due to the imminent eruption of Mount Pichincha. The article stated how the war with Peru was almost at armistice, but renewed fighting was expected. Because of the protests within Ecuadorian borders, the Peruvians would likely take advantage of the chaos by attacking at certain key fronts.

As he sat reading the article, Tómas heard the crickets become silent for a moment, and then resume with the onset of Medianoche's barking and Veronica yelling at the dog to stop. Some men were approaching the front door. Colette yelled for Tómas to run out the back.

"Whatever happens," Tómas said. "We will meet, soon, in Cuzsco."

Veronica emerged from her room with tears in her eyes, the men standing at the front door now. "If you see Montgomery," she said to Tómas. "You must tell him I forgive him for all he has done to me. Because he has given me eighteen years of the most wonderful boy, even though that boy gives me endless trouble ... and I will never leave my home, evacuation, or no. If they come for me, I will hide with mother. They will never make us leave."

As she hugged Tómas there was a momentary comfort in their parting, a taciturn forgiveness, as though the men outside and the realization that he never wanted to leave his Ecuadorian mother, the only mother he had ever known, had faded away into an obscure, distended reality.

There were men at the front, and others at the back now, all in uniform. Medianoche was barking incessantly from the roof, and the evening was brought to life by their flashlights.

This was his most daring moment: more than fighting forced conscription in that courtroom, or wielding the Molotov cocktail and chucking the flaming mass at an army vehicle, and more than challenging his father and earning the disrespect of Eduardo, Padre Pédro and his Ecuadorian mother. He had to fight for his freedom, the same sense of exhilaration overcoming him as when he held the bottle of alcohol with its rag fuse lit, the target in sight. The same as he had done then, he moved without considering any consequences, and without looking back.

In an instant, he slung his backpack over one arm and pushed his way past two officers at the rear of the house. Jumping over the fence, he ran, the men chasing after him. As he scrambled down a muddy road, looking desperately for an escape route, he imagined he was running through the jungles with a Belgian 7.62 mm rifle, being pursued by Peruvians who were adrenalized through recently intensified combat.

Heading toward the campo was his only hope, the only way he could evade these men, the forested jungle he knew so well from his studies taking him away from the main paths.

After a while of running through darkness, energized and with his heart thumping into his ears, his body fumbling wildly, it occurred to him that he was running from duty and responsibility like his father and birth mother had done, but oddly, he was scampering to meet both of them. It was as if he had to experience this same aspect of their lives, to share this common connection before meeting them, to dilute, at least temporarily, his resentment toward them.

Tripping over logs, branches and rocks, he ran, placing his backpack over both arms. The forest was thick with insects. Voices echoed through the trees and he thought he saw lights and people behind him. Whether any of this was real he did not know, but the thought of what might be behind kept him running.

He continued on until there were no longer any lights behind, and he stopped in a small clearing. Up ahead the trees fluttered, and crisp air preceding a rainfall wafted in. All he could see was the outlines of trees moving in the wind. Some birds howled, and dizziness overcame him with the distinctive hum of mosquitoes in his ear. Probing through his backpack, he produced a large water bottle and took a drink. He groped again to fish out his flashlight. Pushing the switch revealed rainfall filtering in through the forest rooftop. The insects were disappearing. Resuming, he tripped over a tangle of roots and fell to the ground. Rainwater trickled down on top of him as the flashlight tumbled from his grip and fell three metres down a precipice. The light extinguished and he was in darkness again. Moving slowly, his knees and hands scratched by the forest floor as the rain subsided and the sound of mosquitoes returned. Some branches gave way and he fell through a few metres of sheer drop. Scratched, cold and wet but otherwise unhurt, he patted the earth around him to reveal an opening in the mud, one that he crawled into. Water splashed over his face as he entered the opening and he lay crouched under the overhang, eventually falling into an exhausted sleep, in this place that seemed only a dream, one in which he would awaken to find himself in a military prison in Guayaquil, awaiting his sentence.

Sunrays cascaded in through the forest rooftop, filtering in to a small cutaway in a mound of earth barely large enough for him to fit into. Reliving the events of the previous night in quick succession, he realized where he was. This was not how he had envisioned this place in the darkness. The flow of water that had been running over the face of the cutaway had reduced to a slow trickle. His body was wet and soaked with mud, and his nose and head were congested with a cold. There was flowing water nearby; the sounds of a river.

With his stomach rumbling, he looked up at the forest treetops to see a flock of green parrots twenty metres in the air. From the direction of the sun he knew the birds were heading northwest, the same direction as he had been going last night. Rising, he retrieved his flashlight and backpack and headed in the same general direction, following the flow of the river.

Hours passed as he walked, listening to the sound of bird and insect song. Laying down to rest, he brushed a few brightly coloured bugs away. Some of the species of orchids he had studied were here: the hanging orchids of Guanderas, looking like the drooping heads of long dead birds awaiting the full rainfall of the wet season to bloom them back into life; the stringy white fingers of the Pululahua orchids stretched out from their central dark branches, their tiny red berries hanging over large green leaves and looking like overripe coffee beans; the Orchids of Pahuma stared back at him like elongated and spindly spider monkeys, eager to begin climbing through the trees. His mind drifted into such descriptions of his surroundings that Montgomery might have written, a career of writing that had transformed into Tómas's lifetime love of reading.

His walk through the rainforest led from sporadic waterfalls, to the occasional cow indicating a house nearby, to chasms traversed by climbing along muddy ledges, to parrots and monkeys and mud-baked termite nests high in the trees. He ate from the yucca plants and plantains. It was as though he had been transformed into his father and, instead of haunting the streets of the capital city like a ghost, he was an animal traversing through the forests on the hunt for Peru, caught between the reality of his past life, now so seemingly distant, and his dream-like present. As though his entire life had been spent in the prison of isolation, and now he was free.

As he walked down the river's length, he began to recognize embankments that collected the river's flow, from his studies of the topography of the region. He was near the Muey Fuentes, an ancient albarrada that fed into Monte Cristo. In his dizziness and confusion, persisting from the night before, he had been heading in the wrong direction, deeper into the forest. Following alongside the embankments, walking for another dozen miles toward the beach and Juan Carlos's boat, which must have departed by now without him, away from Muey Fuentes, his body aching, wet, muddy, scratched, hungry and parched, he arrived in a clearing near the ocean to see Eduardo Delgado, motioning to him from the beach beneath cloudy skies.

35. A Fisherman's Son

" WHAT HAPPENED WITH you?" Eduardo asked.

Tómas retorted, more in shock than in belligerence. "What are *you* doing here?"

"I figured this is where I would find you ... and your friend Juan Carlos. But come ... we must hurry." Eduardo grabbed Tómas's hand and pulled him away from the beach. Then he paused. "Oh, I have this for you."

Eduardo handed over a laminated card, the size of the small cedula document that granted permission to work in the country. "Your military card. We will go to the mainland now. I need to see some people in the government. I need desperately to take a firm hand to this situation that now is out of my control."

"But there is no way to get there," Tómas said, staring at the card incredulously, remembering Juan Carlos's boat which must be on the way to Guayaquil. "Not now."

Retrieving Eduardo's offering, Tómas stared at his own picture and name alongside the gold, blue and red flag of Ecuador with the coat of arms signifying dignity, victory, protection, fraternity of its people, harmony and trade, independence and the blood shed for it, the sea and the sky, ample crops and fertile land. Now he was ready. In his waterproof canvas backpack he had some clothes, books, and all of the money he had saved over the years; all carefully wrapped in plastic, along with his mother's letters. Placing the card inside, still in disbelief of having obtained this document, in such a propitious way, he zipped the lining closed.

Tómas followed Eduardo as he led the way inland, going past the desolated university, carefully avoiding the crowds around the government office, and again down to the beach where they saw protestors gathering. The wind was fierce here, and the waves were high.

"Where do we go now?" Tómas asked.

"I told you already," Eduardo replied, without looking back.

They walked to an isolated area near the Chinchila lagoon at the bottom of the island's only cliff, where they saw the wrecked bow of the ship that had fallen from the apex of the rock formation, the wooden mermaid being pummelled now by waves dashing into shore.

They passed through a narrow cave cut between vertical sections of jagged rock set beneath the cliff. Eduardo led him on, crouching beneath the rocks until they arrived at another view of the water, a wide expanse of ocean northward. The isolated extension of beach was littered with sea lions and blue-footed boobies.

"What is this place?" Tómas asked as they emerged from beneath the cliff.

"We are here," Eduardo said. "At the boat that will take us to the mainland."

Huge waves rocked against the hull of an anchored boat, perhaps 30 metres long, which now appeared a hundred yards offshore. Portholes set in white painted wood dipped beneath the water line. Three masts rose up, not quite perpendicular to the line of the hull, and none of them parallel. Although an impressive sight, it still appeared lower in the water than it should have been. And the bow of the boat appeared to have been removed and temporarily reconstructed using the same sort of wood that littered the construction site.

"She is the Cachalote, 45 metres long," Eduardo said, "and over a hundred years old. Her parts were to be used for my hotel; one of the Galapagos tour boats, she was ready to be sunk off Isabela Island before your father rescued her. Another one of his gifts to me."

He removed his shoes and shirt to reveal a wrinkled yet muscular physique. "We will need to swim," he said, jumping into the water. Eduardo guided himself along a rope extending from a metal pole onshore out to the vessel, the rope anchored to the ocean floor along its length allowing a straight path to the vessel despite the rolling waves. Tómas removed all but his pants, rolling up his clothes, wrapping them in plastic, and placing them in the backpack that he slung across his shoulders. He jumped in after Eduardo, and pulled his weight along the rope.

Climbing aboard the boat, Tómas was able to see the entire hotel construction site: the inactive equipment, the fencing around the site, the tarpaulins covering unused stacks of wood, the immense structure almost complete, wrapped around the cliff as though embracing it. The volcano loomed in the distance behind the hotel, still trickling smoke. But there was more smoke than what should have been produced by the volcano. Looking more closely, he saw flames extending from inside the hotel, and plumes of smoke rising above. The hotel had been set ablaze, and was partially consumed by fire.

Eduardo stared out at the scene, watching the smoke and an increasing sea of flame eating away at his hotel. Then he started yelling at those onshore who were using buckets and passing them along a line of people.

"They will never put that out," Eduardo said fiercely, turning to Tómas. "No matter how any buckets they have. It is too late." He stood observing for a time, shouting a stream of curses as the wooden support beams were devoured, and a framed wall toppled against a concrete post. Piles of unused wood were igniting beside the hotel remnants.

"This boat we are on, she is sinking slowly," Eduardo continued, his voice hoarse, still staring out at the fire. "But she will make it to the mainland. And I will not return for many months, maybe years."

Eduardo began producing sail bags from below deck. The wind began to rise, the waves slamming against the sides of the boat. Steel wires attached to the sides of the masts impacted against them, creating the odd sound of intense, hollow bells.

"Juan Carlos promised to print nothing in the papers, after I was forced to release him," Eduardo said. "I was a fool to put trust in him. And now he has betrayed me, as have so many others who once worked on the hotel."

After handing Tómas some ropes and instructing him to tie them to the sails strewn over the deck, Eduardo showed him the proper way to tie a sailor's knot. Tómas held on tightly to the mast, unfolding the sails as the wind speed rose and the boat began to roll over the cascading waves.

Flames and gravity consumed the hotel as they hauled anchor. Eduardo pulled the sails up slowly and stood behind the wheel of the boat, the noise of the flopping canvas overpowering both the lapping of the sea and the noisy tijera birds in the trees near the Chinchila lagoon. The hotel fire crackled at intervals and the smell of salt, along with burning wood, drifted toward them in a changing wind that filled the sails and pulled them forward. They began heading toward the island.

"We are going the wrong way," Tómas said.

"We will sail by the hotel," Eduardo said, cleating one of the ropes that extended to the mast, and turning the wheel hand over hand. "And inland to the bay."

"Why?"

"No questions."

They sailed past the hotel and over to the bay, now at high tide. Juan Carlos's rusted boat was not there. Eduardo stood at the helm with an expression in his wrinkled eyes that seemed to form so unnaturally on the tanned lines of his face, ferocity and intensity Tómas had never seen before, as they went back and forth for hours, frantically searching for a boat that was not there.

"We must go to the mainland," Tómas said finally.

"We will get there," Eduardo replied.

"When?"

"We will get there. Do not ask any more."

A while later, finally giving up and resolving to leave, Eduardo turned toward Guayaquil.

On the way there, Eduardo tacked back and forth across the huge waves of the ocean for the sails to catch the wind to their destination, the waves rolling up to the height of the masts. They did not say a word to each other, except for what was required to keep the sails full and the lines taut, until Eduardo eventually broke their silence.

"Tómas," he said. "I always wanted to be president, although there may be no chance of that now. Your father's act of helping to fund the hotel, that was the most selfless act anyone has ever done for me. I want you to tell him that."

Then, far in the distance, coming over a crest of waves, another boat appeared, the same colour as Juan Carlos's boat El Coche. But the vessel was too far away to be certain, and saying nothing to Eduardo except to ask for instructions on what to do, Tómas busied himself with the lines, trimming the sails and checking the compass to ensure they were proceeding in the proper direction. Distracting Eduardo with questions about the wind, the waves, and details of their vessel which had now taken on water, Tómas pointed in the direction they were headed, away from the other vessel. But after a while, Tómas noticed that they had moved closer to the other sailboat. The compass showed that they were no longer heading toward the mainland, and their bow was now aimed at the other craft.

"We are off the course," Tómas said.

"You question too much. You must be silent sometimes, and look at what is going on around you. You see, that is Juan Carlos's boat."

As the boat came within better view, the waves rolled over to reveal that Juan Carlos and Colette were on the boat, and were coming about to head further out to sea, back in the direction of Isla de la Plata. But Eduardo was still directing the helm, and the bow of the boat, straight for them.

"You will not get anything from this," Tómas said. "We must go back to the mainland. You can talk to the politicians there. You cannot save your hotel now. But still, you can revitalize the island in a different way. There are other means, other possibilities."

"No more talking," Eduardo replied, trimming the jib by pulling one of the lines in taut, cleating off the rope beside him. The wind caught on to the sail, the vessel keeling over further, the speed increasing in a sudden gust, the hull then sliding downward over the rolling waves at a rapid pace.

"You need to stop this," Tómas said.

"Now I am thinking, in a way, you have betrayed me also. You sent Juan Carlos where I told you to go. I read what I wanted to know, not from your notes, but from the newspaper."

"I *told* him to go," Tómas said.

"And I wonder, too, where that information came from about the transfer of funds between the military and the hotel, the pages he re-printed in the paper. I destroyed the originals. I looked through his office and his boat, and I found no copies. He swore to me there were none. I am very curious if you know anything about that."

"I *gave* those pages to him. I had them in my room. He let me have them for keeping them safe. I only returned them to him, to be printed. I thought that was best. That was my decision, not his. Your anger is with me, not with Juan Carlos."

Eduardo shook his head. "You obviously do not know what is right. You, too, have betrayed me."

They were getting closer to the other boat, rising up with a wave so they were nearly ready to fall down upon them.

"You can do nothing unless you get to the mainland," Tómas said. "We wasted hours searching for Juan Carlos. And now you've found him. Now what? You will hit his boat? What will that do for you?"

"Make better my conscience. Make me think there is justice in this world."

"You do not need to force your own justice. There is a word for that—"

"But you cannot tell me now is a time for thinking, for philosophy. Now is a time for action." There was a maniacal look on Eduardo's face.

"You do nothing for the country by your actions. You talk of action. That would be going to the mainland, not—"

At that moment, their vessel began descending with rapid speed, and they were close enough to see the expression on Juan Carlos's face, Colette sitting in the cockpit and shouting at him.

"Turn around!" Tómas yelled and, seeing Eduardo was not relenting, grabbed the wheel and turned quickly to the right. Eduardo pushed him aside, and corrected back to his previous course. There was a crack and a sudden jolt after the wave slid out from under them, bringing them down on top of the other boat. The bow of the Cachalote had sliced into El Coche.

For an instant, there was the feeling that nothing had happened; as though time had ceased to pass, as though wood had not impacted against fibreglass to produce a hole that now leaked water. Then, after a distended time which must have only been seconds, the two vessels broke apart from each other, Juan and Colette in El Coche passing forward in an increasing wave, Eduardo and Tómas in the Cachalote seeming to pull away but actually remaining in position, both set adrift with sails flapping, both damaged and taking on water, El Coche plowing toward the mainland with water rushing into the side.

Eduardo struggled to control the Cachalote as she rolled to the side on top of another wave, almost toppling over. El Coche travelled further and further away now, pushed forward by the waves, the hull lowered slightly from the weight of the incoming water. Colette splashed into the sea with a life preserver, Juan Carlos frantically struggling to steer away, looking back, and observing that a lull between the waves had reduced his speed and was allowing the Cachalote to catch up.

When the Cachalote was almost upon him, Juan Carlos abandoned the helm, having secured the wheel in one position with a rope. He clambered to the side of the deck, dislodging a spinnaker pole which he quickly fastened to the side of the mast, standing and swinging the long metal pole wildly in all directions. Eduardo stood up, ready to dive onto the other boat when Tómas, with a quick motion, grabbed Eduardo's shoulder to hold him back.

Eduardo immediately pushed him away and Tómas lost his balance, falling back into the cockpit, his back hitting a metal cleat.

At that moment, the vessels collided again, this time with a glancing blow, and Juan Carlos swung the spinnaker pole directly at Eduardo, striking his mid-section and knocking him down onto the deck. Clutching at his ribs, Eduardo rose up again, Tómas regaining his composure enough to grab the wheel and swing the Cachalote away from El Coche.

As Tómas looked up to see the two boats separating, he saw a flash as Eduardo flew through the air. Juan Carlos turned away in an attempted escape, the unsecured end of the spinnaker pole falling limp against the deck of the ship with a crash; Eduardo landed on Juan Carlos, the two of them striking the deck before falling forward together, rolling overboard and disappearing into the wall of a massive wave.

Colette, shouting in the distance, began to wave her hands in the air and swam toward him. Tómas tried to swing the boat around; the front end dragged, and the craft was powerless. After a time, when Colette was close enough, he threw the rope ladder down. The cockpit had begun to fill with water, and the sails were flapping, one of the mainsails punctured by the spinnaker pole. They were adrift, and sinking fast. Looking around, they took the only escape route, descending rapidly into a wooden dinghy lashed to the back of the damaged vessel.

Paddling around, shouting, watching both of the damaged craft descending lower and lower and eventually disappearing behind walls of water, with no sign of Juan Carlos and Eduardo, they were finally forced to abandon their search at the onset of a cold wind, increasing waves and rain, and then evening darkness.

When they arrived ashore hours later, exhausted and wet, informing the police by phone of what had happened, the docks at Guayaquil were abandoned except for a few ocean freighters being loaded in the distance.

36. Journey to Peru

TÓMAS AND COLETTE'S bus passed through Guayaquil to a more mountainous region, through several small towns to Machala where they met with Juan Carlos's family at the bus station and told his short, angry widow what had happened. Tómas promised her, as though his statement might be of some consolation, that in memory of Juan Carlos he would help others file claims of conscientious objection when he returned to the country.

"He may yet be found on my doorstep, there is still hope," she said solemnly, apparently unconvinced at her own words. She seemed impatient to depart with her two boys, perhaps to grieve on their own without strangers' eyes upon them.

Tómas and Colette awoke when they arrived at the Peruvian border that evening. Their bus sat in darkness, motionless, guards with rifles standing beside a tiny wooden shack with dim lights. One of the guards, a man with a moustache who spoke very rapidly, informed everyone on the bus that he would be checking identification. Tómas produced his military card from his backpack.

As the guard approached him, checking passports, Tómas looked to the men with rifles milling outside with lit cigarettes, laughing. The guard on the bus gathered Tómas's Ecuadorian passport and military card along with the others, stepping off the bus to speak with the guards outside. Walking into the shack, he emerged to talk to the others again, pointing at Tómas and a few others as he spoke. Colette and Tómas said nothing.

As he sat waiting, Tómas agonized over internment and incarceration. Confinement in solitude was preferable to one devoid of solitude, as Dostoyevsky had noted when he was imprisoned in Siberia. Among Montgomery's gifts to Tómas over the years was *House of the Dead*, which he said contained everything Tómas needed to know to appreciate freedom; and *Brothers Karamazov*, which he said contained everything Tómas needed to know about religion. These two books were wrapped in plastic and tucked away in the backpack that he now clutched tightly.

Despite the possession of his military card, there was the border war that was about to intensify. He was of age to serve. Additionally, his father was in the news, and he was closely associated with Eduardo, whose death would soon be made public. He was being called out now, just as those cowboys in the spaghetti westerns he had watched with his father when he was a young boy. Those protagonists emerging onto the street, from a saloon or a flophouse to face their antagonizers, was all he once knew about being a man. *Payaso con la cabeza de zanahoria, clown with the carrot stick head,* they seemed to shout out to him as he cowered inside in an unlit corridor, *where is your identification? You are of the age of military service, and you have been called; yet you have not served. Yes or no?*

Anticipating that detention was imminent, Tómas turned to Colette.

"I will not get through," he said. "I leave now to get my passport and military card back."

"I'll wait a week, maybe two, in Cuszco," Colette whispered, her lips close to his ear. "As long as I have money, I'll wait. And if you don't come, I'll go looking for you. I won't let them keep you from meeting your mother, or your father."

Colette kissed him on the side of his face. The weight of the bus shifted once, and then again as two guards boarded the bus. Tómas moved to a seat near the rear entrance, and tried to open the door. The handle was jammed and would not budge despite repeated attempts, and he tried forcing his weight against the sheet metal, which only buckled against his shoulder. When his name was announced along with several others he did not reply, his heart pounding. Then, as though bringing this upon himself willingly, as if atoning for his father's cowardice a generation ago, he slung the backpack over his shoulder and rose resignedly, his eyes focusing on their rifles.

This was just as the instant before an epileptic seizure, the one moment of bliss Dostoevsky said was sufficient for the whole of a man's life, which did not come from a moment of truly experiencing love or faith, as Tómas had anticipated, but from a sudden vitriolic loss of freedom, equivalent to being blindfolded, accused of treason, and sent before a firing squad; then suddenly realizing that the blindfold had been removed, a guard disclosing that the czar had relinquished the sentence in favour of incarceration in a Siberian prison camp.

Along with a few other young men, Tómas was escorted from the bus, contemplating his loss of freedom as the guards stared at him with cigarettes in their hands. The bus pulled away, and they all watched under the moonlit night as the taillights quickly disappeared into the Peruvian night.

A patrolman led them into the shack, pacing back and forth in front of them for an intolerably long time before indicating that unless they came up with a thousand American dollars as a compensation quota, they would be sent to the military base in Guayaquil tomorrow morning.

After a short time had passed, his mind adrenalized, unable to sleep as those beside him now were, he eyed his passport and military card that were on the table among several others. His military service was closer than ever now, unless ... The guards had begun to doze and everyone else was asleep.

The noise of another bus roused the guards from sleep and sent them outside.

Looking out through the openings in the caña hut, Tómas saw that the guards had entered the bus. His heart thumping, he realized that this was the most opportune moment to attempt an escape. Stowing the brown blanket he had been issued into his backpack, opening the door wide enough to squeeze through, he slipped out and into the night as he had done outside his house such a short time ago.

Ducking behind a set of trees, away from the road, he clambered into the moonlit night, his heart racing. Insects and animals hummed and hollered through the forest. Voices and lights behind him, and he ran, thinking they were after him, and he continued running, endlessly running, out of breath and then stopping, then running again until breathless, following the path of the roadway from a distance until the night dissipated into morning.

Exhausted, he welcomed the sight of the hanging orchids of Guanderas, the Pululahua orchids, and the Orchids of Pahuma set among needles of light on the forest floor, noting that this was the same vegetation that had accompanied his freedom on the island, when he had emerged from the forest to see Eduardo Delgado motioning to him from the beach beneath cloudy skies.

37. Devotion

DAYS LATER, TÓMAS arrived in Cuszco, ancient capital of the Inca Empire. He had slept away most of his time on different buses, eaten whatever others had offered, and he arrived hungry, thirsty and stinking. Stepping from the stairs of his bus into the cool, early evening air reminiscent of Isla de la Plata, he thought of how far away the island, and his life there, seemed to be now.

The central square was bathed in artificial light and contained rusty ancient cathedrals, surrounded by mountains littered with homes. He had read of this mystical city before, in one of Montgomery's travel articles. But experiencing this himself was more fantastic than he had imagined, living as though in a waking dream. He realized his breathing was laboured and a headache was pounding at his temples. He sat down at a restaurant and drank several cups of coca tea, using the only two US dollars he had, remembering his father's advice about altitude sickness.

When sufficiently recovered he wandered into an outdoor market with various indigenous items for sale, a place that his father had written about too. He saw what his father meant when he said that the native techniques and products derived from them had not changed in a thousand years. Staring into the faces of elderly women and mothers with their babies, all of them in brightly coloured clothing displaying the same items for sale, he thought that these people, too, their way of life and their means of sustenance, had likely not changed in a long time.

Walking down the Avenida El Sol, he was handed flyers for hostels, an Irish pub, pizzerias and a Jamaican Reggae bar. He used some of these flyers to locate hotels and hostels where Colette might be staying. Unable to locate her anywhere and fatigued at the end of his hunt, he finally checked in to a hotel where he paid using Ecuadorian sucres. The woman looked at him with disgust as he handed her the tattered bills.

"Normally I would not accept these," she said in a quiet Spanish, "with our two countries still at war. But you look ragged and tired, as if you need somewhere, anywhere to stay."

"I thank you very much, Señora," Tómas replied.

Entering his room and flopping down on the bed, despite the discomfort of the thin mattress, he had the deepest sleep in recent memory.

Awakening to a strong light and the familiar sound of a rooster's crow, initially recalling none of his dreams, feeling the cool mountain air and peering out the window at a vista thirty-five hundred metres above the elevation he had slept every night of his life, he recollected that the dreams he had were as strange and surreal as everything appeared to be here. There were visions of dragons flying low over cities and breathing fire over the earth at what he knew to be the end of the world, his disembodied spirit simply witnessing the flames consuming the homes below. An angel had offered him a telephone, set on an ornate pedestal, which gave him a method by which to communicate with anyone, living or dead. He had tried to call his father, and then his mother, and then Juan Carlos and Eduardo. The angel was unable to oblige any of his wishes, as Tómas couldn't definitively tell the angel whether they were alive or dead, which seemed to be the only criteria—other than speaking their names—for talking with them. Upon awakening he was relieved, recalling his Ecuadorian mother's teachings that talking with the dead was abhorrent to God.

That morning, Tómas traveled to the few remaining hostels he had not yet visited. He lost all hope of finding Colette when finally, a hostel desk worker—an elderly woman with an apron who reminded him of Veronica—recognized the name.

The woman escorted him upstairs and knocked on a thick wooden door situated at the end of a long, dark hallway. Hearing no response, she used her key to enter. Colette was on the bed, asleep in short pants and a tight-fitting sleeveless top. As she opened her eyes, she covered herself with a sheet, watching the worker trudge down the hallway. Staring at Tómas, she sat up on the bed.

"You look horrible," she said, smiling, speaking slowly, her voice barely audible. "And you smell awful." Her smile dissipated. "It's true, about your father coming here," she continued. "Some of the locals told me he's near Machu Picchu, in Aguas Calientes. I'll take you there. We need to be careful which path we take, though."

"I know. Over a thousand Inca trails lead from here."

Sitting further upright, she pulled her white, stained sheets higher as she noticed his eyes perusing the curves beneath. "What happened to you after the bus left?" she asked. "I've been so worried."

"I escaped," he replied. "And I found a bus on the Peruvian side. I have not much money, and I am very hungry."

"I rented a tent and some supplies. I can buy us enough food. I don't have much money, either. I bought two airline tickets for Ottawa, so I can introduce you to your mother."

Two young Peruvian boys with hair the colour of midnight, stooped over like pack animals with their huge backpacks, flew up the trail ahead of Tómas and Colette to catch up with their tour group. They walked beside orchids and bromeliads and panoramas of misted mountains all around. It was as though he were simply imagining, or dreaming his presence here among these surreal surroundings, as he had been doing since he left the island. The anticipated joy at the prospect of seeing his father again, and of meeting his mother for the first time, still seemed such an imagined fantasy; the same as those envisioned by the authors he had read having seen the results of their creation.

38. Path to the Ancient City

THREE DAYS INTO their journey along the trail, almost to Machu Picchu, they set up their tent in a clearing beside the charred cinders of a fire pit. Tómas had read and reread his mother's letters, as they hiked the path of the Incas, encountering fortresses, gazing down upon ancient homes, and observing their bathwater that, to this day, still trickled down from the aqueducts. Looking down on the ruins and the clouds blanketing green landscapes below, Tómas thought that he had never seen anything so spectacular. And he could not imagine what other wonders his father had seen and written about, marvels that had never been communicated to him with such clarity.

"We are on the correct path?" Tómas asked, driving some stakes into the ground around their tent. "No one has been on this trail for days."

"We're fine," Colette said unconvincingly, unfurling the tent and spreading the brown plastic over the earth.

The grass outside the tent rustled in the frosty evening air. Tómas opened the tent's zipper to see dusk on the horizon, and he saw the dark form of a woman snaking sinuously by. She was maybe thirty years of age, short with the dark and weather-beaten skin of a Peruvian. She clutched a folded tent tightly in her arms. Pacing over the ground as though surveying it, the two boys with their mighty backpacks released their burdens onto the cold, damp earth beside her. Their groans coincided with the clanging of cooking pots tied to the outside of the packs.

"More campers will be here soon," Colette said, removing plastic cups and a box of wine, with a black cat on its face, from her rucksack. She rolled onto her side to peer at Tómas through dark, tangled hair, opening the spout and removing some foil packaging. "I was saving this," she said, smiling. "We do not need to worry much, any more." She filled the cups and handed one to Tómas. "The tour guides, that woman outside now is one of them, they pay thieves who live near here to stay away from their tour groups. Although, really, we don't have much to steal."

As he drank, he rifled through the entire package of letters from his mother to Colette—all except for the one addressed to him, which he would read when departing for Canada to see her.

In the letters, his mother Violet often asked random questions about Tómas. Colette had gone into San Cristobal from time to time, over the years, to observe him from afar and to provide answers. Colette had written that she had observed Tómas in his primary and secondary school and at the university, walking about with friends, at parties on the beach, walking into the church, often late in the service, with ruffled hair, and when he worked for a short time harvesting bananas, plantains, coffee berries and yucca with his father. There were details that Colette could only have learned from Tómas's friends. And now he seemed to recall hearing through the years of a dark-haired señorita, whom they called the girlfriend he had never seen, which he had regarded as teasing among schoolmates because he had no girlfriend—a teasing that had caused him countless bouts of crying.

Apparently, Violet did not want Colette and Tómas to meet for some reason. But as he read on without questioning Colette, he discovered the reasons why. There was his father's extramarital affair with Violet. Violet had sent notes inquiring about her son, and Colette had gone to the house; but Veronica had sent back threatening and hateful letters in return, and had sent Colette back to the campo whenever she would visit, without allowing her inside. As Colette was Violet's closest friend on the island, Veronica did not let Colette see Tómas. Not until now, after nearly twenty years. So Colette had seen him in the only way she knew how.

An hour passed before a small tour group arrived. Colette was reading a book and drinking her wine as Tómas lay there flipping through his mother's letters, listening as the tourists settled into their tents. His head was swimming from the wine and dizzy with anticipated slumber as he perused his mother's writings and relived the experiences of the past week, in which his entire life had so drastically changed. The sounds of rustling and muffled conversation led to a gathering around the fire pit, where voices could be clearly heard.

In contrast to the heat of the fire outside, there was a chill he had never felt before in an air so completely deprived of oxygen that it rendered the altitude nearly uninhabitable. Even the fire, which he could see clearly now, was wavering, hungry for air.

"What's going on out there?" Colette asked.

"Nothing," Tómas said, closing the tent flap and sitting up. "They sit around the fire and talk. But something bothers me about these letters."

"What?"

"Well, I know you watched me during the years. To give my mother information about my life. I do not know why you never came to me. Veronica would not let you in our house. But why did we not meet sooner?"

Colette paused for a time, finishing her wine before reaching outside the tent to pluck a piece of Peruvian ichu grass, twirling it between her fingers as she spoke.

"She only wanted to know that you were well," she said. "But she didn't want any problems for you or your father. And she didn't want you to know where she was. She thought you might want to search for her."

He looked into her eyes, beautiful now, illuminated by the fire that came in waves of reddish orange through the sides of the tent. The words of his father returned to him: *I don't want you to look for me, or to be concerned with where I am, or why I left. Just know that I've left as a result of a chain of events that I myself, and no one else, initiated.*

"Why she would prefer her son not look for her, I do not understand," he said.

"She said she would come to you when she was ready."

"But I am already a man. And still, she has not come."

"I know. I can't defend her actions."

"She said nothing in her letters about why she left, either. She said only that she was confused and unhappy."

Rolling over in the sleeping bag, rubbing his eyes, he realized how tired he was. Such a long time had elapsed since he had slept in a comfortable bed, and the wine was taking effect.

"What your mother didn't say in those letters," Colette said after a few minutes had passed, when Tómas was almost asleep, "and what she told me before she left was that she wasn't prepared for motherhood at her age, especially with a much older, married man as the father. She's always been ashamed, and all these years she hasn't had the nerve to face you."

Unable to comprehend this in his exhaustion, he looked outside the tent to see the silvery moon encircled by a crimson halo, and the image of so many people huddled around a fire made him think of a gigantic condor: mountains forming its back, its eye the silver in the moon, its body engulfed by a halo of flame. The same as the lion he had once read about representing Babylon, the bear of Medo-Persia, the leopard of ancient Greece, and the nondescript beast of the Roman Empire, this feral beast encapsulated the essence of these Peruvian mountains, an essence that savagely clawed at the brittle air, talons ablaze.

He lay back down again, silent beside Colette who had done the same. His mind was awake once more but his body was fatigued, and he was oddly uncomfortable in the absence of the mosquito's hum at this altitude. The night was dissolving into a slumber induced by the tannins of Chilean wine, as thoughts of his mother, and seeing his father again, intermingled with these paranormal mountain heights, to deliver another evening of the most lucid and spectacular dreams of his life.

39. Ancient Engineers

TÓMAS AND COLETTE had a breakfast of campfire-fried plantains and rice with the tour group before packing up, donning their coats, and trudging for hours along the stone steps.

The ancient Peruvian holy city suddenly appeared as they wound around a stone pathway under the light of the morning sun. They stood staring at the ancient city poised beneath an intensely verdant mountain, all under a cloudless rooftop. A hundred tiny people traversed through its stonework and its temples. Tómas simply stood and observed for a long time, astounded at his father's understatement of this place, before he could begin moving again.

They walked along a pathway overlooking the ancient city, which as Tómas knew had been protected for so long by its remote placement. Those who loved this city, to prevent discovery by the conquistadors, had abandoned the place; and not until five hundred years had passed, along with the invention of the helicopter, was the location finally revealed. Hiram Bingham, the man credited with the discovery, insisted that there were no treasures found at the site. Now eighty years later, the city had been opened up for all to see that Bingham was wrong.

They marched down a recently constructed dirt footpath along a precipice, their feet moving almost in unison. They stopped at the edge of a sheer rock face overlooking the forest treetops. It was an area inundated with the blanched light of the morning sun, the sound of whitewashing rapids flowing somewhere below. Ancient engineers, architects and military men, constructed the great irrigation systems of the past: Mesopotamia (the "land between rivers"), the Tigris and Euphrates region, the Indus, the Nile, Hwang-ho, the canals of Babylonia, and this Machu Picchu. This place that had always been referred to as the "cradle of Andean civilization," had been designated by his father as a city that was saved by having been abandoned.

They took a bus into the town of Aguas Calientes, and walked to the main town area along the length of a railway line. That day they found a man in a bar where all of the furniture, floors and ceiling were made from the same sort of light-coloured wood, a man who admitted to recognizing the name Montgomery Harvey. He was a small dark-skinned Peruvian with a wide face, who claimed to be the one person who was sought when someone needed asylum. He led them down a dark hallway and pointed Tómas to a bedroom without windows, directing Colette to wait in the darkness.

Tómas walked into the bedroom, the only illumination coming from candles and a fireplace. Against the far wall, a man with white hair slept, facing away, in a four-poster bed. Tómas sat beside the bed, feeling the warmth of the fireplace on his feet.

A while later the man, Montgomery, pale and sallow, turned toward Tómas, startled, opening his eyes and staring at the wall as though seeing through him.

Tómas had thought of this moment so many times growing up, the moment where he would voyage to meet his father on his travels. Now this was happening, although not in the south of France, Nice or Monte Carlo, or Spain, Madrid or Barcelona, or in Africa or Indonesia as he had imagined. They did not embrace, as he had imagined they would. This was not the beginning of their travels and their new life together, but instead Tómas had the immediate impression that this was more akin to an end.

40. Ancient Sculptor

HIS FATHER'S CALLOUSED hands moved slowly over Tómas's face, probing its contours, the firelight painting strange patterns on the rugged lines of Montgomery's face. It was as though Montgomery were an ancient Inca sculptor, recreating a visage in clay. His hands moved from the distinctive bridge of Tómas's nose to his forehead to his hair, now straw-like from four days of neglect on the trail, weaving the coarse fibres into the sculpture, now readying the creation to be presented at a festival along with brewed chicha maize beer and sacrificial llamas as homage to Urcaguary the rare, Pachamama the earth, Mamacocha the sea, and Mamaquilla the moon.

"Tómas," Montgomery said in his peculiar Spanish, which was now vocalized with British inflections. Montgomery smiled widely, an expression that Tómas did not expect and did not recognize. "I am having great difficulty seeing, now," he continued, his smile disappearing. "I have a degenerative illness."

His eyes were strange. Looking into them, Tómas was reminded of the boy with the grey eyes in the savannah region of South Africa that Montgomery had once photographed. Montgomery had interviewed the boy's father, who recounted that the boy had approached a spitting cobra too closely. They didn't reach the hospital with its vials of antidote in time to save his son's eyesight. When they arrived, the man carrying his son in his arms, it was too late.

"You shouldn't have come," Montgomery said.

"Father, I do not blame you for leaving," Tómas replied.

There was so much else to say but Tómas remained silent, helping Montgomery sit more upright on the bed. Apart from his well-defined nose with the same distinctive bridge as his own, protruding ears perched forward, the grey speckled hairline and bearded stubble that had all not changed, there was the unusual pallor of his skin, and the emaciated look of his face with his grey eyes slightly sunken into his head.

"You never told me about mother," Tómas said to him in Spanish.

Montgomery said nothing, turning his head away; after several minutes had passed, he closed his eyes. Tómas focused his attention first on the fireplace, and then, reaching into his wallet, he produced the single tattered photograph of his mother that he had carried with him his entire life.

He was still examining the graduation picture when Montgomery began speaking again, taking deep breaths between sentences, his speech slurred, the movements of his hands and head slow as when he used to arrive after a long flight from overseas. But instead of disguising a resentment toward his father, whom he felt had lived as though he did not have a son, Tómas now looked with compassion into the eyes of this man whose movements, speech and sight were an affront to the independence he had always so revered.

"I should have told you before," Montgomery said. "After you were born, I wanted you both to stay on the island with me ... but Violet said she didn't belong there, that the island wasn't her home. She gave you to me as a gift, as if in return for what little I had given her. And I never saw her again. But still, even so many years later, I wonder about the life she has chosen for herself, why she has always chosen to stay away, and about all the time we missed together ... and I wonder about the time you and I have missed together ..."

"I think of that too."

"But life is not for regret," he said, sighing and adjusting his position on the bed. "It's only when close to death that you start wondering how things could've been different, why you didn't question things more when you were still able to make the decisions that could change the course of your life."

"Why was mother unhappy?"

"Well, she enjoyed living on the island for the first months after she arrived. I could tell in the way she was so contented and carefree. There were so many nights that I would simply watch her at parties as she danced on the beach beneath the stars. But after she learned she was pregnant she would often argue with me, mostly for no reason, and she insisted on leaving. What I distinctly remember about your mother was that she always looked at the life she wanted to have for herself, without seeing you, me, and what might have been. I hope she got what she wanted."

"I've thought about her a lot recently," Tómas said. "I read and spent hours on schoolwork to make me not think of her, or you."

"Solitude and loneliness are enduring, constant companions ..."

As Montgomery turned his head to stare into the warmth, his waved and speckled hair illuminated in the fire, Tómas realized that he and Montgomery were more similar than he had ever thought.

"It's strange," Montgomery continued, "feeling alone, despite being in the enormous crowds of big cities. It's worse than being in an isolated area with no one around, because all you see is contented friends and families. But you would not know any of this; you have only recently left the island for the first time."

"I was in Quito at the press forum. I was with Juan Carlos. I saw you there."

"Well, that may be so. But don't live away from your home and your family as I have ... really ... it's only a burden to be a foreigner living in foreign lands. I have always been so busy observing and photographing other people's lives, and it's as though I've never lived my own, with my eye always remaining behind the lens, never in front."

Montgomery pulled himself upright on the bed, rubbing his eyes.

"You had responsibility for taking the money," Tómas said. "I know that now."

"Yes." He nodded his head resignedly.

"Veronica was very angry with Eduardo. She blamed him for your disappearance."

"I left on my own. I did not want shame and disrepute in our family. Do you know the principles the ancient Incan lived by?"

"No."

"Ama sua, ama quella, ama llulla. It means do not be a thief, do not be lazy, do not be a liar. It refers not to actions, but to repeated behaviour ... I have lived by these principles ... not to say that I haven't done any of these, I have. But I have endeavoured never to repeat them."

"Now, I am the one who has brought shame to our family. I escaped the military twice, by running away." Tómas rose, stretched, and then sat down on the chair beside the bed again. After a period of silence, he continued speaking: "Colette wants me to travel with her now, to meet my mother."

"You won't?" Montgomery asked, the fireplace crackling loudly.

"We will. We searched for you after you left. Juan Carlos told me that when you wanted to be found, you would come back to me. But you did not. Just as mother has not."

"I grew too sick, too quickly. Your mother has her own reasons for not returning. I am sure she has regretted leaving you, as I often have when travelling for so long away ... you know, I once loved your mother intensely, and have never stopped. I have wanted to see her again, for so long."

Intuitively, Tómas wanted them all together as a family: himself, Violet and Montgomery. But he thought of

Veronica; and he knew from looking at Montgomery as he closed his eyes, a resignation now apparent in his eyes, his face, and his movements, that his time was short.

"You did not tell me why you left the war in England," Tómas said. "But Diario Hoy did. Whether that story was true, or no, I could not tell."

"I was captured in Spain as a prisoner of war, along with my Uncle Devon. He died of typhoid in our prison camp, but not before getting me a visa to Ecuador. I took his solution, the only way out of that place, and I didn't go back to England to see my family until after the war, when it was too late. I still remember wonderful summers in Northaw with my mother and two brothers, a memory tainted by a collection of rubble at 21 Grove Street in Whitechapel where we lived, and the war office logbook that referred to them as casualties." He paused, the fireplace flickering and popping and accompanied by a dog barking in the distance outside. A tear ran down his face.

"I was thinking only of myself," Montgomery continued, "the same as I have done since; that is, until the time before I left the island, when I thought I was doing some good. But war is sometimes necessary to protect the country's interests, and you can't allow fear to get hold of you like I did. My paranoia extended to you. I didn't want you to have to go into the war, for fear that you would die at such a young age. That's why I asked Eduardo to look after you, to see what he could do to avoid you having to serve in the military."

Tómas produced his military card, and handed the brightly coloured placard to his father who held but did not examine it.

"Eduardo gave this to me," Tómas said. "I fought in court for conscientious objection, with Juan Carlos. We lost. I was afraid of an unnecessary death in an unnecessary war. I was a coward, and not guided well. I did not tell myself that I only objected to the border war between Ecuador and Peru; but I admitted that in the courtroom. That lost the case for me. I am worse than one of the Canadians executed in the First World War for deserting. I never spent a day in combat, so I never knew from what I was trying so desperately to escape ... now, I will go back one day to fight, but not in the way the military wants ..."

Waiting in the room, holding his hand until Montgomery fell into a deep sleep, Tómas had not contemplated that his father and mother might have had regrets about abandoning him; he had supposed that they were not even capable of such sentiments. But the thought consoled him. He wanted to see what his mother would say to him when he stood before her saying nothing.

"Veronica forgives you," Tómas said to Montgomery. "As I do, too."

The noise of Montgomery's weighted breathing resonated throughout the room as Tómas walked outside. Colette was asleep on the hallway floor with a coat wrapped around her, her body contorted, her pose tranquil and oddly seductive.

41. Youthful Photographs

IN THE DAYS that followed, Montgomery seemed to recover, regaining his former colour and eating normally again. But still, Tómas was not surprised when shortly afterwards, the ailing man fell into a coma. Tómas slept in the chair holding his father's hand in his own after that. He awoke early one morning to find Montgomery was no longer breathing.

Montgomery had instructed Tómas that he did not wish for an announcement of his death to be printed anywhere. He simply wanted to fade away, to be out of print for the first time in his life.

They made the necessary arrangements to have him buried at a cemetery beside an ancient Inca gravesite nearby. Tómas telephoned Veronica.

"He did not tell me he was sick," Veronica stated, after realizing what Tómas had said. "He was old, a mule thinking he could fight anything alone, even without doctors..." She paused for a moment, and he could hear her crying on the other end of the phone. "Our island is evacuated, and the military are here like I said would happen. We have been told to leave ... that volcano has gone quiet now ... to get me to leave, they will have to kill me first. Then, they can take my body away, and put it wherever they wish."

I will always remember this day, Tómas wrote in a journal purchased at Aguas Calientes, *the Day of the Dead, el Dia de los Muertos. We walk by children in the streets dressed in both dark and brightly coloured costumes, walking to gather bread and bananas in plastic sacks from any homes able to part with them. In Canada, they celebrate this time of year as Halloween, but here we celebrate both the deceased and the similarities between ancient Inca traditions and Catholicism. For me, it will not be a day of remembering all that my father, Juan Carlos and Eduardo could have been, but a day of remembering what they have given me. This will become my contentment, from gratitude for what I have, and forgiveness for what I do not.*

I think about meeting my mother, removing the photograph I have carried in my wallet, a snapshot taken for a graduation of some sort, her white puffed wrap beneath a young smile, brilliant teeth, and carte blanche promise for the future. I think of how, upon meeting her, I might see the youthfulness sucked from her face, her sad eyes brimming with the sort of wisdom and self-presumed clarity obtained from a lifetime of regret. I think of how she will explain her relationship with my father and describe the person she was at the time she met him, as her eyes remain fixed to the floor. And I contemplate how she will stand there before me, wondering as she has perhaps for my entire lifetime, what I might do next: strike her, walk away, feign congeniality, or shout at her. Any of these would do, but my silence as I stand there will prove intolerable to her.

As we continue down the street, my father, more youthful now, stares back at me from the front page of a Peruvian newspaper. I did not inform them of your death, I tell his stare. We board a huge plane for Ottawa, and I know that the responsibility I have to Ecuador will never, for the remainder of my life, be over. I have a love of the Ecuadorian people and a faith in their inherent morality, and an obligation to help them move toward the acceptance of conscientious objection, and the establishment of a new hotel and improved irrigation systems on the island. Upon returning from seeing my mother, knowing now that she will likely not wish to see me and will be happy at my parting, I will no longer feel alone. I will be at peace, no longer overcome with the desire to know her, and I will be able to fulfill my duties unfettered by a desire to know more about the woman who gave me life.

An hour later, I can see the sea beneath us through a tiny window. This view of the sea is a treasure, as all of its vistas that I've never been far from my entire life.

I read the one letter addressed to me, written by my mother. It is full of requests that I will one day absolve her of her guilt. She was too young, too confused, her thoughts too muddled. One day, she hopes I will understand and forgive her.

The wind moving about the water below seems to whisper the unspoken epitaph of my father's life. Old city squares he has stood in. The crowds of onlookers as he walked foreign streets. Buses and trains he has travelled on, snaking through rolling green hills. Conversations over foreign dinners in foreign restaurants. His comfort in freedom, in solitude, in loneliness, his contentment in a self-imposed exile that he carried with him to the end of his life. His selfless duty to others around him. Random cityscapes of lands described at peace, and at war.

I think of riding on a bus with Colette past the Ottawa River she has told me about, a plethora of farm homes, businesses, coffee shops, a cityscape surrounded by farmland. I can see the rolling hills, the antiquated cottages tucked beneath ivy and age. I can smell the freshness of the country air, the vendors along the streets selling some sort of wares from portable wagons. I see us walking along the shops of the town where my mother lives, to meet her in a park—the tattered photograph alive before me in my one moment of bliss, staring back beside a chattering of birds, nothing less than a splendid, cooing chorus.

-End-

Acknowledgements

I WOULD LIKE to thank my wife Roxanne, the love of my life, who always makes me laugh and who has put up with me through fourteen years of marriage. I would like to thank my son Colin, the capable outdoorsman, and my daughter Abigail, the animal lover, for bringing such joy into our lives.
I would like to thank my parents Craig and Barbara who have always lovingly supported and encouraged me, as well as my brother Benjamin who has challenged me to think critically about my work.

I would like to thank the Humber School for Writers, especially the Artistic Director Antanas Seleika, as well as my writing mentors David Adams Richards and MG Vassanji for their wisdom and guidance.

I would like to thank those who provided valuable feedback on earlier versions of the manuscript, among them David Adams Richards and Sharon Crawford.

To my editor Shane Joseph, I would like to thank you for improving the manuscript immeasurably through your detailed, insightful and thought-provoking comments.

And thank you to Blue Denim Press for publishing this work.

Author Bio

CHRISTOPHER CANNIFF GREW up in Windsor, Ontario. Shortly after completing a Mechanical Engineering degree at the University of Toronto, he moved to Ecuador for a year, where he read over fifty books of world literature, learned a new language and culture, and taught for WorldTeach, a non-profit and non-governmental organization based at the Harvard Institute for International Development. He lived with an Ecuadorian family in Portoviejo and took culture, language and history classes about the country while working with Plan International, an organization tasked with improving Ecuador's faltering rural education system. Christopher has travelled throughout Ecuador, Peru, Columbia, Spain, France, Germany, the Netherlands, Ireland, England and Mexico; as well, he has visited Copenhagen, St. Petersburg, Oslo, and Tallin; places that have fuelled his writing. Christopher is a graduate of the Humber School for Writers in Toronto, studying under the mentorship of M.G. Vassanji and David Adams Richards, both of whom are Giller Prize and Canadian Governor General Award winners.

Christopher has written travel articles for WorldTeach, and his first literary short story publication, *Solitude*, was published by Tightrope Books in 2006. He won the "3 Hour Novel Contest" with LWOT (Lies With Occasional Truth) Magazine in Montreal in 2007, for *Clean Conscience*. In 2008, he was commissioned to write two scripts for Twilight Zone Radio Dramas, a nationally-syndicated radio program produced by Falcon Picture Group in Chicago. Christopher was shortlisted in the 2010 Matrix Litpop Awards for Fiction, for *Songs and Letters of Lost Love*. *The Russian Soldier*, an excerpt from a previous version of *Poor Man's Galapagos*, was published in Descant Magazine in Spring 2011. Christopher's first full-length work, *Abundance of the Infinite* (Quattro Books, 2012), a psychological novella set in Ecuador and Toronto, was shortlisted for the 2012 Ken Klonsky Novella Award.

Christopher was the president of the Canadian Authors Association Toronto Branch for the 2014-2015 season (www.canauthorstoronto.org). He has maintained an active literary life and believes that literary communities are essential for any writer. He is married to Roxanne, and lives with their son, Colin. and daughter, Abigail, in Windsor, Ontario. More details on Christopher's work can be found at: www.christophercanniff.com.

Printed in the USA
CPSIA information can be obtained
at www.ICGtesting.com
LVHW012051210924
791605LV00003B/10